DATE			

ALSO BY EDWARD SKLEPOWICH

Liquid Desires

Farewell to the Flesh

Death in a Serene City

Black Bridge

Edward Sklepowich

Death in the Palazzo

A VENETIAN MYSTERY

SCRIBNER

SCRIBNER
1230 Avenue of the Americas
New York, NY 10020

This book is a work of fiction. Names, characters, places, and incidents either are products of the author's imagination or are used fictitiously. Any resemblance to actual events or locales or persons, living or dead, is entirely coincidental.

Designed by Jennifer Dossin
Text set in Electra

Manufactured in the United States of America

1 3 5 7 9 10 8 6 4 2

Library of Congress Cataloging-in-Publication Data
Sklepowich, Edward.
Death in the Palazzo: a Venetian Mystery/Edward Sklepowich
p. cm.
I. Title
PS3569.K574D45 1997
813'.54—dc20 96–30105
CIP

ISBN 0-684-83031-0

To Dominick Abel

LIST OF CHARACTERS

Barbara, Contessa da Capo-Zendrini—the British widow of an Italian aristocrat

Urbino Macintyre—an American dilettante, Barbara's longtime friend

Gemma Bellini-Rhys—a celebrated painter and member of Barbara's husband's family, the Zenos, daughter of Renata, granddaughter of Marialuisa

Robert—Gemma's son, a medieval art historian

Marialuisa Zeno—the matriarch of the Zeno family

Luigi Vasco—the Zeno family doctor

Renata—Gemma's mother, sister of Bambina, daughter of Marialuisa

Cesarina ("Bambina")—Marialuisa's only living child, now seventy-five

Angelica Lydgate—Robert's fiancée

Viola and Sebastian Neville—Barbara's cousins from England

Molly Wybrow—the uninvited guest

Oriana and Filippo Borelli—Barbara's friends, part of the house party

DEATH IN THE PALAZZO

Whatever happens in a house, robbery or murder, it doesn't matter, you must have your breakfast.

—Wilkie Collins, *The Moonstone*

PROLOGUE

The Contessa's Folly

On this November afternoon everything in the rococo Chinese salon at Caffè Florian seemed burnished to an extreme—the paintings under glass, the wood stripping on the walls and ceiling, the embracing arms and curved backs of the banquettes, the tea service, the bronze amorino lamp, and the parquet floor—and yes, even Barbara, the Contessa da Capo-Zendrini herself.

Urbino Macintyre, a glass of dry sherry in his hand, studied her silently as she gazed out through the glass at the almost deserted Piazza San Marco. It wasn't just her copper-toned dress, gold accessories, and honey-blond hair. It was something about her face as well. In the more than fifteen years of their friendship, the American had seen age make its inevitable, albeit mercifully subtle alterations on that attractive canvas.

But since her extended stay this summer in Geneva, she looked even younger than before—and she had always been a woman who could credibly subtract ten years from what she called "the obscene number" of her age.

After Geneva, she had kept herself aloof up at her villa in Asolo. On the two occasions he had visited her there, she had been masked in large sunglasses, swathed in silk scarves, and obscured beneath wide brims. Today, in fact, was the first time she had cast aside her camouflage, the effect being not unlike that final stripping away of green netting from historic buildings after their months'-long restoration.

"You look so—so"—Urbino searched for the right word, knowing it was essential to find it —"so *rested!*"

Her bright smile showed that he had been successful.

"Why, thank you, *caro*," she said, picking up a petit four. "You know how refreshing the air of Asolo is."

"And the air of Geneva. Mont Blanc, you know."

A frown came and went from the Contessa's remarkably smooth forehead. When she had eaten the teacake and taken a sip of tea, the special first-flush Jasmine that Florian's now stocked for her own use, she said, "It's all for us today."

She made a gesture that languidly appropriated the empty Chinese salon and, by extension, the Piazza outside, so welcomely serene after the madness of high season.

"Thank God it's November," she said. "Almost five months of peace and quiet before the tourists invade."

"Except for Carnevale," Urbino said.

She shivered slightly, for she was reminded of a tragedy that had come painfully close to her during a recent Carnevale. She took another sip of tea.

"It's fortunate that you look so marvelously rested," Urbino said to draw her thoughts away. "Your portrait."

"Ah, yes, my portrait." She said it less than enthusiastically. "How can I forget about that frightful experience hanging over me! Death! That's what a portrait means: She once looked like this. Yes, *once*, but no more! I couldn't be in a worse state! I'm at Gemma's mercy—and everyone will be there to see!"

The Contessa had commissioned her portrait to be begun next weekend. It would be unveiled several weeks later during an intimate house party at her palazzo, the Ca' da Capo-Zendrini. "Gemma" was Gemma Bellini-Rhys, a celebrated painter and the Contessa's cousin through marriage.

"Maybe I should have waited a little longer."

It was a rather outrageous statement, since her reason for having her portrait done was to keep a promise to her husband, the Conte Alvise, dead for close to twenty years.

"But what am I saying?" she corrected herself. "What good would the portrait of a—a crone be on the wall next to that of my handsome Alvise? And that's what I'll be in a few years. A toothless, blind, spotted old crone like the one in that frightening Giorgione at the Accademia!"

Even with the passage of more than a few years—and without any return to the restorative winds off Mont Blanc—the Contessa would be so far from being a crone that Urbino laughed. He spilled a few drops of sherry on his shirt front. The Contessa poured some mineral water on her handkerchief and attacked the spot more briskly than was warranted.

"Men! You don't understand! You never will!"

She finished her assault and, with some of the vehemence of her last words, she flung her glance out into the large square. There, by ill chance, it encountered an old woman with a dowager's hump inching her way across the stones with a cane. When her glance found relief only in a lovely young woman who looked like a fashion photograph, it turned itself on Urbino with something like desperation.

"It's not just your portrait that's bothering you, Barbara," he said, reaching out to touch her hand. "You're worried about the house party."

"And why shouldn't I be?" she threw back at him as she pulled her hand away. "It could be frightful! Everyone gaping at my portrait and—and the Zenos stabbing me in the back! I may never forgive you and Oriana for encouraging me in this folly."

"I don't call it folly when you want to heal wounds in your late husband's family."

"Some wounds never heal! They bleed and bleed and bleed! I'm afraid I might have got carried away with myself. What did the Greeks call it? Hubris? Yes, overweening pride! I thought we might try to carry reconciliation as far as it could go. If I was about to reconcile myself to my age by having my portrait painted, then maybe the Zeno family and I could get reconciled. And since Gemma's a Zeno, too, it's icing on the cake."

Relations between the Zeno and Da Capo-Zendrini families had been bad since the thirties and hadn't been improved by the Contessa's marriage to the Conte twenty years later. Because a tragic house party at the Ca' da Capo-Zendrini during the thirties had been the last time the two families had been together, the Contessa had got the brave idea, of which she was now repenting, of giving her own house party with some of the same Zeno family members as guests of honor.

Urbino had never met any of the Zenos, although he was familiar with Gemma Bellini-Rhys's artistic work. From what he did know of them, however, they were an unusual lot.

Realizing that this was a topic the Contessa needed to talk about, he encouraged her by saying, "Tell me about the Zenos."

"Well, they're not all Zenos by name, as you know. Gemma, the granddaughter, is a Bellini-Rhys and so is her son, of course. Robert is a medieval art historian, with a speciality in relics. Rather appropriate, considering that Marialuisa Zeno—his great-grandmother—is as old as the hills. And even though Marialuisa's personal physician, Luigi Vasco, who is almost as old as she is, *isn't* a Zeno, he's been in attendance on the family so long that he—and they—probably think he is. He had hoped to marry her daughter Renata, Gemma's mother, after she was widowed but that—that didn't work out," she added vaguely, since this was bringing her too close to the troubled waters of the thirties.

"Then last, but certainly not least," she went on a bit too brightly, "is Marialuisa's only living child, Cesarina, or as she's always called—and I suppose *we'll* have to do it too!—Bambina. Never married but supposedly still looking."

"And Bambina is how old?"

"Seventy-five if she's a day! Oh, I've forgotten someone. She's not a Zeno—not yet anyway. Angelica Lydgate, Robert Bellini-Rhys's fiancée."

"Lydgate? Wasn't that the name of the man who was going to marry Renata, Robert's grandmother?"

"Angelica is Lydgate's grandniece. We're going to be an intimate little group." But there was unease in the Contessa's voice. "So that's all of them."

"All the Zenos. But don't forget the two Nevilles."

The Contessa smiled.

"Ah, yes, Viola and Sebastian, my dear, dear cousins."

The Contessa reveled in referring to the Neville twins as her cousins, not so much from strong family feeling—the cousinship was in fact rather distant—but quite simply because it pleased her vanity to have cousins who had recently graduated from Cambridge. She believed it somehow magically took years off her own age.

"I hope you like them. Sebastian's very intelligent but a bit of a *flâneur,* I'm afraid. And Viola—well, Viola is Viola! You'll see. Ah, the whole world before them." She said this with a touch of regret as she looked out again at the Piazza, which—with the fairy-tale city around it—had been a large part of her world for so long. "Their first time in Venice! Aren't they lucky!"

Considering what would soon descend on her home, the Contessa could hardly have uttered a less apt comment—about the Neville twins or any of her other guests.

But neither she nor Urbino had the slightest premonition, despite the dark cloud that chose this moment to pass slowly above the Piazza, dulling all the gold in the Chinese salon and marring the Contessa's well-cared-for face with unbecoming shadows.

PART ONE

The Guests Arrive

1

Sebastian Neville, dressed in loose mauve trousers and a russet cashmere sweater, was the first to alight from the *Orient Express* and step on the fabled ground of Venice—or, more accurately, on the red carpet spread on the pavement of the Venice railway station for the privileged travelers. He turned to help down a lady, not young and certainly not his twin sister, Viola. It was a woman in her fifties, whose dwarflike, deformed body and features and emaciated condition were perfect illustrations of an obscure congenital disease. She gave her clawlike hand to Sebastian and peered around the station from behind thick spectacles that grotesquely magnified her eyes. They gleamed with something more than intelligence.

"A dead girl named Lucy, kidnapped ever so rudely from her sweet, much-needed rest and most secretly and darkly conveyed to this very spot from a long way off. Then her little body snatched again and brought—and brought—" She shook her birdlike head and said, "And brought somewhere near here. Yes, a body of a lovely young Italian girl."

"Oh, hush, Molly, you've been reading your Baedeker again. Don't try to impress us with your hocus-pocus."

The speaker of these words was a young woman whose height and angularity, auburn hair, and green eyes were such a match for those of the young man that she could only have been his twin. Twins of different sex seldom showed such an unsettling resemblance, and these two seemed to constitute almost a race apart, although they might have claimed kinship, if they wished, with the androgynous figures in Burne-Jones's paintings.

"Viola, don't be a skeptic. There are more things in heaven and earth, et cetera and so forth. And don't forget that Molly told you about that terrible fall you had when you were a child."

"Every child has had a terrible fall, although I'll admit that you're not the usual psychic, Molly. You don't jabber on about what's going to happen to a person and hit the mark one time out of ten just by the law of chances."

"No, dearie, I don't, and I'll tell you why," said Molly, whose surname was Wybrow. "The future is as black as a coal bin! Only the past does the trick for me."

"Oh, the past is more than enough," Sebastian said. "At least you're not condemned to repeat it."

Molly gave him a puzzled look.

"I see my reference has gone above your head. Oh, I didn't mean it in that way," he said, suppressing a laugh as he looked down at her.

He directed a porter to have their baggage follow them. The three proceeded along the red carpet and then onto the plebeian stones of the station floor to the top of the broad flight of stairs outside. There they stopped.

Without any warning Venice materialized in all her trickery, a stage set of domes and bridges, windows and balconies mirrored in the waters. It was an improbable scene. It shouldn't have been but it was, and had been for centuries, and just might last awhile longer.

"Now that we've seen it, I suppose we can go back," Sebastian said, impressed but in no way about to show it. "Only more of the same farther down the Grand Canal. But it's a bit chilly, isn't it? And it's been raining."

He indicated the pools of water at the bottom of the steps.

"And from the look of the sky I'd say that we're going to be seeing more of Venice's favorite element."

"Blood everywhere," Molly intoned. "More blood than water."

"Better watch our step, then," Sebastian said. "Blood's a slimy, slippery thing." He took Molly's stick of an arm and helped her down the stairs. "Speaking of blood and consanguinity, what do you think dear old Countess Barbara is going to think about her uninvited guest?"

"Oh, if you think your auntie—"

"Our cousin, actually, but old enough to be our *grand-mère*," Sebastian clarified. "No need to worry. You're a small package. Any nook or cranny will do. And Cousin Barbara loves games. She's planned charades or a treasure hunt or something like that for the weekend. You'll be our little contribution."

Viola took the woman's other arm.

"Sebastian's right. Barbara will be delighted. Oh, look, the gondolas! Barbara said her boat would be waiting for us, but let's not take it. Only a gondola will do!"

In her enthusiasm she came close to dragging poor Molly toward the rocking, coffinlike boats.

Unlike the Nevilles and Molly Wybrow, the Signora Marialuisa Zeno was far from eager to set out for the Ca' da Capo-Zendrini.

At the very moment when the three travelers from the *Orient Express* were making their way to the gondolas, the Signora Zeno was sitting as stiff as a mosaic of Byzantine royalty in a modest pension on the other side of the Grand Canal. One thin hand grasped a black cane with a gold ferrule around its slender wooden shaft. So lost and overwhelmed was she in the dark folds of her dress and the lace wrapping of her head that she gave every appearance of not being able to move at all.

She and her daughter, the Signorina Bambina, had arrived with their physician, Luigi Vasco, the previous day from Rome in their ancient car, driven by a tenant of their palazzo in return for finally fixing his toilet.

What the senior Zeno lacked in movement, her daughter Bambina more than made up for by so much walking back and forth and tossing of her head that her pink ribbons were in danger of being shaken loose. Bambina was a portly woman in her mid-seventies whose pride was her small feet, always shod in the most delicate and expensive of shoes. Her hair, hennaed and tightly curled, framed a face as pink and chubby as that of one of the cherubs floating across the peeling wallpaper.

"I don't understand, Mamma. I'm sorry, but I don't!" She stopped briefly to stamp her tiny foot. "Why couldn't we go yesterday or this morning?"

"We must make the proper entrance. Not like dusty gypsies. It will be plenty of time in a few hours."

A close scrutiny of the Signora Zeno would have left the scrutinizer hard-pressed to detect much movement of her mouth. Now almost a hundred years old, she had long ago given up making any more effort than was necessary. This didn't mean, however, that she was an invalid, but only that she knew the virtue of saving her energies for the important assaults of life, which had become fewer but much more crucial at her age. Like the ruin of a once noble building, her face and form encouraged the eye of the observer to trace the beauty and grace that still remained despite the ravages of time. Her hair might be gray and sparse, her bones sharp and brittle, her whole body peculiarly shrunken like some waxen effigy left out in the Roman sun, but her eyes, dark and eerily undimmed, looked at the world with almost all the hunger and curiosity they had had during the First Great War.

"There's the whole weekend for what we have to do," she said. "And I don't mean make peace with that English witch, Barbara!" She raised her cane slightly for emphasis. "She's a fool if she thinks that's what brings us all the way to a monstrous place like this!"

She sniffed disdainfully. If she was speaking of the pension's room, there was some justice in her comment. Mold arabesqued one wall, and an offensive odor snaked its way from the drains of the sink and the bidet. But as if to compensate for these discomforts—as characteristic of the city, after all, as the span of the Bridge of Sighs or the sweep of the Grand Canal—there was the view from the window: an impressionistic scene of faded brick and tile, obelisk chimneys, and wooden roof terraces, but beauties unfortunately lost on the mother and daughter.

"Can I look at the photograph again?" Bambina asked like an importunate little girl. "Please?"

Bambina grabbed her mother's purse, opened it, and withdrew a piece of folded newspaper. She almost ripped it as she unfolded it. It showed an attractive but uncomfortable-looking man of about forty dressed in a tuxedo. Next to him was a handsome older woman.

"Don't forget what we've come here for! You must leave the man alone! I forbid you!" Signora Zeno said with a force that belied the minimal movement of the thin lips.

Fire flashed in Bambina's dark eyes. Almost sixty years ago her mother had said almost the same words to her. The pain was as sharp now as it had been then.

Bambina nodded her head of curls.

"Yes, Mamma."

But the fire was still in her eyes and she had to put a chubby hand to her face to hide the smile that was starting to crawl across her bright red lips.

Everywhere Dr. Luigi Vasco went, the past spoke to him, but it was absent of doges and Titian and Marco Polo. It was his own personal past, and not his whole past—a formidable contemplation, since he was eighty-seven—only that part which had unrolled in the serene city.

The memories assaulted him. Yes, they were everywhere. At the Bridge of Sighs, which he had drifted beneath in a gondola sixty years ago. At La Fenice, whose mirrored corridors had reflected the passage of two people caught up in something as operatic as anything taking place on the stage. At the parapet of the Rialto Bridge, where he had waited in a pelting rain, not unlike the one yesterday, for someone to keep a rendezvous.

Vasco could have provided a personal commentary of love and loss on almost every major sight in the guidebooks, ticking them off one after another.

His steps inevitably took him to one building, however, that wasn't mentioned in many of the guidebooks. Yet it was a place filled with even more associations than any of the others.

Vasco first contemplated the Ca' da Capo-Zendrini from the opposite side of the Grand Canal, taking in its classical facade of Istrian stone with a frieze of lions, its veranda, its garden wall covered with Virginia creeper. He took the *traghetto* to the other side and spent several minutes contemplating the humble back of the building. Almost sixty years before he had passed through the first of the iron doors into the small, formal garden and then through the doors of the palazzo itself.

Back then there had been a different contessa—an Italian one. Her house party had ended in death. Love and loss all those years ago, and now he was returning.

A face appeared at one of the windows. For a fleeting moment it was Renata's proud, beautiful face. He rubbed his eyes and looked again. The window was empty. He turned away and walked wearily down the *calle*.

Why had he agreed to come back?

A water taxi was speeding in a narrow channel marked out by old wooden stakes. Ominous clouds were reflected in the green waters of the lagoon.

"I think I'm going to be sick. Can't we go back to the airport?"

said a thin young woman sitting in the stern. So muffled and constricted was she in a cape, two scarves, a knit cap, gloves, and leg warmers that it was possible to assume her indisposition could be immediately cured by a merciful loosening of some of the wraps.

Robert Bellini-Rhys, a good-looking, olive-skinned man with short-cropped black hair and penetrating eyes of an unexpected blue, looked at his fiancée, Angelica Lydgate, with an indulgent expression.

"We can, Angelica dear, but then you'll just be bounced in a bus or squeezed into an overheated *vaporetto.*"

"I'll have to endure it, then," she said. She was a plain woman whose heart-shaped face seemed too small for her large brown eyes.

To distract her, Robert pointed out Burano.

"The island where they make lace."

She nodded without interest. In the past few moments she had turned an unpleasant shade of green. Robert had developed the habit of humoring her, but this might be the real thing. He looked nervously at the pilot, who showed no interest in what might be about to happen to the upholstery of his cabin. Instead he was looking at the dark sky and mumbling something in Venetian dialect that sounded foreboding.

Robert, just as much to calm his own nerves as to soothe Angelica, commented on the scene.

". . . more than thirty islands scattered all around Venice, but twenty don't have a soul on them. Completely abandoned, like that one over there, see?" Angelica didn't bother to raise her eyes, let alone her head. "The railway bridge to the mainland is what did it. A direct link with terra firma. Upset the balance and proportion of all the islands. Should have left things the way they were. This is the only way to approach Venice!"

He said it grandly and threw his hand out toward the shining waters of the lagoon. He conveniently had forgotten that they had just stepped off a plane that had left London only two hours ago. But Robert Bellini-Rhys was full of inconsistencies like this. Otherwise why would such a thoroughly modern young man—and one with a great love for what money could buy—have become not only a medieval art historian but also a specialist in relics and the so-called "sacred thefts" of saints' bodies?

"'Far as the eye can see, a waste of wild sea moor, of a lurid ashen gray,'" he went on, warming to his topic and reciting Ruskin. "'Lifeless, the color sackcloth, with the corrupted sea-water soaking through the roots of its acrid weeds, and gleaming hither and thither through its snaky channels.'"

Breaking the spell of Ruskin's hypnotic prose, he said, "That's Murano over there. Glass. The cathedral has the relics of San Donato, and behind the altar are bones. Oh, not of the saint. The bones of the dragon he was reputed to have killed. By spitting at it."

He found this immensely amusing and threw back his good-looking head and laughed.

"Can you imagine that people used to believe such things? Poor souls! But speaking of bones," he went on, "there are plenty of *human* ones in the other churches. For example . . ."

As the boat went across the rest of the lagoon, he threw himself, with both reverence and condescension, into a description of some of the city's saintly remains. By the time they passed the brick walls and cypresses of the cemetery island, he managed to make all the fabled monuments, mosaics, and altars seem little more than mere decoration for a vast boneyard.

Perhaps according to some paradoxical law, Angelica's bilious color subsided during this demonstration of her betrothed's macabre expertise to something closer to its usual pallor. When the boat headed down a wide waterway toward the Grand Canal, she looked around her with more interest. A gentle smile made her face even softer.

"Oh, it's just like a picture."

Angelica was to be forgiven this platitude. It was, after all, her first trip to Venice, and she was a young woman most of whose impressions of life were secondhand. These had been formed, almost obstinately, her friends thought, from the pages of Victorian novels, the sepia-toned photographs of a stereopticon, and a group of painters who belonged to no particular school or period unless it was that of the sentimental.

When the boat turned into the Grand Canal a few minutes later, her raptures weren't therefore particularly surprising, but they were nonetheless sincere.

"Oh my! Just look at it. A real dream! The water's just like a mirror, and the buildings seem to be floating. And the colors! Straight from a painter's palette. It's exactly the way I knew it was going to be. I'm not disappointed in the slightest!"

Robert, vaguely uneasy that she seemed to have forgotten some of the darker associations the city held for her—just as she had failed to notice the inauspicious clouds overhead and the strange quality of the light—patted her hand and said, "I'm glad you're feeling better, my dear. It's going to be a wonderful weekend."

5

Gemma Bellini-Rhys looked at the finished portrait. It was one of her best. Also, probably her last. And from the way the Contessa had fidgeted and complained, it would probably be *her* last, too.

But the Contessa needn't have been apprehensive that Gemma might exact some kind of vengeance through paint. In fact, Gemma was the closest the Contessa might have come to being "done" by Sargent, her favorite portrait painter.

The Contessa was standing in her *salotto blu*, one hand placed on the lid of a waist-high ceramic Chinese urn, the other holding a morocco-bound volume. She was dressed in a pleated silk Fortuny dress weighted with corded pearls of Murano blown glass and with a pattern inspired by Carpaccio. She had been almost as concerned about how it "came off" as she had been about her face. This attribute, as old as the Fortuny, was equally impressive and for the same reasons. Good design and careful preservation.

The Contessa's face, tilted ever so slightly backward with its generous cheekbones, slanted gray eyes, and patrician air, had been rendered without either flattery or cruel, subtle caricature.

The Contessa should be very pleased when she saw it for the first time this weekend during her house party.

Gemma dropped the cloth over the portrait and went to the window. It looked on to the Grand Canal, but for a moment all she could see was her own reflection in the glass. So different from the Contessa's face, although within only a few years of the same age. It had never possessed any of the beauty of her mother Renata's face, and during the past year serious illness, which she had not revealed to any one, had begun to erode much of its prettiness.

She looked past her own disturbing image down at the Grand Canal. Almost sixty years ago she had sat for hours gazing out of another window of this same palazzo with her doll, waving to figures in passing boats and on the opposite embankment. The view had hardly changed in all these years. This was one of the comforts and mockeries of Venice. No matter what different heart and face you brought it each time, it always was the same.

Always the same, she repeated to herself. Someone coming for the weeknd was all too content to have things remain the same—the way they had been for almost sixty years. But Gemma was determined that this weekend she would strike out and put an end to it. Her hand grasped the drape more tightly as she thought of what she would do.

As she looked down at the Grand Canal, a sleek white water taxi pulled into the Ca' da Capo-Zendrini landing. Mauro, the Contessa's majordomo, appeared a few moments later and helped out Angelica. She was a little unsteady on her feet. Gemma hoped she wasn't going to take to her room and stay there the whole time as she had at the country weekend last year in Sussex. Gemma sighed. She had the impatience of the truly ill in the presence of the hypochondriacal. What she wouldn't give for one of the girl's bad days!

Robert emerged from the boat and squinted up at the building. Feeling not unlike the little girl of half a century ago, she waved at her son but he didn't see her.

"And here at last is my dear friend, Urbino Macintyre," the Contessa said as Urbino joined the small group in the *salotto blu*. "This is Angelica Lydgate and Robert Bellini-Rhys. They've only just arrived."

The young woman's eyebrows rose in amazement. She could barely find her voice to say how pleased she was to meet him.

"Are you all right, Angelica?" Robert said. "She got a bit queasy on the boat from the airport."

"Of course she's all right," Gemma said, a touch of irritation in her voice. She moved closer to the plain girl and squeezed her arm. "She just needs a chance to catch her breath. One minute you're in the modern world, the next you're in the time of the Doges."

Angelica managed to take her eyes off Urbino only by transferring them to her hands, covered in demi-gloves as if she didn't quite trust the heating of the Ca' da Capo-Zendrini. Robert studied his fiancée's bent head with a slight frown.

"You and Urbino have something in common, Robert," the Contessa said as she refilled Angelica's teacup. "A morbid taste for the dead of Venice!"

She took only momentary satisfaction in her own bon mot,

however, for the disapproving look on Gemma's face told her how unthinking it had been. The poor woman's mother had died in Venice.

"Urbino's a biographer," she quickly amended. "He insists that his subjects be dead and have some connection with the city."

"That could put you in a strange position," Robert said. His tone was slightly jocular, but his blue eyes were humorless. "You must be waiting impatiently for some choice subjects to die. I doubt that we're in much competition, though. I'm interested in relics of the early Church that found their way to Venice. Barbara said there's the body of a female saint in a church near your palazzo. Santa Teodora. An obscure one. Even less documentary evidence on her than the others."

"There's been quite a bit about her recently, I'm afraid," Urbino said. "Evidence of a different kind."

"Now I remember! The theft of the body from the crystal casket. An old woman was murdered, too, isn't that right?"

"It certainly is!" the Contessa chimed in. "Urbino's our resident amateur sleuth. His first case. Tell Robert the whole story while we women chat about less gruesome topics," she said, apparently having forgotten she had been the one to introduce death into her *salotto*.

She watched Urbino lead Robert over to the bar and pour them both something stronger than tea. When Urbino began his account, she turned to Angelica.

"Excuse me, my dear," she said in a lower voice than was usual with her, "but do you know Urbino from somewhere? He's so mysterious about his past—sometimes even his present!—that I'm reduced at times to the most pathetic bits and pieces."

"Know him from somewhere? I don't know what you mean!"

"Oh, come now, Angelica! I'm not accusing you of anything. Ha, ha! I can see how much you and Robert are in love. But I couldn't help noticing how you reacted when he came into the room. Almost as if you'd seen a ghost."

Gemma's face hardened.

"Really, Barbara, you say the most unusual things!" she said with a nervous laugh.

"Do I, Gemma? To be honest, I thought that you looked at him the same way when you first met him. Oh, don't keep me in the dark!"

Gemma and Angelica exchanged a glance in which there was more than the Contessa could read.

Before the Contessa could decide whether she should pursue the topic further, the door of the *salotto* was flung open and a man's voice said, "Here we are, cuz! Fresh off the *Orient Express!*"

"Sebastian! Viola!"

The Contessa hurried over to them. Behind her angular cousins was a woman she didn't recognize. She knew she could never possibly have seen her before because once seen, how could she have ever forgotten her? The woman was not much over four feet tall, with a twisted body and the thickest glasses imaginable.

She peered into the room and said in a high-pitched voice: "There's blood here, a whole scarlet bath of it."

She nodded her head with grim satisfaction and looked directly at Gemma.

"Of course there is," Viola said. "Meet our blood cousin, the Contessa da Capo-Zendrini! And this, Barbara, is Mrs. Molly Wybrow. Sebastian and I have invited her for the house party. We knew you wouldn't mind. By the way, you look marvelous! I'm absolutely not going to tell Mummy. You look so radiant and—and rested! She'd be pea-green with envy!"

7

The Contessa had a fixed smile, as if she were waiting for her photograph to be taken or posing for another portrait. Viola's compliment didn't seem to register. When her lips eventually moved, it wasn't to thank Viola or to greet Molly but to utter the one word: "Thirteen."

Urbino, who had done his own quick computations and come up with the same ominous number, left Robert abruptly and hurried to the Contessa's side. But once he got there all he seemed to be able to do was to look and feel foolish. Sebastian gave him a lopsided grin, and surveyed Urbino quickly from the top of his head down to his shoes, and then up again.

"Come to kill one of us to even out the number? A bit too drastic, even in the service of a great lady like our Barbara. You must be the local celebrity Urbino Macintyre, who has found his way into our cousin's heart! Maybe Viola and I can accommodate you, too!"

The Contessa, slightly dazed, quickly made all the necessary introductions.

"I tell you what, cuz," Sebastian said. "Why don't we just have one of your many staff mingle with us all? Be very democratic and keep off the old evil eye."

The alternatives the Contessa had been considering in the last few moments hadn't included this, but the more logical if no less desperate one of "disinviting" her friends the Borellis or asking a fourteenth guest at the eleventh hour. However, her loyalty and propriety were stronger—at least at the moment—than her superstition. Also, if she had to be so benighted as to believe in portents and signs—which she did with all the fervency of a medieval peasant—she had little wish to appear to.

"Oh, this is ridiculous. Twelve, thirteen, fourteen, what does it matter?" she said, deceiving no one. "We're all thoroughly modern and enlightened."

This wasn't exactly the most accurate thing to say, since the room contained a specialist in relics, a devotee of all things Victorian, and someone who had turned his back on modern, enlightened America and sequestered himself in a Venetian palazzo.

This latter person—who was of course Urbino—was now

introducing himself to Molly. The deformed woman stared at him through her thick glasses and said in a remote voice:

"Unique child. Only child. And an orphan but not at a young age. Fire and sugar. Car crash."

Urbino paled.

"Don't mind her," Viola said with a touch of embarrassment. "She's been running on like one of the sibyls ever since we met her."

"Wrong, dearie! Those Greek ladies saw the future. Remember, the past's my limit!"

"Modesty in a seer! How interesting!" Robert said.

"I'm not a seer, as I believe I've just explained."

"So sorry. I'm also interested in the past. People like us are often misunderstood. I'm Robert Bellini-Rhys. This is my mother, Gemma, and my fiancée, Angelica Lydgate."

"Your grandmother, a lady of lovely eyes and lovely lines, of sweet and liquid voice, died in this palazzo, Mr. Bellini-Rhys. *Your* sweet mother," Molly said, addressing Gemma, who seemed embarrassed and confused.

"I'm pleased to have you join us, Mrs. Wybrow," the Contessa said, shaken by the unpredictability and accuracy of the woman's pronouncements. If there was one thing she feared in a social situation, it was a person inclined to say whatever might come to mind. Here she was face-to-face with a most aggressive specimen in her own *salotto.* And not only that, but it appeared the woman was to be her guest—her thirteenth guest—for the entire weekend.

"Oh, please call me Molly," said the little woman. "Don't take such a fright to me, Contessa—"

"Barbara. I assure you that I'm not afraid of you in the slightest."

"I wouldn't want to scare a hair off your head, dearie. I mean you no harm. I mean no one any harm. It's just that these—these things come over me. If I tried to keep them in, I'm afraid they'd do *me* god-awful harm."

"We wouldn't want that, especially when you're under my roof—or any other, of course."

"Ah, much dark harm has been done under your roof, but not since the day it first covered your head."

"So Barbara leads an exemplary life and all these Italian palazzi have dripped with blood in the past!" Sebastian said. "You aren't telling us anything we don't already know. Isn't Molly delightful? We struck it off immediately on the good old *O.E.* And how could we help it? We didn't have to tell her a thing about our pasts! It got us to the intimate stage long before we finished our first drinks. Speaking of which, I'm as thirsty as the Ancient Mariner!"

"Oh, excuse me!" the Contessa said. "Would you like some tea?"

He eyed the teacup cradled in Angelica's demi-gloved fingers.

"How Elizabeth Barrett Browning! If I were sporting my colored gloves like the Baron de Montesquiou, I just might consider a cup of *thé à la bergamote*—just!—but considering my shabby state, I'll settle for a simple gin."

"That suits me down to the ground, too," Molly said. She seated herself next to Angelica on the sofa. "So, my dear, tell me all about yourself, and then I'll tell you if you're right!"

As Molly burst into peals of laughter amazingly robust for such a small person, the Contessa gave Urbino a quick look that screamed for help.

Half an hour later, everything seemed to be going smoothly. The twins had made brief visits to their rooms, where they had freshened up. Molly, whom the Contessa hadn't assigned a room yet, had refrained from making any more pronouncements, and now sat on the sofa with her gin. She was listening, with many smiles and few words, to Sebastian, who was giving the women his impressions of their circuitous gondola ride from the railway station. On the other side of the room Urbino, at Robert's insistence, had resumed his account of his first murder case involving the relic of Santa Teodora, but was half-listening to Sebastian's account and watching Viola.

"The great laundry room of Venice!" Sebastian was saying. "Everywhere we looked, it was plastered against buildings, strung across streets, and crisscrossing from window to window. It was even draped over wellheads and benches, with a couple of cats squatting on it for clothes pegs—which was a good thing, considering the wind that's kicking up. Really, Gemma, you should take your easel out into the wonderful world of Venice and capture the scene. You could be to laundry what Van Gogh was to chrysanthemums!"

"Sunflowers, you mean," Gemma said.

"He knows very well. One of Sebastian's sly tricks," Viola said with a laugh before sauntering over to Urbino and Robert. She was wearing a dark green wool-velvet dress with long sleeves. Her crisp auburn hair was massed at her temples. Tall and lithe, she had an exotic air and seemed meant to be hung with amulets and to read poems of her own fashioning in overfurnished rooms.

She had done very little since arriving, but, without any effort, she had captured Urbino's imagination, and not least of all because of her striking physical resemblance to her brother.

"And God was back in his place and all was right with the world," she said when Urbino came to the end of his story about Santa Teodora. Her thick eyebrows hovered above eyes that were melancholy and emerald. "That's a literary reference, in case you missed it! You don't know how valuable it is in social situations to have read English at Cambridge."

"Barbara said you did a special project on Rossetti, but she didn't know if it was the brother or the sister," Urbino said.

"Christina, of course! No sister should ever be in her brother's shadow—especially when he's her twin, as in my case."

All three of them looked over at Sebastian, whose thick auburn hair, strong features, and green eyes somehow served to feminize him whereas they had the opposite effect with his sister.

"You're rather Pre-Raphaelite yourself," Urbino said.

"I've been told that." She said it as if she didn't do everything to enhance it, like wearing the kind of dress she had on or the pendant patterned after stained glass around her longish neck. "My tutor found it amusing—and also a little distracting, just as you seem to."

Robert, who had been feeling increasingly left out of the conversation, said, "So your parents named you after the twins in *Twelfth Night*."

"Mummy's doing! She's wild about Shakespeare. Sometimes I think it's condemned us to a life of mistaken identity, role-reversal, and cross-dressing—but maybe also the triumph of true love, who knows?" she said, addressing this last more to Urbino than Robert. "Oh, our twinship is the bane of our existence! That's why I envy you, Urbino. Molly knew what she was talking about with you, didn't she? You *are* an only child. I could tell by your reaction. And your parents were killed in a car crash?"

"A few years before I moved here."

"I seem to remember that Barbara wrote and told Mummy that you inherited your palazzo through your mother. But what's this about fire and sugar?"

"Perhaps he wants to keep it to himself," Robert said, but his blue eyes bore into Urbino as if he would search out the answer if Urbino didn't give it.

"To himself? Molly knows, and she's a complete stranger!" Viola looked at Urbino silently for several moments, with much more gentleness than Robert had. Her strong face turned serious. "Perhaps you're right. I can see that whatever it is, it's very painful even after all these years."

She touched Urbino's hand with her long, narrow fingers and smiled at him sympathetically.

"Molly's comment just took me by surprise," he said. "What happened to my mother and father isn't a secret. They were killed when their car burst into flames after being hit by a sugar-cane truck. It was outside New Orleans."

He had tried to say it matter-of-factly, but he was betrayed when his voice quavered slightly, and he averted his eyes from Viola's to consider the Contessa's Veronese over the fireplace.

"Molly should show more self-control," Viola said and threw an angry glance at the woman. Molly was peering with a smile at the Contessa, who, now that Sebastian had finally finished, was describing how enjoyable her sitting for Gemma had been and how she herself couldn't wait to see the portrait tomorrow evening. "People with Molly's kind of gift, if that's what you call it—curse is more like it!—should keep it to themselves."

"Don't be so hard on the little lady," Robert said. "Remember what she said about the damage it would do to her if she held herself back."

"There's no need to be upset on my behalf," Urbino said. "I appreciate it," he gave Viola a smile, "but the death of my parents isn't something I try to hide. And the story's there for anyone who wants to take the trouble to find out about it."

"Are you saying that you think Molly doesn't have a gift?" Viola asked.

"I believe what Urbino is saying is that someone might have put the bug in the little lady's ear," Robert said. "Maybe—"

"Oh, my God!" Viola interrupted as she looked at the door. "The Zenos and their doctor, I'm sure! What a ghastly crew! Oh, excuse me, Robert, you're related to the Zenos. Great-grandmother and great-aunt, isn't it? I wonder if Molly will have anything to tell us about them!"

Viola, who seemed to have reverted back to her earlier cavalier attitude to Molly and her controversial gift, grabbed Urbino's arm.

"I'm *so* glad you're here this weekend!" she said. "We're going to have a marvelous time. I'm just the kind of person to draw you out! Wait and see. Come on!"

And she led Urbino across the room to the new arrivals.

Signora Marialuisa Zeno had insisted on hiring a gondola from the pension, and had sorely regretted that the Contessa hadn't been at the landing to see them all alight.

The strange trio had been the cynosure of everyone else's eye, however, as they had floated down the Grand Canal to the dark building of their past: Dr. Vasco, gaunt and severe, melancholily contemplating the passing scene from beneath his shaggy gray brows; Signora Zeno, a shrunken doll peeping out from dark garments, her black walking stick gripped in her hand; and Bambina in a beribboned gondolier's hat, sprawled magnificently against the cushions like some superannuated Cleopatra and casting condescending glances at anyone on foot or in lesser craft.

The three of them now silently surveyed the field of the *salotto blu* as if unsure of whether they wanted to venture farther in—that is, until Bambina caught sight of Urbino. She started forward involuntarily, a coy smile on her brightly colored lips, but was restrained by what seemed to be a sharp pinch from her mother. She then took out a small silver flask from her pocket, unscrewed the lid, and liberally applied perfume to her neck, wrists, and inner elbows, all the while staring at Urbino.

The Contessa, the strain revealing itself in her voice and face, introduced them to everyone except, of course, Gemma and Robert. Then she gave them no time to say anything for several minutes as she ran on nervously about their trip up from Rome and how pleased and honored she was to have them here at the Ca' da Capo-Zendrini.

"And once my friends Oriana and Filippo arrive this evening," she finished a bit breathlessly, "everyone will be here so we can get on with all the fun!"

Her comment fell flat despite the enthusiasm of its delivery.

Signora Zeno and Dr. Vasco stared back at her with weary, long-suffering looks. Bambina kept shooting Urbino the kind of glances that would have been overdone in a silent movie.

Signora Zeno installed herself on a sofa with some help from Dr. Vasco.

"You look different, Barbara," she said as she laid her cane across her knees. "What have you done to yourself?"

Considering that she hadn't seen the Contessa for decades, it was a strange comment until Bambina clarified it by saying, "She means compared to your photograph in the *Gazzettino.* And she's right, Barbara. Maybe it's the company you keep."

Viola assessed Bambina with an amused grin as she squirmed and kept smiling in Urbino's direction.

"You seem to have an admirer. Other than me, I mean."

Gemma seated herself next to her grandmother and managed to find one of the old woman's hands up in her sleeve. She held it and said in Italian:

"It's so nice to see you, Nonna. It's been a long time."

Her grandmother—in fact, her aunt Bambina and Dr. Vasco also—were fairly fluent in English, but it was only natural to speak Italian with her grandmother even though Gemma felt more comfortable in English. The only persons in the room with a slight disadvantage of language were Angelica, whose Italian was still at the textbook stage, and Molly, whose command was more spirited than correct.

"You don't look well," the old woman said with the candor that often accompanies the elderly.

Dr. Vasco nodded his head grimly and said with a worried frown, "Your color is very poor, my dear."

"It's all this dampness!" Signora Zeno proclaimed. She looked around the room as if searching out damp spots, mildew, and mold among all the bibelots. Her lively eye became arrested by the Veronese. It showed a stout, golden-haired, barebacked Venus dividing her attention between two handsome bearded swains beneath a lush tree.

"That's new," she said with a touch of contempt, pointing to the painting with her black cane.

"Only about four hundred years new! It's a Veronese!" Sebastian said.

"Don't be impertinent, young man," she responded in thickly accented English. "I'm well aware of the age of this painting, and the real name of the painter is Paolo Caliari! What I meant was that it's new since I was here last."

Her voice had a tendency to fade out slightly at points, yet it had a command in it. It almost made her weakness seem less a disability than a form of restraint.

"And when was that?" Sebastian asked.

"The month of May in the year of Our Lord 1938."

The response was made by none other than Molly. Every pair of eyes turned to her.

"Molly claims to know the past," Gemma said.

"Claims to know!" Molly said. "You tell me, Signora Zeno, was it May 1938, or wasn't it? And was there a gala here then, or not?"

Various degrees of shock and surprise showed on everyone's faces. Dr. Vasco stared at Molly with cold fury.

"About the Veronese," the Contessa said quickly. "It was a wedding gift to me from Alvise. That's why it's—it's new to you, Marialuisa."

If the Contessa had thought she was smoothing things over she couldn't have been more wrong, for this reference to her marriage and her husband, Alvise, was just the sort of thing to irk Signora Zeno and Bambina. They had hoped, actually even expected, Alvise to marry Bambina herself, his distant cousin, who was much closer to him in age than the Contessa. For a brief moment hatred seemed to gleam in the eyes of mother and daughter.

"More than a little strange for a wedding gift," Signora Zeno said. "A practically naked woman between two men." She added something indistinguishable because of the fading out of her voice, then: "I wonder what Alvise was thinking of? But then, he did have his lapses of judgment."

The Contessa colored. No one said anything for a few moments until Angelica got up.

"It's a bit warm in here, don't you think?" she said to no one in particular.

"Oh, God, here comes the swoon," Sebastian said.

Angelica seemed not to have heard him but Robert had. An effort at control was clearly visible along his jaw line.

"Do you mind if we go out on the loggia for a breath of air, Robert? I'll fetch my shawl."

When she had left, Molly said to Robert, "Your sweet fiancée is afraid I'm going to say something about her, but she's poor in vibrations. Won't you please tell her?"

"She should be very glad to hear it. Excuse me."

As he went out into the hall, he glared at Sebastian.

"I hear you have a lovely palazzo near the Pantheon," Urbino said to Signora Zeno, thinking he would make his contribution to keep the conversation going smoothly. "I met a man last year living in one of the apartments."

Signora Zeno seemed to subside farther into her garments. It was understood among her friends and family that no one would mention that the Zenos had been reduced to carving up their palazzo into flats and living in a few rooms on the third story.

"Well, I hope he wasn't the one who drove us here yesterday. A terrible driver."

"Today. We came today, Mamma, remember?" Bambina said. She smiled at Urbino and shook her curly head in patient understanding of the old and feeble.

Signora Zeno, infuriated that she had no choice but to come off as either deceptive or senile, said sharply, "You're not very far behind me, Bambina, and don't you forget it. I had you when I was barely a child."

"Oh, Mamma, you do say the silliest things."

Urbino, having failed with Signora Zeno, turned to Dr. Vasco, who had seated himself in a Brustolon armchair.

"I understand that you know London."

"I've spent some time there—before and after the war," he said in English in a thick accent. "Not recently, however."

From Sebastian's corner floated the comment, "I wonder which war he means?"

Either Dr. Vasco didn't hear him or chose to ignore the comment.

"You loved a beautiful woman who came to the end of her days in this house," Molly said without any preamble, as was her way.

Signora Zeno's wrinkled face tightened and diminished even more. Bambina gasped.

"Do not talk about something you do not know about!" Dr. Vasco said, his grim face having turned grimmer.

"Oh, but I do! I can't help it." She turned to Bambina. "Your little pussy died. Dido, Queen of Carthage, was her name. She suffered a lot, but not flames, no, no, not flames like her namesake of long, long ago."

Bambina sat down on the nearest chair. She put a chubby hand in front of her face.

"Dr. Vasco is right! You don't know what you're talking about!" she screamed at Molly.

Molly tossed the rest of her gin down and held her glass out to Urbino.

"To the top, dearie." Then, peering at the Contessa through her thick spectacles, she added in a more refined tone: "It's such a pleasure to have the distinct honor of drinking such topflight gin in the presence of such a gracious lady."

The Contessa gave her the further honor of a smile and a slight bow of her head.

"I never thought Molly would be this much fun," Viola said to Urbino, apparently having forgotten how upset she had been on his behalf earlier. Urbino said something noncommittal and went to fix Molly another drink.

"Really, Molly," Sebastian said, "you should be more careful. You could get hit over the head with an andiron or stabbed with a letter opener. Then how would Viola and I feel for having brought you here?"

"You're the one who should watch your words!" Gemma said with a strange vehemence. She went over to Molly's side. "Don't listen to such rubbish!"

"Believe me, dearie, after all these years I'm as impervious as my mackintosh! And from the sound of it, it seems as if I'll be needing it."

She cocked her little head toward the window. They all listened. She was right. The rain was beating forcefully against the pane from the direction that boded the least good for the city.

10

The group in the *salotto* was about to retire to their rooms until dinner when Sebastian reminded the Contessa of something she had forgotten about in all the commotion.

"I hope you don't think Molly is going to squeeze in with me or Viola, small though she is, Barbara. Where's the room she can call her own for the weekend?"

The Contessa took a quick breath of utter astonishment, as if he had just asked the most embarrassing of questions. This was followed by a look of fear. She didn't answer for so long that everyone stared at her, increasing her discomfort.

"Don't tell me we're going to have to board her out?" Viola said with a nervous laugh. "Surely there's another room free?"

"Of course there is! Molly, why don't you go to the conservatory until we make the arrangements. It's at the far end of the hall. It's especially delightful when it rains, and there are some lovely plants and flowers."

"There always used to be lovely ones in the old days," Signora Zeno said. "But you've probably ripped them out."

The conservatory was a source of pride to the Contessa. She spent many hours there and occasionally entertained the local botanical society among its blooms and fronds. Far from having ripped anything out or changed the conservatory it was much the way it had been in the past—not just many of the plants themselves, but also the furniture and accoutrements, even down to the tins of rose spray made up from an old nicotine formula from the thirties by a retired pharmacist in the Dorsoduro quarter.

"Not at all, Marialuisa," the Contessa said, trying to control her irritation. "Most of the plants there go back a very long way. What's the point of having a conservatory if you don't—don't conserve the best plants of the past?"

Signora Zeno didn't allow this to mollify her. As she moved slowly toward the door with the help of her cane, she said, "I would like to see what you consider the 'best' plants from the past! I remember the conservatory very well."

She said something more, many of the words of which faded away, but enough was audible to indicate that she and Bambina intended to show Molly the way to the conservatory.

Molly got up, gripping her glass of gin, and was shepherded out of the *salotto* by Signora Zeno—two small forms, one shrunken, the other stunted. Behind them, considerably rounder but on much tinier feet, came Bambina, who managed to cast several final glances back at Urbino before the door closed behind her.

Dr. Vasco didn't seem to know what to do with himself. He got up from the armchair and walked to the opposite side of the room to the window. He spent a few moments looking out, then devoted his attention to the labels on some of the bottles in the liquor cabinet. Giving this up, he strode toward the door, excused himself, and left.

Only the Contessa, Urbino, Gemma, and the twins—posed for maximum effect against a collection of medieval tapestry altar cloths—remained.

"You're thinking of putting Molly in the Caravaggio Room, aren't you?" Gemma said. "It's the only unoccupied bedroom."

"Then you understand my dilemma."

"After all these years, you'll have Molly stay there?"

"Barbara has been ruled by superstition and a casual promise made to Alvise," Urbino said, coming to the Contessa's defense. "I've been trying to make her see the sense of using the room. It's ready to be used now, isn't it, Barbara?"

"More or less," the Contessa said without enthusiasm. "It's been ready for a year. I just haven't had the—the occasion to use it."

"What are you all going on about?" Sebastian asked. "Did Caravaggio sleep in one of the rooms here? Why didn't I ever hear of it? Did you, Viola?"

"No. What is the Caravaggio Room, Urbino?"

"One of the bedrooms on the second floor. It has a Caravaggio painting."

"I say! That's interesting!" Sebastian said. "He's more to my taste than Veronese."

He cast a dismissive look at the painting over the fireplace.

"This is the worst time to open up the room!" Gemma said. "It's bad enough that Robert is next door to it. I don't want to be unreasonable! But the room itself? It was my mother, don't forget! And—and Molly is so impressionable!"

"There's no point in our even discussing it. There's nowhere else to put her! There's more staff than usual for the weekend and they're already doubled up in their quarters. You're not suggesting that I move your grandmother or Bambina! Or even Dr. Vasco."

"What about Oriana and Filippo?"

"Oriana? She'd never spend a night in there. She pretends not to be superstitious, but I've seen her go hysterical if she spills olive oil, and God forbid you should put shoes on the bed!"

"Urbino, then," Gemma persisted.

Throughout the exchange between the two women, Sebastian and Viola had been looking more and more puzzled. Viola came over to Urbino.

"What *is* going on?" she whispered. "If you don't tell me, I'll go mad!"

But he ignored her and said, "She's right, Barbara. I can switch my room."

"Never! You might not be family, but you're too close to it. You never know how these—these curses work out, all in tricks and deceptions. Oh, listen to me! You would think that I was superstitious myself!"

"I hope you don't think it's superstition in my case, Barbara." Gemma's haggard face looked frightened, however. "It's just that I don't think it would be—be proper for Molly to stay in the room. You saw how she was picking up vibrations or auras or whatever she calls them. She was right about Urbino and about what she said to me and Robert, remember. Putting Molly in that room would be the wrong thing to do. Have her stay with me!"

The Contessa pulled the cord to summon Lucia.

"Molly will stay in the Caravaggio Room!" she said obstinately. "I don't want anything to spoil this weekend, Gemma. I thought that if we all spent a civilized weekend here, we might be able to conduct the rest of our lives together with more good sense. Bad blood doesn't have to stay bad! If we make too much of a fuss about this room—if we put too much emphasis on Molly, who, after all, wasn't invited by me or anyone on your side"—she looked sharply at the twins—"why, then, we're just fools looking for pain and grief. And I assure you, my dear, I am nobody's fool."

When Lucia entered the room a few moments later, the Contessa continued to show how determined she was by asking that the Caravaggio Room be made ready immediately.

"Yes, Lucia, the Caravaggio Room! Will you please see to it? Oh, the key. Very well, then. Let's go together."

The Contessa went out with Lucia, much with the manner of someone escaping to less odious duties—even if they might be the turning of a mattress or the beating of a rug—than those she would find if she stayed behind in the *salotto.*

Gemma, her face set and ashen, quit the room a few moments later without a glance at its three remaining occupants.

Urbino looked at the twins and said, "Of course I understand. You want to know—"

"I *need* to know," Viola corrected. "The Caravaggio Room is close to mine."

"How do you know that?"

A flush came into her face.

"Despite your and Barbara's attempts to mystify Sebastian and me, it wasn't difficult to figure out. A locked room. The room diagonally across from mine next to Robert's is locked. Every other bedroom is occupied. Ergo—or should I say *demonstratum est?*—it's the Caravaggio Room."

"And how did you know it was locked?"

"Because I tried the knob. I wanted to see what everyone else's accommodations were like. The door to that room was the only one locked."

"Curiosity killed the cat!" Sebastian said. "Maybe that's what happened to Bambina's pussy."

He burst into laughter, which earned him a withering look from his sister.

"Men are so adolescent! Don't you ever grow up?"

She directed this rhetorical question not at her brother but Urbino. Urbino gave Sebastian a quick smile before answering.

"Proust said men don't develop emotionally after the age of sixteen."

"Well, there you are then!" Viola said, a spark of pique in her eyes.

Sebastian, with a self-satisfied expression on his good-looking face, brought things back to the matter at hand: "I think it's pretty rum of Barbara never telling us she had a haunted room in this place."

"It isn't haunted." Urbino quickly added: "There's no such thing as haunted rooms or houses."

"Yes, Daddy, and now would you look under the bed? But, seriously, tell me this: Why is Gemma so bent out of shape about the room and so afraid of Molly staying in it, and why won't this Oriana woman sleep in it? Though *you* said you would."

"And Gemma didn't make any objection to your staying in it the way she did about Molly," Viola pointed out. "Strange."

"Maybe it wouldn't be quite so strange if Urbino finally filled us in on this room's dark history."

"Would you like some drinks?"

"So it's going to be one of *those* kinds of stories!" Sebastian said. "All right, then. I'll take Molly's kind of poison, and if I know Viola, she'll have a glass of very dry sherry."

When they were seated with their drinks, Urbino read them the story of the Caravaggio Room. He had gone over it so many times before in his own mind and with the Contessa and their closest friends that he had memorized it like some bard of old.

It was a disturbing tale and most of the actors in it were gathered together at the Ca' da Capo-Zendrini on this stormy night.

PART TWO

The Caravaggio Room

1

The Contessa had been married only a week and was already in tears. If she had known that they would be among the few tears she would shed in her marriage because of the Conte, they might have been far less bitter. At the time, however, they seemed a catastrophe.

It had all happened because she had been too eager to play the chatelaine. She had gone through the Ca' da Capo-Zendrini from the *pianoterreno* with its water entrance and lumber rooms to the wooden *altana*, or terrace, perched on the roof. The building was in need of repair, severely damaged as it was by the recent war and industrial pollution from the mainland. It had only been in the family for the past seventy years, the Da Capo-Zendrini family having moved from a smaller palazzo in the San Polo quarter.

She was confronted by that most intriguing and disquieting of situations. At the far end of one of the two wings devoted to the bedrooms was a locked room, the only one in the palazzo. It was on the side where the broad loggia overlooked the Grand Canal. When she went out onto the loggia and examined the louvered doors of this particular bedroom, she found that they too were locked.

"You will have to ask the Conte for the key," the housekeeper said when the Contessa had asked her about the locked room. "I don't have it."

"What's in the room, Vittoria?"

"It's just another bedroom, Contessa." She paused, then went on nervously: "It hasn't been used in twenty years. Excuse me. I must see to something."

That evening the Conte refused to answer anything about the room and forbade Barbara to ask him or other members of the family any more questions.

"And don't ask the staff either. If I learn that you have, I'll be very upset. It might lead to my giving them immediate notice. The room is no concern of yours!" When he saw the tears in her eyes, he added more softly: "My father made me promise on his deathbed to keep it locked as long as I live and to exact the same promise of my children. All you need to know is that it's not a happy room. Someday it will all be explained."

"But what do you mean by an 'unhappy' room, Alvise?" Predictably, the story of Bluebeard and his wife had flashed through her mind. "You frighten me."

"That is exactly what I do not want to do, my dear. It is for your own good to forget the room exists. It cannot harm you if you do."

The Contessa, whose understanding of psychology was more advanced than her husband's, was well aware of the harm that can be done when we try to bury our fears or unhappinesses. But she sensed that her husband, reasonable so far in all his behavior and expectations, would brook no opposition on the locked room. She never broached the topic again, telling herself that it was just another idiosyncrasy of the Italian family she had married into. As the years of their marriage went by, she didn't so much forget the room as accommodate herself to living with yet one more mystery and to meeting one more obligation.

When her husband died almost twenty years ago, the Contessa found a large, thick envelope among his private papers. Written on it in his hand in Italian was:

For my beloved wife, Barbara
To be opened after my death

With fear and curiosity, the same emotions that she associated with the locked room, she opened the envelope. Inside were many sheets of paper. The top sheet bore the cramped handwriting that had become the Conte's near the end of his life.

My dear Barbara,

I hope I have not caused you much sorrow in our life together, for you have been the light of my life, my beloved English rose, as I call you. But I know that there was one time, when our marriage was very young, when I did, and I fear it has been a continuing sorrow. I hope you have forgiven me long before this. If you haven't, perhaps you will be able to do it once you've read this.

It's about the locked room on the second floor. It's been called the Caravaggio Room since the nineteen twenties when I was just a boy. I told you that I promised my father never to open it in my lifetime. I would have exacted the same promise from the son or daughter we never had, who would have inherited the Ca' da Capo-Zendrini.

I should have spoken about it to you long ago but the happiness of our life together made it more difficult to recount its sad history. I felt that its blight would fall on our marriage.

It's for you to decide what to do, now that I am gone and after you have read the following pages. Whatever you do, however, never sleep in the Caravaggio Room or have any blood relative of the family do so—or anyone you truly care about.

I love you with all my heart and will be with you forever.

The Contessa laid aside this page and began to read the others.

I am writing this in my forty-fifth year upon the occasion of my marriage. It is a time to take the measure of the past and to look forward to the long future I hope to share with my beloved wife. I hope and pray that our future will be blessed with at least one child and that this child will, in the course of events, inherit the Ca' da Capo-Zendrini. It is to this child that I address these lines, which explain in as full a fashion as I can remember them certain events of extreme importance to our family. I cannot trust that I will not be taken away suddenly by the will of God, or that my memory will not fail me.

There is a room on the second floor of the palazzo which has come to be called the Caravaggio Room. It has been locked since May of 1938, nearly twenty years ago, a day I remember very well.

Less well remembered, since I was only a boy of nine at the time, was the discovery made by my father, the Conte Amerigo, may God rest his soul, that eventuated in the designation "the Caravaggio Room."

One winter—the year was 1922—my father made an unusual discovery in one of the rooms of the Ca' da Capo-Zendrini. The family had moved to this palazzo on the Grand Canal thirty years earlier. The previous owner, a man sadly without any heirs or immediate family, in my estimation a form of living death, fell seriously ill and was eager to make a sale to move to a warmer climate. My grandfather was in a position to meet this ailing man's rather outlandish financial expectations. The building in the San Polo quarter was sold and the family moved to the "new" Ca' da Capo-Zendrini. Our family finally had what they had wanted for centuries: a splendid palazzo, this one designed by Cominelli, on the Canalazzo.

Following the death of my grandfather, my father was taking stock of the palazzo from top to bottom. He was rummaging through one of the lumber rooms on the *pian-oterreno.* He said that he had a premonition when he found a bundle wrapped in canvas in a trunk large enough to contain the body of a man.

When he unwrapped it, he found a painting of sixty-six by fifty centimeters. It was dark with age, and mold had invaded one whole lower corner. It was a portrait of a round-faced youth holding a mandolin, and with lipstick, rouge, and a white flower in thick auburn hair that resembled a wig. At first my father assumed, with good reason, that it was a young woman. On closer examination, however, he determined that it must indeed be a young man, strange though he looked with his makeup and in a green robe that slipped provocatively off one shoulder. This young man stared at my father with a mocking kind of smile.

For no other reason than that my father played the mandolin, he immediately liked the painting. Nothing identified either the name of the painting or its painter.

The next day my father took the painting to one of the good Armenian monks on the island of San Lazzaro in the lagoon. The monk was a man who loved art and who was a master at cleaning paintings. When he saw the painting, he blessed himself. "By our Blessed Mother," he said, "this is either a Caravaggio or a devilish imitation. It could be very valuable." The name of this painter meant nothing to my father, whose knowledge of art was limited to the great Leonardo and Michelangelo and the obscure painters of the portraits of the Da Capo-Zendrini family that hung in our portrait gallery. Neither did he care for its possible value. He wanted to hang it in the Ca' da Capo-Zendrini.

In due course the painting was cleaned by the monk. Then through his contacts in Florence and Rome, it was authenticated as a Caravaggio. Many impressive offers to buy it were made but my father refused them all without a thought and did as he had originally intended. The painting was installed in one of the bedrooms on the second floor.

I remember the excitement in the house. Family and friends came to look at the famous picture of the mandolin player in his makeup and wig. One old man said that it would have been more appropriate if it had been hung in our former palazzo in San Polo, since this building was near the Bridge of Teats. There, during the days when the city was a Sodom of the sea, courtesans often dressed as boys in doublet and hose to attract Venetian men into their rooms when they had no success exposing their breasts.

My brother Amerigo and I were the first to sleep in the room. We sneaked in late that night after the party was over and had our own fun. To say we slept, though, is not exactly true. We spent most of the night laughing and making up stories about the boy in the painting, and during some friendly fisticuffs broke a Chinese vase. Perhaps one of the maids noticed next morning that the coverlet had been disturbed, but no one ever said anything to us, and because we had broken the vase, we kept our silence.

When Amerigo died three years later of a disease of the kidneys that made his body swell, I looked at his bloated face in the coffin and thought of the boy in the painting. The mortician had even put a faint coating of rouge and lipstick on his face. I have often wondered if my father noticed the faint similarity in his profound grief over having lost his eldest son.

Perhaps I was the only one to make an association between my brother's death and the painting in what had by then come to be known as the Caravaggio Room. Certainly it was a childish fancy.

The room was put into occasional service and no one complained of anything more serious than a night of tossing and turning.

Then, two years later, Nonna Teresa, my father's mother, slept there. Her regular room needed to be repaired because of water damage.

Her maid, Giuseppina, found her dead in bed the next morning. The doctor said her heart, which had troubled her for the previous twenty years, had given out during the night and that she had died peacefully in her sleep.

Just because Nonna Teresa had died in the room was no reason not to use it again, of course. Death in those days almost always took place at home. Families couldn't become overly sentimental about the rooms where their loved ones breathed their last breaths. With rare exceptions they were put into use as soon afterward as was decent, given the demands of mourning.

A year after Nonna Teresa's death, my cousin Flora slept in the room. She chose it herself, precisely because of the Caravaggio, which she had heard so much about.

Flora was a beautiful girl of fifteen, a year younger than I was at the time. She was my father's grandniece, thus my second cousin, as such things are calculated. An only child just as I had become since the death of Amerigo, Flora lived with her parents in Naples. She would visit us for several weeks most summers, when her parents were obliged to make a circuit of the spas with an aged, wealthy relative. Flora was an asthmatic, and Venice, though subject to its own *malaria*, was within occasional reach of the cool breezes from the Dolomites.

Whenever Flora visited, my mother, who loved her like the daughter she hadn't been blessed with, would take her to her friend Don Mariano Fortuny's studio. There Flora would select whatever patterned fabric caught her eye while I wandered through the rooms and marveled at all the paintings of nymphs. On Flora's last visit she selected, after her usual pleasurable indecision, a lovely *pezza* of green silk velvet which reminded her of the robe of the boy in the Caravaggio painting.

That afternoon Flora and I spent in the conservatory of the Ca' da Capo-Zendrini. With its jungle of plants, smell of damp soil and fungus, and humidity, it wasn't the best place for someone with her affliction. But Flora, although she loved my city, was nostalgic for her own Naples, and she felt a kinship with the profusion of plants. I often thought that her name had created some mysterious link between herself and the blossoming world.

She would insist on inhaling the fragrance of the flowers and even take it upon herself to spray the roses, her favorite flower, with the special concoction kept on a shelf. My father had warned everyone in the house about this spray, made up by a young pharmacist in the Dorsoduro quarter, for it contained a deadly poison. Whenever one of the staff or my mother picked up the can, they wore gloves and covered their mouth. But Flora was fearless and deaf to my warnings. Perhaps her name gave her not only an affinity for the conservatory but also led her to believe that she had some special immunity to its dangers.

On that afternoon Flora and I read passages from books aloud to each other and played cards. My mother had gone to pay a visit to a friend in the Castello quarter. When she returned to find us in the conservatory and learned that we had been there for the whole of the afternoon, she berated me for encouraging Flora in such foolhardy behavior. Flora, after telling my mother that she shouldn't blame me for what had been her decision, retired to her room.

When the dinner bell sounded, Flora didn't appear. We waited for a few minutes, then my mother asked me to fetch her. Obviously the poor girl had tired herself out in the conservatory—this with a sharp look at me—and had fallen into a deep sleep.

I knocked on the door of the Caravaggio Room. When there was no answer, I knocked again and called for her, but still with no response. I opened the door slowly.

The room was dark. Flora or one of the maids had drawn the drapes so that whatever light was still available outside didn't penetrate the room.

I switched on the light. My eyes immediately went to the painting, which dominated the room more than anything else in it. The mocking smile of the boy in wig and makeup flashed at me. For a moment it seemed as if he was alive. I shivered. Then I saw Flora.

She was lying at the foot of the bed, grasping the piece of Fortuny material. I went over to her.

"Flora?" I whispered. She didn't respond. I looked down at her and knew that she never would again.

Her eyes stared up at me. Her mouth was open. Her lips were blue.

I remember very little after this. My mother and father came up. I was sent to my room. I sat there, stunned, unable to cry. Flora was dead.

Dead, the doctor said, because of an attack precipitated by her hours in the conservatory, smelling the flowers, breathing the oppressive air, and spraying the roses. But I didn't believe him. It wasn't that I didn't want to admit some responsibility for her death for not having discouraged her from staying in the conservatory.

No, Flora had died because of the Caravaggio painting. The smile of the strange-looking boy had told me that.

Soon what was only the fancy of a boy saying good-bye to his childhood became the talk of the family, and then of friends and neighbors, as they remembered the death of Nonna Teresa in the same room. The Caravaggio Room was "bad luck." It had the "evil eye." There was a "curse" on it. And it was all because of the painting of the young man, which was baleful in some way that couldn't be explained by reason.

I kept my own counsel, but had many nightmares. Some of them were of my brother Amerigo with the face of the boy with makeup.

Almost ten years passed. No one had forgotten what had happened in the Caravaggio Room. No—but the mind and the heart can become dulled and deadened with time. Even the face of a departed loved one dims over the years and the memory needs to be refreshed by looking at a photograph. This was the situation with my mother and most of our family and friends, but not with me and not, as I eventually came to realize, with my father.

My own uneasiness about the Caravaggio Room remained as keen as ever. There was not a time I passed its door—not locked, but always closed—that I did not think of Nonna

Teresa, Flora, and my brother. I could feel the boy smiling at me behind the door.

My father's response was different, as befitted a man of his mature years and unusual sensibility. He was troubled as much—if not more—by his fear, and what it meant to him as a religious man, as he was by the room itself. In his youth there had been some expectation that he would enter a monastery. He was always a model of saintly, though never overly pious or self-righteous, behavior.

God, he had been taught, did not manifest His love or justice in heathenish fashion. Nor should a believer put any faith in the power of objects, except those blessed by Mother Church, like the miraculous body of Santa Lucia near the Ca' da Capo-Zendrini or the icon of the Virgin and Child at the Salute. In other words, my father's faith was at war with his cold fear of the room in which his mother and his grandniece had died.

He consulted a friend who was a priest attached to the Congregation for the Causes of the Saints at the Vatican. This priest examined the room several months after Flora's death, said some prayers, burned incense, and assured my father that he need have no fear of the room.

Despite the priest's visit and my father's fervent attempt to follow the revealed truths of the Church, the Caravaggio Room remained in limbo for almost ten years. It was cleaned seasonally and used for storage, but no one ever slept there again until May of 1938.

My mother's way of dealing with difficulties was often to pretend they didn't exist. With the world around us so confused and becoming more so, thanks to Hitler and our own Mussolini, my mother decided to forget all troubles and have a big gala at the Ca' da Capo.

My father was less than enthusiastic. He feared that my mother was inviting so many guests that the Caravaggio Room would probably have to be used.

"What are you afraid of, Amerigo?" my mother said. "Father Olivieri blessed the room years ago, not that such a thing was necessary. It's ignorant superstition, and this is 1938. We're all modern and informed—*and* we trust in God."

My father could disagree with neither the advanced date nor with what were surely my mother's far from artless comments on God and superstition. He said no more about the upcoming gala, although I detected in him an increasing uneasiness as the day drew near.

I was twenty-five and had finished my studies at Bologna with no great success and no prospects for the future. Everything seemed bleak around me—my immediate world and the larger world outside.

There were two guests coming to my mother's gala who, I hoped, would be able to lift my spirits. One was Luigi Vasco, a chum from my days at Bologna. He was a few years older and had successfully completed his medical studies. The other was my third cousin on my father's side, the beautiful Renata Bellini, a widow of only twenty-five. Despite all the warnings of my mother, I was hopelessly in love with her. It made no difference to me that she had an eight-year-old daughter and a questionable reputation since the death of her husband—along with her father, Signor Zeno—two years before in a boating accident.

My mother's patience with Renata, whom she wouldn't have found sympathetic even if I hadn't been interested in her, was tried from the first half-hour of her arrival.

"But Gemma can't possibly stay in the same room, Bianca. She's becoming such a big girl, aren't you, my love?"

Gemma, a sweet-faced girl with chestnut hair, nodded her head. Cradled in her arms was a doll. Perhaps it was because I had always wanted a little sister to love and protect or because she reminded me of Flora. Whatever it was, I felt an immediate bond with the little girl, whom I had never seen before. She looked at me directly with her large brown eyes and smiled, then whispered something to her doll.

"As you wish, Renata, but we are a little short of rooms . . . " My mother trailed off and cast a nervous glance at my father, who was talking to Luigi, the doctor, and Renata's mother, Marialuisa Zeno.

"Short of rooms? You make the Ca' da Capo sound like a *pensione*. Ah, but I understand! You're not still locking up that room where Cousin Flora died! Gemma and I needn't suffer because of some medieval superstition!"

My mother was silent for a few moments and gave the appearance of considering the possibilities.

"Very well, Renata. I'm sure we can make arrangements to accommodate your sweet girl."

What transpired because of Renata's insistence on a private bedroom was that Gemma was given the room that had been set aside for them both, and Renata was installed in the Caravaggio Room. What my father had feared had happened. The Caravaggio Room was going to be used after almost ten years.

As soon as Luigi and I were alone an hour later, he made it clear why Renata didn't want Gemma in the same room. He was a close friend of the Zenos and claimed to know everything about them.

"She wants to entertain the Englishman," he said. "She wouldn't care if she had to sleep in a closet as long as it's private and she can be with *him*."

He indicated an attractive man in his thirties who had arrived in the company of Signora Zeno, her younger daughter, Bambina, and Renata and Gemma. He had met the Zenos through an English friend married to a Roman, who had been tutoring the family in English for the past several years. I had exchanged only a few words with him earlier and had summed up Andrew Lydgate as one of those Englishmen with an abundance of money and leisure time and a deep love for all things Italian. That this deep love might extend to Renata had not occurred to me until Luigi made his comment.

I don't know if I was more surprised at what Luigi said or the way he said it. He sounded bitter and disappointed. He went on to explain that Signora Zeno was determined to secure Lydgate as Renata's husband.

"Even a woman as beautiful as Renata has her liabilities," he said.

"The child?"

"Yes, and she has almost no money. You know Bellini squandered what little he had."

I observed that surely many men other than Lydgate would be very happy to take on the responsibility of Renata and her daughter. My comment had the effect I intended. Luigi could now be in no doubt that I shared his admiration for the beautiful Renata. He became all scowls and glowers, not all of them directed against me, by any means, but mainly against Lydgate. And when Luigi scowled and glowered, he did it like no man I had ever met before or have since.

Before dinner that night I pointed out to him that rather than being at odds because of our admiration for Renata, we should feel a brotherly kinship, all the more so since neither of us seemed to stand any chance because of Lydgate.

"This isn't a game for me, my friend," he said. "I don't intend to be made a fool of."

What he meant by this I don't know, other than that Renata might have given him reason to hope. If she had, it would have been against the wishes and advice of her mother, who, despite her regard for Luigi, would not want a husband for her daughter who had little more than his medical degree and a good heart to recommend him.

Then Luigi said a strange thing.

"Tonight during dinner Lydgate will spill wine all over the front of his shirt."

I started to laugh, but caught myself when I saw Luigi's stern look. I remembered then that he had an interest in hypnotism and the power of suggestion, and had often entertained me with stories of how by the power of his own silent will, he could occasionally affect a response in people's behavior. To me it was all nonsense and coincidence.

It didn't occur to me that I was being inconsistent, considering my own superstition about the Caravaggio Room.

We were a relatively small group for dinner—just my parents and myself, Luigi, Signora Zeno, Renata, Bambina, Lydgate, and half a dozen assorted cousins and friends. Little Gemma was in the kitchen with the staff. A storm had swept in on us from the sea, and the rain was beating against the windows of the dining room. It seemed to make us enjoy the comforts of our table even more.

I had Lydgate on my right and Bambina on my left. Bambina wasn't her Christian name, of course. She had been baptized Cesarina, but had always been called Bambina by friends and family. What started as an endearment soon became her name, and as inextricable a part of her as her round little body and sharp mind.

As sometimes happens in siblings, Bambina and Renata were as different as different could be. Bambina was rosy-cheeked and plump, with dark Medusa locks that she tossed in her enthusiasms—and there was a considerable amount of tossing because she was full of enthusiasms. Ten years later, when I was still unmarried, she turned some of these enthusiasms toward me, but without any result. Perhaps she will still find a suitable husband.

At my mother's gala, her enthusiasms were all for Lydgate, however. Placed as I was between them, her clever comments either flew past me to their intended target or artfully rebounded from me to him. I enjoyed her display, for she was intelligent, with a knowledge of history and art. She also had some talent as an artist and had kindly made my mother a hostess gift of a charming sketch of our cat, Principessa. She insisted that Mother have it fetched so she could show it round.

"Absolutely beautiful," Lydgate said. "Look at those eyes. You can almost hear her purr, can't you?"

But as he spoke, he wasn't looking at the sketch in his hands but across it at Renata. She returned his look with a smile.

Bambina suddenly hurled herself into an extended account of the life of Petrarch, who, it seems, was also a cat lover, and was about to recite one of that poet's sonnets to his beloved Laura.

Renata, however, interrupted her, not very graciously. She said that her sister's head was full of silly thoughts. She indicated the sketch of the cat and with a cruel smile said that it was good that Bambina had made a sketch of her beloved Dido, since she had lost the cat itself.

"So unlucky in things you love, Bambina dear," she said and then smiled at Lydgate.

Tears came into Bambina's eyes. She grabbed her sketch from Lydgate and excused herself. She didn't come back for the rest of the meal. Renata's behavior had revealed a cruel streak that a lover should take note of. I certainly was fast revising my original opinion of Renata, which, like so many strong emotions of its nature, was based on limited contact. But Lydgate appeared as infatuated as ever, and joined in Renata's laughter.

Luigi stared morosely at Renata. She seemed annoyed and said, "If you wear a face like that with your patients, Luigi, you're going to scare them to death, not cure them."

It was to Lydgate's credit that he didn't laugh this time, although the ghost of a smile twitched at the edges of his mouth. A few moments later, when he was raising his glass of my father's finest merlot, his hand slipped and the ruby-red liquid stained his starched white shirtfront.

Luigi neither looked in my direction nor said anything, but it was clear that he believed he himself had been the indirect agent of Lydgate's accident.

My mother had been growing more uncomfortable. To smooth things over, she started to tell a story from her childhood in Naples. It was about a tribe of gypsies and their stealing of a beautiful little boy—one of a set of twins—from a neighboring family. I had heard the story many times, and so had my father, who had become increasingly less patient with it over the years.

After my mother's recital, one of our cousins from Milan matched it with a tale that somehow also managed to involve both gypsies and twins. From then on the pattern was set for the rest of the evening as many of the guests recounted stories, which soon began to take on a distinctly ribald flavor when we passed from the dining room to the salon overlooking the Grand Canal.

I couldn't help but be reminded of Boccaccio's ladies and gentlemen killing time in the countryside while the plague ravages Florence.

Half an hour after we retired to the salon, Bambina, looking even more lively after what must have been a good cry, returned. Renata was finishing a story about a sailor and a mermaid, which despite its risqué elements, she had delivered in a listless way. In fact, as the story had progressed she seemed to lose more and more energy and become paler and paler. No sooner did the thought occur to me that Luigi might have had some mesmeric influence over her than I quickly banished it as ridiculous.

When Renata finished, Lydgate indulged in a story of even more dubious taste about a coal miner from the north of England and his two daughters.

After I had acquitted myself by telling an innocuous anecdote about the rivalry between Giorgione and Titian, Bambina, who was becoming increasingly restless, made her contribution.

It was about the peacock brooch of gold and precious stones my mother was wearing. Most of us knew the story. It was part of the history of both the Da Capo-Zendrini and Zeno families, but Bambina told it as if to an audience hearing it for the first time. She made the most of its mystery and high adventure—the Turkish assault on old Constantinople, Venetian merchant ships sailing defiantly through the Bosphorus beneath the cannons of the Turks, near escapes from barbarous forms of death, and the rivalry between the Da Capo-Zendrini and Zeno families.

Throughout the account our attention was divided between Bambina and the brooch sparkling on the front of my mother's Fortuny dress. Of everyone there the most fascinated by the brooch seemed to be Signora Zeno, who considered it with her dark eyes slightly narrowed.

It wasn't perhaps the wisest choice of a tale because of the bad blood that existed between our families due to the brooch, but Bambina carried it off in such a light, amusing spirit that even my parents didn't seem offended.

No sooner did she finish than Renata emitted a loud cry. She had become even paler and a slick film of sweat coated her face. She stood up abruptly and seemed dizzy, but she strode to a far corner of the room and pulled Gemma and her doll out from a shadowed recess.

When Renata asked her how long she had been there, the frightened child said that she had come down with her aunt Bambina. Whereupon Renata turned to her sister and started to berate her for her stupidity in not only having dragged Gemma from her bed at such an ungodly hour but then making it worse by having Lydgate go on with his story when she knew that Gemma would be all ears.

Although I had to agree with Renata, I sympathized with Bambina, who, for the second time that evening, was suffering from her sister's sharp tongue. I had the sense that Renata was about to say more when she reeled slightly, let go of Gemma's hand, and seemed about to fall. Lydgate was next to her in a moment and led her to a chair. Luigi went over. She was given water and a few minutes later Lydgate and Luigi carried her up to the Caravaggio Room.

Gemma began to cry. She said that it was her fault her mother was sick and that she wanted to take care of her as she always did. Bambina took Gemma from the salon.

Quite understandably, our group then broke up and we retired. My mother, trying to put the best face on things, said that she was sure Renata would be fine after a good night's rest. Tomorrow we all had an outing to Torcello to look forward to, not to mention the ball in the evening, which was to be the highlight of the weekend.

But there was no outing to Torcello and no ball, for by morning Renata was dead.

Signora Zeno found her body lying at the foot of the bed. She immediately summoned Luigi. I followed him to the Caravaggio Room.

Renata's beautiful face was contorted. There was blood on her mouth, and her hands were like two claws. The scent of perfume hung in the air and, with my seminary training, what came into my mind was: the odor of sanctity. The pleasant scent that we have been told surrounds those blessed in the service of our Lord.

I looked up at the Caravaggio. It was tilted slightly to one side, and for a few moments the boy seemed to smile at me again with living malevolence as he had when I discovered Flora's body.

Renata's death was said to have been from a cerebral hemorrhage. With the help of Luigi's connections and a large sum of money from Andrew Lydgate, Signora Zeno prevented an autopsy. She claimed she didn't want her daughter's body violated.

Little remains to be told. Gemma was raised by her father's parents in Perugia. Rumors reached us that Signora Zeno believed Renata would never have died if she hadn't been "forced" to sleep in the Caravaggio Room. Our two families gradually drifted apart. There was a brief rapprochement when Bambina took it into her head that I might be interested in marrying her. When it became apparent that I wasn't, Signora Zeno and Bambina cut off all relations.

A week after Renata's death my father decided to remove the Caravaggio painting from the room, put it back in the lumber room, and find a buyer as soon as possible. He no longer cared what this said about his faith in God. Three family members dead in the Caravaggio Room, all of them women and all on his side of the family, was too much to blame on coincidence. The room was cursed.

But as my father was reaching for the painting, a sharp pain stabbed him in his chest, and he stopped. He didn't need another warning. He immediately left the room. He gave instructions for the panes of the doors to the loggia to be painted black. All the doors were to be locked. Then he gave orders that no blood relatives of the Da Capo-Zendrini family were ever to enter it.

During the rest of his lifetime, and up until now in mine, none ever has. I promised my father that I would respect his wishes and not "tamper with fate," as he came to express it to himself.

I no longer know what I myself believe or suspect. All I do know is that the Caravaggio Room has been directly associated with three deaths—Nonna Teresa, Flora, and Renata—and indirectly with that of my brother, Amerigo. I would be lying and deceiving myself if I didn't admit that the painting has a power over me, as does my promise to my father.

And so the room has remained, hidden away, locked, with its sad and dark history. Someday I hope I will do what my father tried to do. Remove the painting. Make the room over into one like all the others at the Ca' da Capo.

When and if that day comes, then this letter to my future child will no longer be necessary—unless it be as a warning that even those of us who believe in God and the saints are as weak in the grip of superstition as the most faithless heathen.

PART THREE

The Brooch

1

When Urbino finished reading the Conte Alvise's memoirs, he put down the sheets of paper he had fetched from the library. They were a copy of the originals the Contessa had first read over twenty years ago. For a few moments the only sound was that of the violent rushes of wind against the windows.

"Isn't Barbara the deceitful little devil?" Sebastian said, breaking the silence. "A locked room! A malevolent painting! Mysterious deaths! A jewel with a dark past! If we had known about all this before, we would have come a long time ago, wouldn't we, Viola?"

His sister didn't share his excitement.

"Poor Barbara," she said. "Now I understand what she meant when she spoke of bad blood between the families, but surely no one holds anything against her?"

"You know how these Eye-talian blood feuds are, Viola," her brother found it necessary to remind her. "No one rests until both sides are destroyed. Barbara is right in the line of fire. Don't forget she's an interloper, being a Brit and all, and this Bambina wanted to marry her husband. I say she's in for it, and maybe we are, too, being *her* blood."

Viola gave him a weary look.

"But what about the rest of the story, Urbino?" she said. "I mean, what happened after she read the Conte's letter? By the way, I hope you're not breaking any confidences."

"I'm not—and I wouldn't. Barbara has long given up keeping any of this a secret. She would have told you both under the right circumstances."

Urbino freshened their drinks and told them the rest of the story.

"Strange as it might seem, Barbara didn't immediately examine the room. Not for at least a week. When she did she found a dusty, moldy bedroom with some fine pieces of furniture and, of course, the Caravaggio, which far from having suffered from neglect, seemed to gleam with life. As a subject and composition she didn't find the Caravaggio in any way pleasing, but Caravaggio has never been one of her favorite painters.

"She was in a quandary. Should she renovate the room completely? But what would she then do with the Caravaggio? Sell it? Donate it to the Accademia? Put it back in storage? Or should she leave the room just as it was? In the end that's what she decided. From both fear and the inability to make a decision. Better, she thought, to keep things as they had been since 1938.

"The only member of the staff who had been here at the time of the house party was Mauro. The others had long since died or left the Da Capo-Zendrini service. Mauro had been only fifteen and had worked in the kitchen. He told her nothing that she didn't already know from the Conte's letter—in fact, far less, of course—but she felt that there were things he wasn't saying. She didn't press him, however, because she knew his loyalty over the years to the Conte and remembered how the Conte had forbade her to ask questions of any of the staff. She made some tentative inquiries among members of the family but got nowhere.

"She decided to end her halfhearted attempts to learn more. She felt as if she was betraying the Conte now that he was dead, despite his final wish for her to know the story of the Caravaggio Room.

"And so the room was relocked.

"Then I came into the picture. I met Barbara a few years after the Conte died. You know I write biographies, and I got it into my head that it would be interesting to write the biography—a history—of the Ca' da Capo. I had toyed with the idea of doing the same thing for my Palazzo Uccello but put it aside when I learned that the centenary of the Da Capo-Zendrini family's possession of the building was coming up in a few years. It would make a nice gift to Barbara and could be presented to the state archives and the Marciana Library. I detected that she was less than eager but thought it was because she felt it was an imposition on me.

"In the course of my research I came up against the locked room. At first Barbara was evasive, said it was closed off because it was in severe need of repair. I persisted, however, and eventually gained access to the room and its history, at least what Barbara knew from the Conte's letter. Needless to say I was intrigued, and with her reluctant permission began to make inquiries to learn more about the painting and the room itself. I promised that nothing detrimental to Alvise or the family would find its way into the monograph I was putting together.

"I had very little success learning any more than was already known. The family was even less willing to speak with me than they had been with Barbara. The only contact I ever had with the Zenos was a brief note from the signora in response to my detailed letter. It said that she, her daughter, Bambina, and her granddaughter, Gemma, had no wish to review an episode of the past that was so disturbing to them all. Understandable, under the circumstances.

"I decided to contact Gemma directly. She was living in London, where she had acquired a reputation as a portrait painter. Barbara had met her several times, both before and after the Conte died, but they had never progressed beyond the state of acquaintanceship.

"I had little hope of learning much from Gemma since she had been only eight at the time of her mother's death. As it turned out, I was right. The few memories she had, she found difficult to sort out from what she had overheard or was told by her family over the years. The main thing she conveyed was a pathetic sense of the confusion and fright she felt that weekend. After all these years she's still bitter about the death of her mother. It changed the direction of her life, although she certainly has turned out well. But inside she still seems to be the little girl abandoned by her mother when she died so suddenly.

"I had more success with the provenance of the painting. The family of Signor Ugo Rigon, from whom the Conte's father bought the house, was given the painting by a dissolute nobleman who lost heavily at the Ridotto gaming tables to a Rigon in the middle of the eighteenth century. How the nobleman came to have the painting and who owned it before he did I don't know, but it appears to be one of the paintings commissioned by Cardinal Francesco del Monte, a highly cultured but somewhat dissolute ecclesiastic who took Caravaggio under his wing. I didn't come across anything that associated the painting with bad luck or violence, but the fact that it was consigned to a lumber room in the palazzo and never mentioned to the Da Capo-Zendrini family when they bought the building a hundred years ago might indicate that it wasn't considered a desirable object. Of course, there's the possibility that the painting was forgotten by the former owner, who seems to have been a bit of an eccentric.

"That's about it. I wrote the history of the building, but never felt happy with it because I had so many unanswered questions about that room. I admit I'd become somewhat obsessed with it and felt that all the mystery had to be brought to an end. I prevailed upon Barbara to have the room restored, not to change anything in it, and to treat it just like any other room. She eventually agreed and the room was fixed up a year ago, but she's never used it. She saw no need to make a point of having guests stay in it when there were more desirable rooms available—more desirable, that is, even apart from the history of the Caravaggio Room."

Viola had a pensive look on her face when he finished.

"You have a lot of influence with Barbara," she said.

"Influence? Well, we think a lot of each other's opinion. We try to help each other in whatever way we can."

"And you think it was a help to her to encourage her to treat the room like any other?"

"It was my intention." Then, as this seemed to leave too much open to question, he added: "I still think it was the right thing."

"But no one has slept in it yet, have they?" Sebastian said. "You won't be able to breathe easy until then—until Molly wakes up raring to go in the A.M." A troubled look came into his eyes, however, and his grin faded. With peculiar forcefulness he added: "And I'm sure she will!"

"I'm sure she will, too," Urbino said. "I don't believe a room can cause someone's death. I can understand a bad luck room, so to speak, but when you get down to it, most rooms in a building of this age must have their sad stories, as the Conte himself said in his memoirs."

For a few moments each glanced around the comfortable room with its furniture, art, and bibelots that reflected the Contessa's sensibility so clearly. The exception was, perhaps, the flagrant Veronese over the fireplace, the wedding gift from the Conte Alvise.

"'Blood everywhere,'" Sebastian intoned in a deep, sepulchral voice. "That's what Molly said as soon as we came down the steps of the railway station, didn't she, Viola? She probably saw us all wading through the sticky liquid in just about every room in this place. God, can you imagine the brutality even here in—what does Barbara call it—her *salotto blu?* Poor souls knifed by pointed comments, bludgeoned by turned backs, poisoned by false smiles. The Murder of Reputation! The Slaying of Trust! The Death of Innocence!"

Urbino gave a little smile of agreement which he hoped Sebastian didn't misinterpret. He had often thought along similar lines himself about the dangers of the overly socialized life. Under other circumstances he would enjoy pursuing the topic with Sebastian, if the young man could abandon just a little of his archness.

Viola, with a look of sufferance, said to Urbino, "You said that you don't believe a room can cause someone's death."

"Unless he's extremely susceptible and believes that it can. In that case, he can be frightened to death."

"There's another possibility, of course. Someone could take

advantage of the idea of a curse to cover his own villainy," Viola suggested in a matter-of-fact way.

Urbino found her gaze somewhat disconcerting.

"But that would mean that the police would have to accept the death as caused by a curse and not open an investigation. I don't think superstition is one of the traits of the police."

"Perhaps not, but maybe the Italian police are different. Things seem to suffer a sea change when they cross the Alps. And, yes, Sebastian," she added, turning briefly to her brother, "I'm quite aware I'm mixing my metaphors. I may even have done it deliberately to show Urbino how caught up I am in this whole story."

She smiled at Urbino as if they had a secret.

"But the police don't seem to have been concerned about looking into this femme fatale's death—what was her name? Renata? What do *you* think happened? A mysterious death in the thirties! Just the kind of thing someone like you would love to sink his teeth into. I'm sure you have theories."

"I found no reason to think anything other than what was determined at the time—that she died of a cerebral hemorrhage," Urbino said, an element of caution creeping into his response.

"But you have your suspicions, don't you?" Viola asked earnestly, as if her opinion of him was riding on his answer. Urbino, however, was relieved of having to make one when, once again, her brother plunged ahead:

"Maybe she was murdered! Old—or rather young—Dr. Vasco shot her with poisoned darts of mesmeric suggestion! You saw the way he looked at Molly when she was dipping into the past. Or maybe Bambina had finally had enough of being in the ravishing Renata's shadow. Then again, Mamma Zeno could have knocked off her own daughter for some twisted reason. Or maybe it was matricide: Gemma, the bad seed, giving her mother the old heave-ho! No! I've got it. It was the Conte, and the Zenos have gathered to take their revenge against Barbara.

Hmm, why does that sound familiar to me? Ah, yes, *Murder on the Orient E!* How appropriate that we came chugging in on it ourselves with little Molly."

"But not the authentic one that went all the way to Istanbul," Viola took some pleasure in reminding him.

"Not a tinplate replica, either. And here we are, safe and sound, and ready for anything. I know I am! What I'm going to do now is take a peek at the C.R. before it gets cleared of cobwebs."

He hurriedly downed the rest of his drink and left.

Viola was in no way as eager to leave as her brother had been. She rearranged her long limbs and dress with a self-conscious air. Urbino was struck by that correspondence between a person's appearance and interests that occasionally comes along to startle you. Viola had said that she had done a project on Christina Rossetti, and here she was looking as much like Dante Gabriel Rossetti's favorite model, Mrs. Morris, as it was possible to look without intentional caricature, and of this he didn't silently accuse her. Her affectations lay in other directions.

She looked at him with eyes that, through no visible effort on her part, became even more Swinburnish and melancholy. Their green color had a trick of darkening startlingly. He almost expected her to break out into an exotic mélange of anapests and spondees but instead she said in her deep voice, "Sebastian was acting a bit strangely, don't you think?"

"How can one tell?"

"Well, he was," she said with a laugh. "Take it from someone who knows. For one thing, he's recovering from one of his love affairs. He always chooses the wrong kind of man, poor boy. And he probably feels guilty for bringing Molly here. He's the one who struck up the acquaintance first. If she even has indigestion during the night—or if there's any contretemps at our dinner table of thirteen—he'll take it hard. Beneath that bantering surface he's really quite sensitive."

"Not unlike you," Urbino ventured.

"I don't exactly know how to take that. I've become suspicious of comparisons between myself and Sebastian."

"Inevitable, aren't they?"

Urbino wondered if Sebastian and Viola had ever deceived people by pretending to be the other, an easy enough trick for fraternal twins, but somehow not completely unbelievable in these twins of opposite sexes. He absent-mindedly started to trace out Sebastian's features in Viola's face, until he saw that Viola was staring at him. He was embarrassed and folded up the Conte's letter and put it in his pocket.

"We make you feel uncomfortable, and you don't quite know why, do you?" she said with an ironic little smile. "Well, we won't pursue the topic. Let me ask you something easier to answer. Am I mistaken or is Angelica's last name the same as Renata's fiancé?"

"Angelica is Andrew Lydgate's grandniece—and his heir. He died a few years ago."

"How intriguing! Death prevents two people from marrying and two generations later their heirs consummate it. It's romantic, but also a little bizarre, you have to admit. Is this a marriage of love or convenience?"

"They look as if they're very much in love."

"Ah, appearances! Who can trust them?"

She was silent a few moments as if contemplating her own comment, and stared down into her glass. When she looked up, she said, "So we're a cozy group, aren't we? Even a bit incestuous. Maybe it wasn't such a bad thing for us to bring a thirteenth guest to the feast. Molly and Barbara's two friends will help to thicken up the blood."

Suddenly a woman's scream shattered the air. Urbino and Viola jumped up and went out into the hall.

Right on the heels of a surprisingly sprightly Dr. Vasco, they followed a second scream to its source in the conservatory at the end of the hall. There, Gemma, pale and frightened-looking, was sprawled on a sofa set among a sea of lush foliage. The conservatory, so little changed from the past and with its incongruous scattering of sofas, chairs, footstools, and little tables, was like some colonialist drawing room in the process of being reclaimed by the jungle. Or—at the moment—destroyed by the boisterous gale crashing against the glass.

"She went all white and almost fainted, poor thing," Molly said.

Bambina emerged from behind a screen of artificial-looking plants. She was holding a glass.

"Here's some water, Gemma dear."

She held the glass out to her niece, who made a determined motion of pushing it away. Vasco hurried over to the sofa and said sternly to Bambina, "What are you trying to do? Get away from her!"

He reached out in a gesture intended as both a rebuff of Bambina's ministrations and a protection of Gemma, who now looked even paler than she had a few moments before.

Bambina gave a good appearance of being amused instead of offended.

"No reason to waste good water," she said.

She was about to pour it on one of the plants encroaching on the sofa when she shrugged and quaffed it herself. She put the glass down and went over to her mother, who was sitting in an armchair, the large ostentatious flowers of a hibiscus shrub gleaming behind her with a sickly efflorescence.

"My poor little Gemma," Vasco said, moving closer to her and reaching out for her hand. "Why don't you lie down and put your head on a pillow?"

Gemma shrank from him.

"I'm perfectly all right! It's—it's just the air in here. My God, you can't even breathe!"

The old physician retreated a few steps. A look of guilt crossed his lined face, but was replaced by one of anger when Molly broke out in the poetical manner reserved for her retrospective statements:

"In the sweet long ago, a lovely girl of innocent ways died after she breathed the air of all these shrubs and herbs and *fleurs*. Roses, there must be roses."

At this moment the Contessa appeared, a bit out of breath, with Sebastian at her side.

"Who screamed? Gemma! You look like a ghost!"

The Contessa rushed over to Gemma and threw her arms around her. She looked up at Vasco, who continued to stare at Molly, now with an unmistakable glaze of fear in his eyes.

"Dr. Vasco, can't you see that she needs attention?"

"Here come the leeches," Sebastian said to Urbino and Viola. "He probably carries them in his pocket."

"I don't need him or—or anyone else fussing over me!" Gemma insisted. "Is that Robert?" she asked expectantly when footsteps sounded outside the conservatory.

But it wasn't Robert. It was Oriana and Filippo Borelli and Mauro, followed by two of the staff laboring under enough luggage to take the Borellis on a world cruise.

Oriana quickly surveyed the scene from behind her large-frame eyeglasses. She was an attractive middle-aged woman known throughout the city, and as far as Rome and Milan, for her histrionics and extramarital affairs.

"I must say, Barbara dear," she said in her throaty voice, "that you've chosen the strangest place to entertain your guests. I've always suspected that you keep a snake or two slithering around for atmosphere in this mad jungle! And tonight of all nights!" She made a wide gesture that included not only the wind and the rain immediately outside the windows but also the storm-tossed waters of the Grand Canal and, beyond them, the Adriatic crashing against the Lido barriers. "The only worse choice would have been the loggia! Can you believe it, Filippo?"

Her husband, a tall, handsome man who managed to make his total baldness look like an adornment, said in impeccable English, "Barbara always surprises me. That's what makes her a magnificent woman. *Buona sera,* Barbara. Maybe we can shake ourselves off on your plants."

"My God! You're both soaking! You must change immediately." The Contessa hurriedly made the necessary introductions—Oriana and Filippo knew only Urbino and Gemma. "Lucia, show the Borellis up to the Longhi Room and have Tonio and Carlo bring their things."

Oriana went over to the sofa.

"Let Filippo and me help you to your room, Gemma dear," she said. "Your son can find you there and you can introduce us."

Seeming anxious to leave the conservatory, Gemma nodded her head weakly and put herself in the care of the Borellis.

"What happened to her?" the Contessa asked Urbino after Oriana and Filippo had helped Gemma out.

"I don't know. Viola and I were in the *salotto* when we heard a scream."

"That was me," Signora Zeno said, obviously proud that she could still scream loudly enough to summon practically the whole house. "Gemma was sitting normally one minute and the next she fell over. It's a shock to see one's own granddaughter look so ill."

A shock, but also a gratification, if one could judge by the self-satisfied look on her small, wrinkled face.

"It was right after Signora Wybrow—that is your name,

yes?—right after she said something about plant diseases," Signora Zeno clarified.

"Plant diseases?" the Contessa repeated.

"I was merely saying that I could feel all sorts of diseases growing around me," Molly explained. "And perhaps I said something about aphids and slugs. I don't always know what I've said after I've said it," she added, looking at them all as if she expected immediate and abundant praise. When none was forthcoming, she said, "Is my room ready, Contessa Barbara?"

"I'll say it is, Molly!" Sebastian said.

"Why don't you show her, Sebastian? We'll see you for drinks before dinner, Molly dear."

The Contessa's voice held a note of weariness.

When Molly and Sebastian had left, Viola leaned closer to Urbino and whispered, "Barbara looks knackered already. She's going to need you this weekend. And you can count on me—and Sebastian. It'll be our penance for having added Molly to the brew."

The Contessa was peering into the dense screen of plants behind the sofa.

"'Aphids and slugs,' is that what she said? And 'diseases.' She must be mistaken."

"Of course she is," Bambina said. "She hasn't got the slightest idea of what she's talking about—ever! Nonsense from start to finish!"

"I hope so," the Contessa said, but she didn't look convinced.

"The weekend has barely begun, *caro,* and I'm about to snap," the Contessa said to Urbino half an hour later in the *salotto.* "I should have just had Gemma come here and paint my portrait. That would have been enough stress."

"But you were prepared for much of this."

"Not for Molly! Not for a thirteenth guest! And I certainly wasn't prepared to throw open the Caravaggio Room after all these long years!"

"Don't let superstition ruin your weekend."

"Superstition! You heard that woman. She does have a gift, of one kind or another. She knows *things*, and people who know things are—are—"

"Molly is a harmless sort," Urbino said, not quite believing his own words.

"She's done quite a bit of harm already. She must have said something to upset Gemma. I certainly don't believe she almost fainted because of plant diseases and aphids and slugs." She sighed and shook her head slowly. "You can try to minimize things, but you know and I know that Molly is in possession of some disturbing pieces of information. She got them somewhere, and if it wasn't from the ambient air or halos or auras or whatever in creation they're called, then from where? No one here knows her."

"There's Sebastian and Viola."

"They met her on the train." She considered for a moment, then went on: "She's a stranger who knows more than a stranger would or should. I don't pretend to understand it. You're the rational one."

"Which means you're irrational?"

"Which means that I'm confused and frightened and looking to you for some guidance!"

"I've never let you down, have I? And this time you have your cousins, too. Viola said that she and Sebastian would be whatever help they could be this weekend. She's concerned about you."

"I don't think you should be so quick to rely on Viola—with or without Sebastian. I know they're blood, but they're just children! They could be *your* children!"

"Perhaps, if I had been much more precocious in that area than I ever was. But I disagree with you. Viola might be young—

Viola and Sebastian might be young," he amended, "but they're not dullards. Sebastian is a bit of a poseur but I doubt if he means anything by it."

"On the contrary! The boy means everything under the sun by it. It's his whole identity! You're more attracted to that kind of behavior than you should be."

Urbino didn't disagree but told her that he had taken it upon himself to relate the history of the Caravaggio Room to the twins and had read Alvise's letter to them.

"They didn't need to know! It's not any of their business. Whatever will they think of Alvise?"

It was only to be expected that this would be her first concern. Urbino felt uncomfortable as he remembered how Sebastian had joked about the Conte having "done in" the beautiful Renata.

"Well, the damage is done already," the Contessa said with a resigned air. "I'll tell them to be as discreet as someone their age can be. All we need is for them to put ideas into Molly's head when she's already buzzing with them! *And* sleeping in the Caravaggio Room! You saw how Gemma takes it as a personal affront! And Marialuisa Zeno and Bambina can't be too happy, either. Who knows what Molly said to them? Remember! You're the unofficial host this weekend. You should have been seeing that things were running smoothly instead of telling tales out of school and having tête-à-têtes with Viola. You were alone with her when Sebastian came up to the Caravaggio Room!"

He ignored the implications of this and said, "Maybe it wasn't Molly who upset Gemma, it could have been Mamma Zeno or Bambina. Those three don't exactly make an ideal grouping. Rather—rather odd, wouldn't you say?"

"And would you call it even odder when you throw Robert, Angelica, and Dr. Vasco in, and then—just for good measure—*me*?"

"Viola called it a cozy group," Urbino risked saying. "She even described it as incestuous."

"Filled with the wrong kind of imagination, that girl, and don't forget it! Well, whatever you want to call our little group, there are too many balls in the air for me to juggle. I'd retire to my room for the weekend if the idea of three ailing women under one roof wasn't too absurd."

"Three?"

"Me, Gemma, and Robert's pale and wan Angelica. Speaking of her, I wonder where she and Robert disappeared to? Gemma won't take it too lightly that her precious son was off with Angelica somewhere when she needed him."

"Doesn't she like Angelica?"

"Let's just say that she doesn't approve of the family connection, despite all the money. She would have been happier if he had foraged more distant fields. And I think she's nervous about the precedent."

"The precedent?"

The Contessa had temporarily lost him.

"The death of a future bride, her mother, so many years ago. In this house, and in the very room that our little Molly is even now making her own. We're in for quite a weekend! And this weather won't make things any better. We'll be thrown even more on each other's company. No chance for Torcello."

She cast an apprehensive glance toward the window, against which the wind and rain beat with increased force.

A few minutes later Urbino watched the storm with alarm from the window of his room. The water level in the side canal had risen considerably. The pavement across the way was awash with water not only collecting from the rain but seeping from beneath as well—a very bad sign.

When he called his housekeeper to double-check the security of the Palazzo Uccello, he had difficulty getting through. First there was no signal on the line, then it crackled several times and almost went dead.

"Everything is fine, Signor Urbino," Natalia said when he reached her, but there was an undercurrent of worry in her voice.

He hung up the receiver and continued to stare, broodingly, out the window at the gray sheets of rain.

"Aren't you a sly one, Countess Barbara! Trying to test me like that," Molly said when she joined the rest of the party in the library for drinks. Her grin twisted her face all to one side.

"Testing you? Whatever do you mean, Molly dear?" the Contessa said, unnecessarily rearranging her Grecian-drape Grès dress, then shooting a look at Urbino. He was standing next to Dr. Vasco, Sebastian, and the Borellis.

"To find out if I'm a charlatan or not! I don't blame you! There are plenty around. But I'm the real, honest-to-God thing." She seated herself in a green lacquer chair. "If someone will favor me with a gin, I'll tell you what I mean about testing old Molly."

Urbino poured her a generous portion.

"Thank you, dearie. I hope you don't hold anything against me." She took a sip of the gin and fixed the Contessa with her magnified eyes. "There's blood all over that room, Countess Barbara, and don't try to tell me no! Someone has been clawing at the walls. And a crumpled body of a woman was lying on the floor by the foot of the bed! Eyes of an innocent doe, staring up at the blessed orb of the world she'll never see again."

Dr. Vasco gave Molly a glare of resentment. Gemma started and seemed about to repeat her collapse earlier in the conservatory. She had come down a few minutes before with Robert and Angelica, assuring everyone that she felt much better. Angelica sat on a nearby walnut divan, a quilt arranged around her. She appeared unmoved by Molly's comments—if she had indeed heard them, for she had her heart-shaped face nearly buried in a novel by Miss Braddon. Robert, however, who stood between his ailing mother and fiancée, asked his mother if she was all right. Gemma was now staring at her aunt Bambina, whose eyes were turned down in what seemed to be admiration of her small, patent-leather shoes.

"I—I'm fine, Robert."

Robert then turned to Molly, his olive skin becoming a shade darker.

"You should watch your tongue! Stupid woman!"

Molly flushed.

"Molly doesn't mean to upset anyone," Gemma said. "She—she's just doing what comes naturally."

The woman in question beamed.

"I don't know what your game is, Mrs. Wybrow," Robert said, "but I don't like it. My mother is too polite to tell you what she really thinks—and so is everyone else!"

His sharp blue eyes swept the room, pausing briefly but pointedly on Sebastian.

"Oh my," Sebastian said, standing up straighter and adjusting his purple cravat. "I may be in for it. And Viola, too. We brought the ghost to the feast!"

Viola, now dressed in a plum-colored robe with deep sleeves, gave Urbino a questioning look. It was as eloquent as any words could be, asking if it might not be time to give the help she had offered earlier. Thus reminded of the help he himself should be giving, he stepped forward.

"Let me freshen your drink, Robert. Then I'd like to show you a book I'm sure will interest you."

"My drink's fine," he said with less than good grace.

"It's something the Conte found in Cairo about the theft of St. Mark's body," Urbino went on, hoping to distract Robert by appealing to his medieval side, so often at odds with his up-to-date skepticism. "Privately published by a Coptic priest. In Coptic, but the Conte had a monk from San Lazzaro degli Armeni do a translation into the Italian. Both versions were bound in the same volume by the printing press there."

Since another monk from this lagoon island had been the one to clean and authenticate the Caravaggio, Urbino wondered how much he was doing to smooth things over. But Robert didn't give any indication that he associated the island with the Caravaggio Room.

He said, somewhat begrudgingly, "I hope the translation can be trusted," and opened the book at random.

He seemed on the point of temporarily losing himself in the account of the miraculous transport of the corpse of St. Mark to Venice, when Molly said to the group at large, "A young lady's body, I said, but—but actually there were two. The bodies of two most sweet and lovely ladies, both young, but one in the true beginnings of her verdant spring. It was almost as if—as if they were competing for my attention. Sometimes the impressions come so thick and fast they're like a whirligig!"

Almost regretfully Robert pulled his attention away from the book and closed it.

"There are too many distractions at the moment," he said. "I'll read it up in my room, if you don't mind."

He rejoined Angelica, who was grasping her own choice of reading material with tense fingers and gave him a tremulous smile.

"Venice is called a serene city, Countess Barbara," Molly was now saying, "but it's very violent from what I feel and see."

"Or *read* about in a guidebook," Sebastian said.

"I was looking down at the two faces switching back and forth," Molly said, "and then I saw pieces of another woman's body, a woman not young at all. In a sack and lying in the lagoon."

"The murder near the Casino degli Spiriti," Filippo said. "The two *gondolieri* who murdered the old woman and stole her money."

Molly peered at him blankly through her thick lenses and said, "I could see from the shape of the woman's head that she was generous and trusting, probably prone to walking in her sleep."

Dr. Vasco, who had been looking at Molly with a combination of bewilderment and uneasiness, now said in a strained voice, "You're interested in phrenology, signora?"

"Oh yes, Dottore. And also somnambulism, mesmerism, and—and all the untapped powers of our minds."

"I've studied them for decades myself."

"A marriage made in heaven, it seems," Sebastian said not too quietly.

"The young don't understand these things, Dottore," Molly said. "Don't let it bother you."

"It doesn't, I assure you, signora. Shall we go over there," he indicated a corner dominated by a papier-mâché Buddha, "and talk over what we have in common?"

He bestowed a quivering smile on her. Dr. Vasco, who had so obviously disapproved of Molly earlier, now appeared to exude only congeniality as far as she was concerned.

"Delightful, Luigi, if I may be so bold as to call you by your first name! But first a wee bit more Beefeater."

With a brief detour to the liquor cabinet they went to the Buddha's corner, where they soon became involved in an enthusiastic but inaudible conversation.

Gemma and Bambina both watched the couple intently, as if they might be able to make out what they were saying if they only concentrated hard enough. Mamma Zeno showed an equal, although more covert, interest from the folds of her clothes.

The Contessa, Urbino noted with some discomfort, was looking at him with a frown. Surely she couldn't hold him responsible for Molly's disturbing comments to the group earlier and possibly now to Dr. Vasco? Short of removing the woman completely, perhaps locking her up in the Caravaggio Room, what could he do?

"Barbara dear," Oriana said, "why are you frowning like that?"

"Oh, was I frowning?" the Contessa said and relaxed her face. "It must be this storm. Pounding and whining away like this."

The storm had indeed not let up in any way, but if possible had become worse. At this moment something more substantial than the rain hit against one of the windows. Urbino suspected that it might be something dislodged from the garden beneath the windows. The same thought must have occurred to the Contessa, for she said:

"I'm afraid the garden is going to get all torn up. But I suppose that's the least of my—or anyone's worries. The Ca' da Capo was severely damaged back in sixty-six. It took years to make the repairs. I pray God we're not in for another bad time."

"But this place seems solid," Sebastian said. "Little chance it'll break off and float down the G.C."

"We don't joke about floods in Venice. Solid, yes, but I have nightmares about the pilings. I see them slipping and sliding and breaking like matchsticks!"

She involuntarily shivered.

"Ah, yes, the *acqua alta* of sixty-six," Oriana said with a little smile. "I spent it in a tiny apartment on the Riva degli Schiavoni with a wisp of an artist I thought would blow away. Filippo and I weren't engaged yet—or were we, dear?"

Filippo smiled at her indulgently.

"Who knows?" he said.

Angelica was looking with disapproval at Oriana as she continued her description of the charms of the *acqua alta* in sixty-six. Robert, now seated next to his fiancée on the divan, seemed lost in his own thoughts—rather unpleasant ones, to judge by the expression on his good-looking face.

Urbino, seeing a way to help divert attention away from Molly and her visions or flashbacks or whatever they were, decided to carry on in the manner started by Oriana. When she finished her anecdote of the storm, he began one of his own. It was secondhand, however, for he had moved to Venice more than fifteen years after the *acqua alta*, but he had heard it so many times from his housekeeper, Natalia, that he had come close to making it his own.

It was about an eccentric old woman who persisted in believing that her treasured Tintoretto had floated to safety from her decrepit palazzo in San Polo and not been stolen by thieves and later recovered in a storage room on the other side of the Grand

Canal. For the rest of her life she lit votive candles in front of the painting, which despite its subject—a bare-breasted, fiery-haired Mary Magdalene—became known as *"The Miracle of the Flood."*

When Urbino finished, it seemed that things would continue smoothly. Filippo next described his own impressions of the *acqua alta,* spent in the company of more than a dozen cats that had sought shelter with him in his palazzo and refused to leave afterward.

It soon became clear as one tale followed another that they were the group's way of exorcising their uneasiness over the growing intensity of the storm. Urbino was reminded of the diverting stories of the lords and ladies in Boccaccio, which in turn inevitably reminded him of the house party in the thirties that had ended in the mysterious death of Renata Bellini, four of whose blood relatives were now in the room.

It was therefore with some renewed nervousness that he pulled himself away from his own thoughts and looked around the room. Everyone showed varying degrees of interest or its absence, from the intense look on Molly's pinched face to the bored one on Angelica's pale one. Mamma Zeno now seemed half asleep, sunk into the cushions of her chair, and Dr. Vasco, with a fixed smile, kept nodding at what were all the inappropriate places.

When Urbino looked at Viola, he was startled to find her staring at him, and he got the eerie impression that she, too, was thinking of Boccaccio and the other house party. His suspicions were proved correct when she slipped over to him and whispered, "Déjà vu."

Gemma, speaking in a weak voice, had just made her own contribution about her experiences in Florence, where the *acqua alta* had been even worse, when Molly, her eyes behind the thick glasses opened wide, burst out:

"Fiddling while Rome is burning! Dancing when the barbarians come sweeping in! Chatting away with the plague outside!

It all comes down to the same thing in the end. This isn't the first time this building of noble lines and noble residents has listened to stories while a storm was building up. And why do I think of the name Boccaccio? Does it mean something? And Signor Urbino mentioned a stolen painting! Is it the one in my room? And—and Signor Filippo, you spoke about cats! Are there cats in the house? Are they dead or alive? Oh, everything's all mixed up in my mind!"

"No wonder about that," Sebastian said in a stage whisper to Oriana. "The girl has drunk half a bottle of B.E.! It's a wonder—"

"You're saying too much!" Gemma cried. At first Urbino thought she was speaking to Sebastian, but she stood up and glared at Molly. An expression of discomfort then came over her face. It was as if Gemma had spoken involuntarily, or at least without thinking, and was now regretting it.

"I'm sorry, Molly."

She went over to the little woman and took her hand. She bent her head and said something to her in a voice inaudible to Urbino, who was standing the closest of anyone to the two of them. The Contessa's face was white and strained as she watched the two women.

Gemma squeezed Molly's hand, and in the several moments before the dinner bell blessedly sounded, the two women gave every appearance of understanding each other completely.

Dinner was, at first, a surprisingly calm affair. It was as if everyone was weary from what had gone on in the library and was determined to get through the meal as smoothly as possible. There was little general conversation, and the diners broke into shifting patterns of talk, avoiding anything disturbing—and this included the bad weather, which continued to assault the Ca' da Capo-Zendrini and, beyond it, the vulnerable city.

It was a sign of the Contessa's foresight, as well as her uneasiness, that she had had the table set with her own Pembroke family china and crested glasses and not the Cozzi china that had been in the Da Capo-Zendrini family since the eighteenth century.

Urbino remembered her comment about three ailing women under one roof, and considered them now in turn as they went through the ritual of dinner. The Contessa herself looked weary as she addressed Mamma Zeno, who, although the oldest person at the table, seemed in many ways the most vital. It was all in her quick dark eyes, eyes that were still hungry, and in the way that she seemed to relish her food.

Angelica, by contrast, looked out at the dinner table with a dull, uninterested gaze and picked at her food. She probably couldn't wait to get back into the cozy intrigues of *Lady Audley's Secret*. Most likely she had another Victorian novel or two stashed away in her room, along with several boxes of bonbons. Every once in a while Filippo, who was sitting on one side of her, would address her, but her responses were so minimal—weak smiles and even weaker nods—that he soon gave up to bestow his attentions on Viola.

Robert, the thoroughly modern man of relics, had the pleasure of listening to Sebastian rant on about Canterbury and materialism like some latter-day Chaucer. Robert said as little as possible, which was more than enough for Sebastian's diatribe.

Gemma was very still, and kept observing everyone around the table in an almost furtive manner. Her face had a grayish cast and there were dark smudges beneath her eyes and in the hollows of her temples that even the Contessa's carefully calculated lighting couldn't conceal. Although she was eating more than Angelica, it seemed to be only to keep up appearances.

It fell to Oriana's lot not to have the attention or the ear of any of the gentlemen, but instead that of the energetic Bambina, who both ate and spoke with a kind of nervous avidity. Her eyes darted all around the table in an almost desperate manner, and her gestures were so dramatic that at one point Urbino feared she was about to fling some *petits pois* into Oriana's inviting décolletage.

The only people who genuinely seemed to be enjoying themselves were Molly and Dr. Vasco. They forgot all about the food and drink for long minutes as they earnestly—and in low voices—conferred on topics they obviously felt were of little interest to the group at large or to Viola and Mamma Zeno, who sat on either side of them. Vasco gave every appearance of being fascinated by the little Englishwoman.

"I must say, Urbino," Oriana declared, escaping with evident relief from Bambina's nervous volubility, "that our dear Barbara didn't keep the proportions right for the weekend. All too many women and all too few men."

"We're a perfect mixture," Urbino said, marveling at his cool ability to stretch the truth to such thinness. "Besides, it's not a dance. We don't need to be paired up. But if we did, you wouldn't end up a wallflower."

"Ever gallant, Urbino, managing to defend Barbara and pay me a compliment at the same time. What would we women do without you?"

"Indeed," said Viola, who had been listening to their exchange. "He makes himself indispensable."

"True enough, Viola dear," Oriana responded, "but I warn you: Barbara is equally indispensable to him."

"Only Barbara? That puts the rest of us women out in the cold."

"Out in the dark, I'd say," Oriana corrected with a laugh. "Urbino has his intentionally inscrutable side."

"Perhaps," was the limit of Viola's agreement, although she might have committed herself further if at this moment Oriana hadn't suddenly shrieked and stood up. Everyone broke off their conversations.

"Thirteen! We're thirteen for dinner! Thirteen for the weekend! How could you do this to me?"

She collapsed back into her chair and reached for her water tumbler. She knocked over her wineglass. A red stain crept across the cloth.

"Déjà vu *encore*," Viola had time to say to Urbino with an arched eyebrow before the Contessa responded to Oriana's outburst. For a moment he didn't know what Viola meant, then remembered the wine Andrew Lydgate had spilled across his shirtfront at the original house party. He looked over at Vasco, who, back then, had predicted to the Conte that Lydgate would do just that because he wanted him to. Vasco's mouth was tight and grim.

"Don't take it as a personal affront, Oriana," the Contessa said with a nervous laugh, her eyes on the growing stain. "These things sometimes happen."

"Thirteen for dinner doesn't just 'sometimes happen'! Not with you! And not when you've been as nervous as a cat for months about this house party."

The Contessa colored deeply and gave Urbino a silent plea for rescue.

"Let poor Barbara off the hook," Sebastian said before Urbino could step in. "Viola and I are the guilty ones. *We* added Molly to the feast," he said with an unmistakable air of pride. "She was so irresistible."

From the look Oriana gave Molly it was evident that she found the woman as resistible as poison in the present circumstances.

"But we're really not thirteen," Sebastian went on, trying to suppress a smile. "There's Lucia, Mauro, and about half a dozen other staff."

"They don't count in situations like this!" Oriana snapped back, as if there existed a book of rules on superstition. "Believe me, if there wasn't a deluge out there, I'd leave immediately!"

"We'll just have to take our chances, dear," Filippo said. "There's no turning back now."

After they retired to the *salotto blu,* their ominous number was diminished by one. Mamma Zeno no sooner heard there now would be a bridge game and charades than she pronounced herself ready for bed and made it clear she wanted Bambina to accompany her.

"Charades, Mamma! You know how much I love charades!"

"You do?"

"Of course." Bambina laughed her girlish laugh. "I played them every summer when we used to go to Bellagio. In English! With all those Americans and English that stayed at the Hotel Grande Bretagne. *You* remember."

It didn't seem that her mother did or, if she did, that at the moment she didn't choose to. She insisted that Bambina see her up to her room, and mother and daughter left.

As they waited for Bambina to return, conversation was desultory until Angelica discovered the Contessa's collection of Venetian paperweights. She picked up one of the *mille fiori* balls and stared at it with an almost rapt expression on her thin, pale face.

"That one belonged to Colette," the Contessa said. "It used to be in her bedroom."

"Ah, La Colette," Oriana apostrophized. "You are my soul mate! *Chéri! The Last of Chéri!*"

Under the amused glance of her husband, she enthused at great length over Colette's novels about the love affair between an aging courtesan and a young man.

"Did you know Colette?" Sebastian asked, trying to restrain a grin, when she had finished.

"Bosom buddies, my charming young man! We went around Paris together in the twenties! I'm joking, of course!" she said with evident irritation when he seemed about to ask her something else. "Where is Bambina? She's taking forever!"

She no sooner said this than the round little woman appeared at the door, looking flushed and strangely self-satisfied. She gave the Contessa a glance and seemed to be repressing a smile as she bustled across the room to Molly and Dr. Vasco, who were once again ensconced in a corner together, whispering furiously.

"I want to be on your team," she said to Molly. "You must win all the time."

"Quite the reverse, dearie."

"Don't let Molly fool you," Sebastian said. "She's ingenious at them, I'm sure. First rule of games-playing is never to believe a word of what the opponent says."

"Urbino, why don't you get the charades organized?" the Contessa said quickly. "I'll see to bridge."

But she had some trouble getting four players. Only Oriana and Filippo showed an interest in joining her.

"I suppose we can play dummy bridge," the Contessa said when still no one volunteered to join them. "Oriana, you can play the dummy hand, if you don't mind?"

"But I do! Have we got our group down to twelve just to play dummy bridge? You know what it is in Italian!"

"What's she talking about?" Viola asked Urbino.

"*Morto.* It means to be the dead person. Same in French."

"Now I see why Father always told us to beware of the Continent! Dangers lurk even in the tongue!"

"Won't someone rescue us from this silly situation?" the Contessa threw out to the room at large.

"Perhaps a game of bridge will be a fitting end to a wonderful evening," Dr. Vasco said.

"Our knight of the evening," the Contessa said.

"Don Quixote is more like it," Sebastian said loud enough for everyone to hear.

"I assure you, young man, that I would recognize a windmill for what it is, and I see none around here," Dr. Vasco said as he went over to the bridge table. "Nor any ordinary wenches, either," he added as he grinned at Oriana, looking like a death's head.

Oriana gave an involuntary shiver, only marginally less pleased to have the cadaverous Vasco as her partner than to be the dummy. Even more disturbed by the arrangement, however, was the abandoned Molly, who glared the full force of her ill will at Oriana through her impossibly thick spectacles.

Despairing of any smooth interludes that lasted for longer than a few minutes this evening, Urbino quickly explained the rules for the charades.

"All topics will be in English, since Gemma and Bambina obviously know English better than the rest of us do Italian," he began.

"Spoken ever so humbly for yourself," Viola said with a smile.

"Except for proper names, of course, like—like Vivaldi or Veronese," Urbino went on. "Also, all topics will be on a Venetian theme. For example, the Bridge of Sighs or Grand Canal. We're going to need a timekeeper." He looked at the group, which included himself, Viola, Sebastian, Bambina, Gemma, Robert, Angelica, and Molly. "Is everyone going to play?" he asked, feeling more and more like a master of ceremonies for a less than enthusiastic group of celebrants—except for Bambina, who was close to squirming in anticipation.

"I'll just watch," Angelica said and drew her limbs more closely to her on the sofa.

"I will, too," Robert said.

"Oh, not on my account, Robert. I'll cheer you on."

A less energetic or mirthful cheerleader Urbino could hardly imagine, unless it were Mamma Zeno, who had already retired.

"I'll be timekeeper," Molly volunteered and raised her arm to display her watch as if its outrageously colored bands and stars alone qualified her for the job.

Urbino wrote the names of the six players on slips of paper and had Angelica draw for the teams. It fell out that Sebastian, Gemma, and Bambina composed one team, and Urbino, Viola, and Robert the other.

Urbino went to the library and gathered up half a dozen books on Venice and brought them back to the *salotto.*

"To give us some ideas. But please, let's not be too esoteric."

"Most definitely not," Viola mocked him with a smile.

They spent ten minutes selecting and writing down their topics. Urbino was pleased to see that there was at least some of the usual giggling—although all Bambina's—and self-satisfied nods and stares, which were brought off with theatrical aplomb by Sebastian.

Molly sat in a chair placed between the two facing sofas on which the rival groups sat.

Urbino's team got off to a bad start. Robert, despite his original reluctance, gave an energetic impersonation of a crazed bull, enacted an assault on a woman he carved in the air with his arms, and then pointed furiously at the painting over the mantelpiece. It was only a few seconds before their time was up that Urbino identified the painting as Veronese's *Rape of Europa* at the Doges' Palace. Sebastian's smirk identified the topic as his own.

Sebastian's moment of victory was short-lived, however, for it fell to his lot to draw "Giorgione," his sister's offering. He spent many long precious moments trying to act out the syllables but he—and Gemma and Bambina along with him—became completely confused as he switched without any indication from English to Italian words and back again. Then his face lit up and he started pointing repeatedly to Bambina, pulled the skin of his face down with his fingers, and gave a slow, labored walk between the two sofas.

When he pointed again to a bewildered and increasingly uncomfortable-looking Bambina, Gemma leaned forward and, in a voice that managed to contain a strong suggestion of both reproach and victory, said, "*La Vecchia!* It's 'Giorgione'!" She had identified the artist from one of his most famous paintings, *La Vecchia*, or *The Old Woman*, which hung in the Accademia.

Gemma's eyes took in Bambina's shocked expression, and the ghost of a smile played across her lips.

"Thank God I remembered the painting!" Sebastian cried.

It would have been better—and easier, considering the storm outside—if he had remembered Giorgione's *La Tempesta* instead, thought Urbino. Bambina was totally discomposed. Her painted face had collapsed and there were tears in her eyes. At the moment, if you ignored the vivid, curled hair and imagined a white cloth cap on her head, she did indeed resemble Giorgione's painted warning of what we all would become with time.

She glared first at Sebastian, then at Viola, who was proudly acknowledging that "Giorgione" had been her choice. It was obvious that Bambina considered the twins to have been in league to humiliate her. With an abrupt gesture she reached deep into the pocket of her dress, took out her little flask of perfume, and proceeded to douse herself with a liberal amount.

Molly, who had followed all this with a bemused expression, announced that "Giorgione" had been guessed in three seconds less than "*The Rape of Europa.*"

Fortunately, Urbino next had an easy time with "*The Love of Three Oranges,*" the play by the Venetian dramatist Carlo Gozzi. He was tempted to use Viola as a convenient prop for love but instead settled for a ridiculous but convincing display of his two hands interlocked over his heart. Bambina's dudgeon was increased by the rapidity of Viola's correct guessing, for "*The Love of Three Oranges*" was her own selection.

She wasn't so upset, however, that she couldn't throw herself back into the game. In good time, through a blowing out of her rouged cheeks and furious gestures at the roaring fire and the pagoda chandelier hung with glass and beads, she left Gemma and Sebastian in no doubt that she was making all this effort on behalf of "Murano."

But despite her performance and the quickness of the others' response, Molly announced that their rival team was fifteen seconds ahead. When Sebastian started to protest that Molly might have been distracted or, as he put it, "roaming around in the past," Angelica revealed that she had been keeping time on her own wristwatch, and that Molly was dead right. Robert, who was responsible for "Murano," gave her a smile of gratitude.

Only two clues remained. Viola, with a few flowing strokes of her hands, conjured up a bed hung with drapes and placed herself within it, only to writhe and try to remove something from her face. It seemed to Urbino that Molly, Bambina, and Gemma—whose clue it was—watched with just as much nervous attention as did he and Robert.

"Desdemona!" Robert cried.

"Right you are," Viola said. "I absolutely refused to take out my handkerchief and drop it or point to a cushion. That's cheating, the way I look at it."

Molly, corroborated by Angelica, told them that the other team would have to guess their clue in ninety seconds or less. Gemma got a little unsteadily to her feet and managed to confound what Urbino had intended as a difficult though not "esoteric" clue by simply sketching a Star of David in the air and getting Sebastian to cry out in considerably less than the needed time: "The Ghetto"!

Encouraged by his victory, Sebastian suggested that they play another round, this time with "the gloves off," whatever that might mean. No one seemed inclined. Bambina stood up and said she should see to her mother. Her earlier enthusiasm more than a little dampened, she had perhaps decided that she had already suffered enough buffets for one night from the gentle version of the game and wanted to avoid risking a more robust contest.

After saying good night to the Contessa and the other card players, she left.

The bridge game was far from over, but from a look the Contessa threw Urbino it appeared that she wished it were so that she could call it a night. He had noticed that she had at times shown as much interest in their game as her own, straining to catch the clues and to access the dynamics.

As often happens when one guest leaves, most of the others

acted like lemmings to the sea. Gemma, looking more fatigued than before, followed quickly on the heels of her aunt. A few minutes later Angelica and Robert left, then Sebastian, but not before he tried to persuade Viola that she was more tired than she claimed she was.

"I'll stay awhile longer," she said, "and keep Urbino company."

"He still has Molly."

"Not for long, he doesn't," the little woman said. "I think I'll go up with you, Sebastian. Time to rest these weary bones. Good night, Countess Barbara, and all the rest of you. Sleep tight, and don't let the bedbugs bite—only in a manner of speaking, of course!"

Dr. Vasco watched her retreating figure with intensity.

"Alone together again at last!" Viola said when Urbino had furnished her with a cognac and they were sitting on a sofa by the fire. She looked at the bridge players. "Except for the others caught up in *their* game."

She accompanied the emphasis with a smile that she quenched by bringing the cognac glass to her lips.

"I got the sense this evening that a lot was going on that I didn't catch, and I don't consider myself a particularly dull-witted girl."

"I'd say that you're very much the opposite."

"But still not witted enough to catch what might have been going on," she pursued, deflecting his compliment.

"Perhaps you're just being hard on yourself because you feel guilty."

"Of what?"

"Of having stirred things up by bringing Molly along."

"Yes, it has something to do with that, but I don't feel guilty." She gave him another smile, but it was a pensive one that quickly faded. "I'm a little bit apprehensive. I get this way from time to time and usually it means nothing but—but sometimes it means a great deal."

She looked down into her glass and seemed to be considering

all the times her uneasiness had presaged something disagreeable. She laughed nervously and looked at him. Her deep green eyes held no glint of humor.

"Don't tell me that you're psychic, too."

"Just call me susceptible," she said with an attempt at lightness. "I keep getting the feeling that I've been through all this before—all our talking and squabbling and drinking and eating this evening. Déjà vu, as I said. I guess the Conte's memoirs made a strong impression on me—or maybe it was your incomparable skills as a raconteur," she added, once again trying to be light.

But her face revealed that she was uneasy. She looked at the bridge players again and her eye momentarily caught Dr. Vasco's.

"That man gives me the creeps!" she said in a carefully guarded voice. "He reminds me of Dr. Caligeri. He's even interested in mesmerism! I wonder if the victim who does his evil bidding is Mamma Zeno or Bambina? Or maybe he's preparing Molly for the job, judging by the attention he's been giving her."

As if by some sixth sense, Dr. Vasco suddenly lifted his head and looked in their direction. Viola gave a shiver when the physician turned his eyes back to his cards.

"I'm definitely going to lock, bolt, and bar my door tonight," Viola said. "His room is right next to mine. Whatever was Barbara thinking? I thought she was the type to put all the men in a bachelor wing. Well, Sebastian's on my other side, thank God." She took another sip of her cognac and put the glass down. "I think I'll call it a night. Oh, no need to accompany me through these dark and drafty halls. Just see that Dr. Caligeri doesn't steal up after me. Besides, there still might be services you have to render Cousin Barbara."

As it turned out, Viola's parting comment proved to be true, but not until an hour after the bridge party broke up and everyone had retired for the evening.

Alone in his room, a copy of E.T.A. Hoffman's *Doge and Dogaressa* lying ignored in his lap, Urbino at first sat mulling things over.

Viola, he felt, had been right. The atmosphere of the Contessa's house party was charged with something he himself was unable to understand. It had been in the air all afternoon and evening, and wasn't only—or even largely—attributable to their thirteenth guest and her sallies into the past. If he believed in strange correspondences, he would have said that the storm crashing outside his windows now had been conjured up in some fateful way by the bad weather within.

Almost everyone seemed to be on edge. He could understand the Contessa's nervousness. She had been dreading this get-together for months. As for the others, they were all related, directly or otherwise, to the tragic death of Renata almost sixty years ago—all of them, that is, except for the Borellis, Molly, and the twins, unless there was some hidden connection he was as yet unaware of.

Urbino, not only as a biographer but also as a sensitive—sometimes, according to the Contessa, a too-sensitive—man, was well aware of the chill breath that past sorrows and tragedies could blow across the decades. He didn't need to go any farther than himself to find an example of this. Hadn't the death of his parents in the car accident, which Molly had referred to this afternoon, dropped a pall on him that still hadn't quite lifted after all these years?

This question led him to another: Where had Molly's information about his parents come from? That it could have originated from some power or "gift" that she was blessed or cursed with was too difficult for his logical mind to accept. But if not from there, then from where? And what of her other pronouncements? How much on the money had they been? To judge by the startled reactions of almost everyone, she had hit the mark as precisely with them as she had with him.

What game, if any, was she playing?

At this point in his ruminations there was a quiet knock on his door. It was Lucia, the Contessa's maid. She handed him a note and left. He opened it and read:

Urbino,

Would you please come to my room at once? And whatever you do, don't draw any attention!

This somewhat intriguing and vaguely troubling summons sent Urbino out into the hall within seconds, his caftan and Moroccan felt slippers giving him a stealthy feel as he in fact crept stealthily to the Contessa's bedroom door.

Out here in the hall the sound of the storm was muted. A light showed under the door of the Caravaggio Room at the end of the wing, where Urbino imagined Molly convening with the resident spirits of the place. Vasco's room was directly across from it, and Robert's was adjacent to it. Their rooms were dark, as were those of Sebastian and Angelica. Viola's room was the only one other than the Caravaggio Room that showed a light under the door.

Urbino had to pass by the broad stairway to get to the other wing of bedrooms where the Contessa's suite was. Here were the rooms of the Borellis, Gemma, Mamma Zeno, and Bambina. All were dark except Bambina's, near the head of the stairway.

No sooner did he give a muffled knock on the Contessa's door than she opened it and practically pulled him into the room. She wore a blue dressing gown and patterned Moroccan slippers.

"It's gone! My peacock brooch!"

"Gone? What do you mean?"

"Gone! Taken! Stolen! Please keep your voice down!" she said loudly. In fact she had been almost shouting ever since he came into the room. "Look."

She brought him over to the jewel cabinet. The drawer held a glittering assortment of jewelry and little boxes. The peacock brooch wasn't among them.

"It was with the other pieces. I took it out of its box before dinner. I was going to wear it and then remembered the bad blood between the Da Capo-Zendrini and Zeno families about it. No point in flaunting it, so I put it back. But not in its box," she added, anticipating his question. "I just laid it on the top of the other things. It was taken sometime between when I came down for drinks and when I returned after the bridge game."

"Why didn't you lock the cabinet?"

"This isn't a hotel!" she shot back at him. "I never imagined there was a thief in the house!"

"But who?"

"I refuse to speculate! And I don't want anything said about this. It's embarrassing."

"But don't you want to retrieve it, if possible?"

"How? By calling in the police? By locking everyone in the library and frisking them? Isn't that what it's called? And then we can search their rooms. No, let it be! At any rate, it's insured," she said, but he knew it was more for his benefit than because she was concerned about the monetary aspect.

"But whoever took the brooch might take something else. Shouldn't we warn the others?"

"I absolutely forbid it! Everyone would probably assume that it's one of the staff, and then how would that make me look?"

"I assume you've ruled that out? Don't forget that there are some new staff here for the weekend."

"And each one comes highly recommended. No, it was one of the guests, but farther than that I can't—I won't!—go."

Urbino looked down at the jewelry, some of the items worth a great deal more than the peacock brooch.

"Was anything else taken?"

"No." She seemed to wait for him to say something, then went on: "That's why I don't think that we need to be afraid that anyone else will—will lose anything. The person grabbed the peacock brooch because it was lying right on top. If he or she wanted anything more, it was all here for the taking. Probably whoever it was thought the brooch might not even be missed." She looked with a wry smile at her jewels. "There *are* a great many."

She had said several things that Urbino didn't agree with, but he kept quiet. This was her house party and he would let her conduct it the way she wanted to. To be honest, he didn't relish the idea of having everyone accused of theft tomorrow at the breakfast table.

"As you wish, Barbara."

She looked drawn.

"Now just try to get a restful night's sleep. I'll have Lucia bring you some chamomile tea."

He was closing the Contessa's door behind him and had walked only a few steps down the hall when he saw a figure standing near the stair landing. It was Viola.

"I was afraid I'd find only Dr. Vasco creeping around making night calls," she said when he reached her. "I believe that's Barbara's room?"

An exaggerated, sweeping glance took in his robe and slippers.

"She had a problem she needed your services for?"

"Making a night call yourself?" he countered.

"Turn about is fair play—and, in this case, a good way of evading a difficult question. It so happens that I wasn't able to sleep and was on my way to the library to find something to dull my mind."

"Ah, yes, that so very *un*-dull-witted mind of yours." He now made as exaggerated a point of taking in her attire as she just had his. She was still wearing what she had on earlier in the evening. "Do you always go to sleep—or try to go to sleep—in your clothes?"

"Only in strange houses. It's very compromising to be seen in your nightclothes by complete strangers, even if *my* nightclothes are far less outré than others you see these days. Good night."

She returned along the corridor to her room, having either forgotten about seeking out a book or now gauging herself sufficiently fatigued to have a good night's sleep. Urbino went downstairs to help assure the Contessa's own restful night by seeing Lucia about the chamomile tea.

As he was returning to his room, he noticed that the light was still on under the door of the Caravaggio Room. All the other rooms were now dark.

Urbino, who shared with Viola a mind unwilling to be laid to rest, read *Doge and Dogaressa* for a while. The story of Doge Marin Falier's treachery against the state and his eventual beheading was, however, so overwrought that it excited rather than wearied him. He put it aside and instead listened to the storm assaulting the city.

This was an equally poor soporific. In fact it proved much more excitable to his imagination than the Hoffman tale.

He went to the window. Although he could see very little, the night was full of noises. Sirens wailed, thunder crashed, rain and broken branches beat against the windows. Trees creaked in the Contessa's garden, and tiles slid from the roof and shattered on the ground.

He had experienced storms in Venice, but none had come close to this one.

Disturbing sounds came from the direction of the Grand

Canal. Not human or animal sounds, for surely every soul had long ago sought shelter, but the keening of the wind and the mad rushing of water taking possession of the Grand Canal and turning that usually placid boulevard into a raging gorge between frescoed marble walls.

Like a parent with a child out in the storm, he thought of the Palazzo Uccello. When he tried to call Natalia again, hardly heeding the lateness of the hour, he was dismayed to find that the phone was dead.

He could imagine only too well, from reports of the great flood of sixty-six, what was happening to the besieged city. Buoys were rocking madly all around. Water was seeping up into the ground floors of palazzi and working its way through all the cracks and spaces.

Steps down to the sea must now be drowned and inaccessible. So high had the waters risen that, if you were looking from a window above the broad sweep of the Riva degli Schiavoni, it would seem as if the sea had finally invaded the entire city, with no boats floating upon it except those wrenched from their moorings.

And there was the fog, swallowing with frightful silence Romanesque capitals and Baroque cupolas, Byzantine friezes and loggias, classical balconies and pediments.

Yes, Urbino's vision of chaos and destruction was most vivid and complete, but not, he feared, in any way exaggerated.

Suddenly, as if conjured from his imagination, a white hand, with its fingers splayed, flew past his window, driven by the wind. He shuddered, thinking of the old woman whom the *gondolieri* had murdered and then cut into pieces and thrown into a sack.

The hand disappeared. A few moments later his fringed lamp and those lights still burning in the windows of the palazzi suddenly died out, then came back to life. This was followed by a terrible stillness at the end of which the storm returned with greater force and a newfound malevolence.

With an effort he tried to separate the sounds of the storm from the sounds of the embattled house. The walls themselves seemed to groan, and somewhere glass shattered. He thought he could almost hear the trickle of the water seeping persistently under the door from the loggia and forming a puddle. He rolled back the carpet a foot and wondered if he should push some of the pieces of furniture off so that he could roll it farther from danger.

Thank God the Contessa had replaced the rotten pilings of the Ca' da Capo two years ago. One of his constant worries about his own palazzo was that its pilings weren't strong enough to weather a severe assault like this one.

He tried the telephone once more. Still dead. The lights flickered off and on again, then went off and didn't come back on.

He sat in the dark, surrounded by all the sounds he could hear and those he thought he did. Earlier he had felt like a parent worried about an endangered child. Now he felt like the child itself.

He thought of the Contessa and hoped that, exhausted after today's events, she was sleeping through all this.

But he doubted it. Only the dead could sleep through a storm like this.

PART FOUR

The Shrouded Portrait

1

The strained, weary looks at the breakfast table next morning revealed what Urbino had suspected during the night: that he hadn't been the only one kept up. In fact, it looked as if there had been an entire houseful of insomniacs, for even the staff were walking around like zombies.

Except for Bambina. If she had been up all night, it had apparently done nothing but energize her. She was full of her quick movements, and the bows in her hair seemed almost charged with static electricity.

The Contessa looked around the table as if making an account of those who were still absent: Gemma, Angelica, Filippo, and Molly. "Lollygaggers," she would have considered them under other circumstances, but this morning the storm could excuse just about anything.

For those who had the energy, the general topic of conversation was, predictably, the storm still battering the city.

"All that whining and banging!" Oriana complained as she rubbed her temples. "I must look a fright."

When no one denied it, she said angrily, "I don't know how I'm going to stand it much longer!"

"The way the rest of us will have to," the Contessa said. "And try to remember that this storm is more than just a personal discomfort! Think of what's happening out there!"

"You both have the wrong idea," Sebastian said as he refilled his coffee cup. "We have gallery seats on the ark!"

In an oversized periwinkle cashmere sweater, loose wool trousers, and black velvet slippers, he seemed more than ready for hours of snug and casual viewing.

"Don't be an ass," his sister said. "Barbara's right. This storm is serious." She looked at Urbino. "Isn't it?"

"I'm afraid so. It's not at all a good sign that the electricity has been off since the middle of the night."

"And the telephone is still out," said Oriana. "Filippo is sitting in our room upstairs dialing our number over and over again. I told him to come down here with the rest of us and act in a civilized way. But I see he's not the only one keeping to himself. Gemma, Angelica, and Molly aren't down yet either."

Robert informed them that Angelica wasn't feeling well and had decided to keep to her room. As for his mother, he had thought it best not to disturb her. He wanted her to sleep as long as possible.

"Such a good boy to his mother," Bambina said with an attempt at an affectionate smile at her grandnephew. Lipstick marred one of her yellowed front teeth. "I'm sure you were, too, Signor Urbino. By the way, I got caught up in the pages of one of your books after our game of charades. There it was, right on the bookshelf waiting for me. It was my companion for much of the night."

"Which of his scandalous tomes was it?" Sebastian asked.

"His life of Vivaldi. I cried at the end. To think he died a pauper! Such beautiful music." She hummed some bars of *Autumn*. "You have a gift, Signor Urbino."

"Equal to Molly's, doubtlessly," Sebastian said. "By the way, where *is* the old girl? We're all dying to find out how she passed *her* night!"

"No better or worse than the rest of us, I'm sure," the Contessa said. "Perhaps this is she," she added hopefully as footsteps sounded in the hall outside.

But when the door opened it was Gemma. As white as wax, she gave no greeting but went over to the Contessa and bent down to whisper something urgently in her ear. Her scalp, vulnerable and shockingly exposed, gleamed through her hair. For a brief moment it wasn't Gemma's head Urbino was looking at but a skull almost ready to give up its camouflage. How she seemed to have changed since the previous evening!

"Mother!" Robert cried, starting to get up from his seat. "What's the matter?"

Gemma looked at him blankly. The Contessa stood up and took her arm.

"She's fine, Robert," the Contessa said in a strangled voice. "Will you all excuse us?"

Bambina's hand—the one holding her coffee cup—stopped halfway to her mouth. When she put the cup down, she raised her napkin to her mouth to conceal the beginning of a smile that, judging by the slight heaving of her bosom, was accompanied by a giggle.

The Contessa and Gemma left hurriedly. Dr. Vasco only barely seemed to hold himself back from getting up and pursuing them. His face was tense and strained.

"I wonder what that's all about?" Viola said to Urbino in a low voice, but not low enough that her brother, who seemed to have his ears especially pricked when she spoke to Urbino, said:

"Maybe it has something to do with the portrait. Oh, not the Caravaggio," he clarified with a smile that hinted he had been intentionally ambiguous. "The portrait of Barbara. Today's the great unveiling. They must be as nervous as hell. Gemma certainly looks it."

Mamma Zeno sat silently, lost in her sea of material, looking at no one.

Long moments of silence reigned at the table. It was as if Gemma's entrance and her hasty departure with the Contessa had thrown them into their own private thoughts.

Only Bambina and Oriana appeared immune to the somber, reflective spirit that had overtaken the others. Bambina somehow managed to combine an air of nonchalance with coy looks at Urbino. As for Oriana, she introduced one topic after another with no result until, with a sigh of exasperation, she stared moodily out the window as if she had been personally affronted.

They were still drifting through the doldrums of conversation when Mauro entered. He came over to Urbino and said in a low voice that the Contessa wanted to see him upstairs immediately.

Sebastian, who had been unsuccessfully straining to catch Mauro's message, said, "Summoned to put your finger in the Ca' da Capo's dike like the little Dutch boy?"

Urbino excused himself and left the breakfast room. He hurried up the broad staircase ahead of Mauro to the next story, where he found the Contessa collapsed against the red-and-gold upholstery of a divan outside Gemma's bedroom, drained of all color. He knelt down beside her.

"What is it, Barbara? Are you all right?"

"It's Molly," she said in a strangled voice.

He got up and went to the other wing to the Caravaggio Room. The room was closed but not locked. He opened it slowly, somehow expecting to find Gemma within.

But the only person in the room, partly kneeling, partly sprawling near an overturned low table and an armchair, was Molly. She was still dressed in her nightclothes and her feet were bare. Her thick spectacles were on the carpet, one of the bows bent.

Her head was thrust through one of the open doors to the loggia, fixed by jagged pieces of glass still lodged in the frame. Blood stained the door beneath her head and formed a pool diluted by rainwater. The louvered doors were also open. The soaked carpet and the floor of the loggia were littered with shards of glass.

Dead, just like little Flora and Renata before her, ran through Urbino's mind.

The thought was followed by an awareness of a slight scent, driven by the air blowing from the loggia. A woman's perfume or a man's cologne, vaguely familiar.

When he looked up at the Caravaggio, it seemed as if the epicene boy was smiling at him with the same living malevolence supposedly bestowed on the young Conte so many years ago in the presence of another dead woman.

Urbino closed the door of the Caravaggio Room behind him and crossed to the other wing, where Mauro was standing beside the Contessa, still sitting on the divan. She exchanged a brief look with him filled with sorrow and fear.

In response to Urbino's quick questions Mauro told him that Gemma had been helped to her room and that, no, the telephone was still not working.

"And the motorboat?"

"Milo secured it yesterday but something—a barrel or a piece of timber driven by the storm—staved the side in. But even if it were in good order, Signor Urbino, with this storm—" He broke off and shook his head.

"Is something the matter?"

The voice, weak and wispy, belonged to Angelica, whose head appeared farther down the hall at her door.

"No, Angelica, it's just the storm," the Contessa said with much more calmness than veracity. Urbino wondered if she were in shock or just trying to put off the inevitable.

Angelica pulled her head back into her room and closed the door quickly, as if afraid of learning any more.

"We should get Vasco up here," Urbino said.

"Why?" the Contessa said sharply. Urbino feared that she had no idea of what was happening until she said, "That poor woman is dead! It doesn't take a doctor to figure that out!"

"Things have to be done properly. There's been a death in the house," he went on. "It appears to be an accident—"

"Appears to be!"

"And the body in any case must be examined. We're fortunate in having a physician here, cut off as we are for the time being. It makes everything official."

Weariness replaced the Contessa's defiance.

"Do what has to be done, then. We'll both do what has to be done. That poor little woman."

Tears filled her eyes. Urbino sat down on the divan next to her and put his arm around her.

"I know, Barbara," he said consolingly. "It's a terrible thing. I found her endearing, in her way. I admired her honesty."

The Contessa, drying her tears with her handkerchief, looked up at him strangely.

"I don't necessarily mean her—her pronouncements," he clarified, "but her directness. She was without pretensions when she wasn't pontificating. That was her real self."

He thought of the little woman's preference for gin and the colloquial, and then of her body sprawled on the floor of the Caravaggio Room. He sighed and patted the Contessa's hand and stood up.

He told Mauro to ask Dr. Vasco to come upstairs but to say nothing to the other guests about what had happened. When Mauro had left, the Contessa got slowly to her feet.

"I'll see how Gemma is doing. Then I'll tell the others after Luigi has had a chance to—to examine poor Molly. She died through my negligence. I must face that. If she hadn't slept in the Caravaggio Room she'd be alive."

"This isn't the time for self-indulgent superstition."

"Is it superstition that I didn't have the doors looked after properly? Superstition that if I had, they wouldn't have blown open? Molly is dead because of me."

"We don't really know what happened to her."

"You stop right there, do you hear? Right there! I didn't want anyone to know my brooch had been stolen. Do you think I want to have it bruited about that one of my guests might have been murdered and that—that someone under this roof is the murderer? That poor, defenseless woman died because of *me*, I tell you, and I won't have it any other way!"

Vasco turned away from Molly's body with a face that looked more frightened than anything else. His emaciated body was trembling slightly.

"A terrible accident! We should remove her head from the door and lay her on the bed. I'm sure if we call up Robert or Sebastian, we can manage it."

"I don't think we should touch her," Urbino said.

Vasco raised one bushy gray eyebrow.

"And why is that?"

"The police will want to have everything kept just as we found it."

"For decency's sake! She can't be left like that!"

"You're right, of course. Photographs will have to be taken, then. We'll move her after we take them."

Vasco looked down at the twisted body of the woman who had begun by irritating him yesterday but who, by the end of the evening, had seemed to strike in him a sympathetic chord.

"As you wish." Vasco made a stiff little bow. "And what about little Gemma?" he asked as if she were still the eight-year-old girl she had been when her mother had died in the same room. "She saw this, didn't she? I must go to her."

Urbino followed Vasco out into the hall and closed the door gently behind them. The Contessa hurried over to them.

"Gemma doesn't want to see anyone, not even Robert, but I think you should see her, Luigi."

Silently Vasco set off for the other wing.

"How bad is she?" Urbino asked.

"Very bad. The shock of finding Molly is reason enough, but something else seems to be behind it."

"What do you mean?"

"I don't know. Just a feeling, and God knows I can't trust my responses right now. And she's not a well woman. You must see it!" She looked toward the other wing as if considering something. "But I must get myself together. I have to break the news."

"Do you want me to do it?"

"I should be the one. Let me get it over with. Why don't you ask Angelica and Filippo to come down? We'll all meet in the library."

"I have something very unfortunate to tell you all," the Contessa said to the nine guests gathered uneasily in the library. "It's about Molly. She's had an accident."

She was restraining herself from looking at Urbino.

"An accident? What kind of accident?" asked Angelica.

Scarfed and demi-gloved, she sat near the fire in a deep armchair. Robert was beside her, holding her hand. One of the locks of his short-cropped black hair fell across his forehead, giving him a slightly vulnerable look. His improbably blue eyes were troubled.

"I—I'm afraid, my friends, that she's dead."

"Dead?" Angelica repeated, her heart-shaped face looking lost and bewildered. "That's impossible."

"Molly is most definitely dead," Vasco said sadly.

"My mother!" Robert said and dropped Angelica's hand. He appeared ready to bound from the room.

"She's resting," the Contessa said. "She prefers to be alone right now, Robert."

"There's nothing to worry about," Vasco said, not convincingly. "She said to come to her room later."

"Please don't leave me, Robert," Angelica said. She took his hand again. "I—I'm afraid."

"There's no reason for you to be afraid, Angelica," the Contessa said emphatically. "It was a freak accident."

This time she did look at Urbino, as if challenging him to disagree with her.

"Most freakish," Vasco said. "The balcony doors blew open from the force of the wind and—and hit her in the head. An obvious and tragic accident."

"How ghastly!" Viola said. She was sitting on the sofa between Urbino and her brother. Her green eyes darkened and became more Swinburnish. "Poor Molly!"

"Poor Molly? Poor *us!*" Oriana almost screamed. "Can't you see? The number thirteen! And this storm raging around us, cutting us off from any hope of help!"

"Maybe all the bad luck has been used up, Oriana," Sebastian said and gave a nervous laugh. "The Caravaggio Room has taken the thirteenth guest as its victim. Rather economical when you think of it."

All too obviously and most inappropriately he was straining to recapture his characteristic manner, but his heart didn't seem to be in it. Neither could he count on an appreciative audience unless it was, briefly, Bambina. She suppressed a giggle, of which she seemed to have an abundance to be bubbled out or held back, as the occasion demanded. Her mother, however, sitting next to her on the sofa, frowned her disapproval of Sebastian's comment.

"If you don't know what to say, Sebastian," the Contessa reprimanded, "it would be best to keep quiet."

"She's right, young man," said Vasco. "This is no moment for humor with little Molly lying the way she is upstairs, her life snuffed out by such a sad accident."

Sebastian got up and went over to the liquor cabinet.

"My sincere apologies to you all. My humor wasn't meant to be irreverent. To steady the nerves, you know. Now I think I'll indulge in something a bit stronger." He poured himself a whiskey. "I don't think the rules against drinking before a certain hour apply when there's a dead lady lying in the house."

Viola was staring at him without her usual ironic affection, but instead with a look of distinct dislike.

"You've become very unfunny of late, Sebastian. How can you say such things when we're the ones who are responsible for Molly's death? Yes, us! We invited her here. We imposed her on Barbara. If we had let well enough alone, she'd be alive now in some hotel or other, entertaining people with her—her gift."

A look of embarrassed guilt came over Sebastian's face. He took a big sip of whiskey and retreated to the other side of the room.

"If any of us should feel in any way responsible for poor Molly's death, it is I," the Contessa said. "And not because I set her up in the Caravaggio Room. It was because of the loggia doors that she died. If they had been looked after properly, this would never have happened. I accept full responsibility."

She looked around at the group as if defying any of them to dispute her claim to guilt and responsibility.

She was about to go on when Mamma Zeno startled them all by raising her cane and saying loudly, "An act of God! He's the only one responsible. The only one!"

Urbino was confused as to whether this outburst was to be taken as a pious expression of faith in Providence or a condemnation of the whims of the Deity. The way Mamma Zeno looked briefly at her daughter—as if searching her face for some validation of what she had said—gave him no clue. Bambina's only reaction was a great deal of shifting about, followed by a concentrated playing with the lace at the wrists of her dress.

The Contessa, who probably thought it best neither to agree or disagree with Mamma Zeno's ambiguous comment, took a deep breath and said:

"Under the circumstances we'll just try to get through the rest of our time together as best we can and as respectfully as we can, remembering that poor Molly is lying the way she is upstairs.

Let's hope that things will soon be back to normal." This must have struck her ears as a bit naive, if not fatuous, for she added, "I mean the electricity and the telephones and—and everything like that."

As if to warn them all of just how long things might take to return to this questionable state of normality, the storm howled and hurled itself against the frail barrier of the windows. The drapes ballooned inward toward the group, huddling together in their fear and uneasiness.

5

When Urbino returned to the Caravaggio Room ten minutes later after getting a camera from the Contessa's room and a pair of rubber gloves from the cabinet beneath the sink in the conservatory, the rainwater was now pooling more deeply and widely around Molly's body. Some of the blood had become a fainter pink.

He looked down at the body and silently uttered something that was both a prayer and a promise. He would find out why the little woman had ended up like this. Even if he hadn't grown fond of her in the short time he had known her, he owed her this.

He started to take photographs, thankful that the Contessa had supplied the camera with film in anticipation of her house party. Photography was far from his forte. Fortunately, however, the Contessa's camera had proven itself amenable to his inexpert manipulations on those rare occasions when he had wielded it, once or twice in situations and conditions he had been sure would yield up only embarrassing oblongs of black.

He began by photographing Molly's body from every possible angle. It was a distasteful task, more so for him than for most other men, for if the truth were told, Urbino was unusually squeamish when it came not only to the sight of blood but even to the sound of his own heartbeat. As he maneuvered around the body, he once again detected the scent of perfume or cologne interlaced with the odor of blood. It was vaguely familiar, and seemed to be more concentrated near Molly's body. He bent down and sniffed. Yes, it definitely was stronger. Either perfume or cologne had been spilled near her body or she had put on some perfume before her death.

He next took photographs of the room: the bed, with its bedclothes turned down but apparently not slept in. The chair and overturned little table. Molly's clothes and possessions scattered about. Her spectacles lying twisted on the floor. Her felt slippers, which seemed to have been kicked off violently or carelessly. The walls, the carpet, the drapes, the loggia doors.

And the blood.

He looked for signs of more blood other than what had dripped down onto the loggia door beneath Molly's pierced head and formed a pool. He couldn't find any.

When he realized he was photographing even the Caravaggio, he put the camera down. Certainly he was carrying things too far. The room would be locked after they moved Molly's body. But what of the loggia doors? How secure were they now? Should they be kept open or should he close them and try to secure them? The wind was occasionally moving them back and forth, the motion of the broken-paned door limited by Molly's impaled head.

Carefully stepping around Molly's body, he took several photographs of the loggia, so awash with the rain driven in by the storm that the drains were inadequate to deal with it. The wind whipped at him.

He noticed something in the water and picked it up. It was a piece of silk ribbon, as soddenly pink as the blood mixed with water. He took out his handkerchief and unfolded it, placed the ribbon in it, refolded it carefully, and returned it to his pocket.

He began his search of the room, wearing the gloves that made him feel both furtive and foolish.

The Caravaggio Room was one of the few bedrooms without its own bath, since the locked room hadn't been included in the renovations after the Contessa's marriage.

However, at some point after coming upstairs last night, Molly must have been to the bathroom across the hall next to Vasco's room, for a bath towel, hanging from a wooden rack, was damp. She could possibly have mopped up water coming into the room from the loggia, but it wasn't even slightly soiled, as it probably would have been if it had been used for this latter purpose. If she had taken a bath upon retiring to her room, it would seem that she had then applied perfume. It wasn't something one usually did before sleeping—unless, that is, one was expecting a guest.

Molly's only medication was a half-filled bottle of aspirin. There was a rather Spartan collection of toothpaste, creams, and an inexpensive perfume. He sniffed the perfume. It wasn't the scent that seemed to be emanating from Molly's body.

He next looked through the clothes in the armoire and the chest of drawers. The dead woman appeared to fall into the category of the sensible, perhaps even the seasoned, traveler, for she had brought only a modest wardrobe, with interchangeable pieces. Two pairs of comfortable shoes were neatly lined up in the wardrobe.

No Ouija board, no Tarot cards, no crystal ball stored away—but, after all, Molly had insisted that her gift was one for the past, not the future. He looked at her body lying so exposed and undignified on the floor. No, her gift, if she had had one, certainly hadn't included the future. Otherwise she might still be alive.

On the bedside table were a paperbound copy of a popular guide to Venice and a lacquered lap desk of vaguely Oriental design.

He thumbed through the guidebook. He read a few underlined passages and quickly a pattern emerged. Each of them dealt with some aspect of Venice's sensational side. The stabbing of Paolo Sarpi on a bridge not far from Urbino's Palazzo

Uccello. The *acqua alta* of sixty-six. The intrigues of the Council of Ten. The theft of St. Mark's body from Egypt. The Black Death. The skinning alive of a Venetian general by the Turks. The cholera plague of the nineteenth century. The beheading of the traitor Doge Marin Falier. The ghost legends surrounding the Casino degli Spiriti.

Molly's ticket from the *Orient Express*, quoting the high fare, was between the pages of the guidebook. Molly hadn't seemed the kind of person with that kind of money. Her humble collection of belongings attested to this.

He put the book down and opened the lap desk. It held pens and pencils, a letter opener, stationery with Molly's Northwest London address, British postage stamps, an address book, a checkbook, a small notebook, a packet of file cards fastened with an elastic band, and an envelope with the address of a London literary agency. Urbino opened this latter and found a standard literary contract, duly signed, for a "nonfiction book, tentatively entitled *The Blood of Venice*," by Molly Wybrow. A modest advance was quoted, as was the delivery date of the manuscript nine months from now.

He removed the elastic band from the file cards and shuffled through them. About a dozen were written on in a small cramped hand. They appeared to be notes—quotations and summaries about Venice, with once again Venice's frequently dark history as their theme.

He put everything back in the lap desk to take to his room. His slight nausea of before was now replaced by a more general uneasiness and discomfort.

He looked down at Molly's body again. He rejected the possibility that the source of his discomfort was the feeling that he was violating her privacy. After all, as a biographer, he had had many occasions to settle this particular qualm. If he didn't quite subscribe to the maxim that the dead had no claim to privacy, he nonetheless knew the dangers of being overly scrupulous. And certainly those who had died under mysterious circumstances could claim no privacy—and neither could anyone who had been associated with them.

No, the uneasiness was coming from somewhere else, perhaps from the fact that, in the absence of the police, he was acting without authorization and setting himself up for censure. Yet, didn't the present situation—the storm, the isolation, the need for immediate action—call for something more than just sitting back and waiting?

Urbino thought that he had resolved—or was it "rationalized"?—his feelings, until something else occurred to him. It was the possibility that his uneasiness came from another quarter entirely. From fear. The circumstances that might excuse his present behavior were the very ones that contributed now to his apprehension.

For if his suspicions were correct, he was in the palazzo with a murderer.

Urbino wasn't a physically brave man. He would be the first to admit it. But physical bravery wasn't something particularly required in that small, floating corner of the world that he had so comfortably sequestered himself in. Even his amateur sleuthing had required no heroic efforts. What he did have, however, was moral courage and a cold fury against almost all forms of injustice. These things, along with his intelligence and tact, hadn't failed him yet, and he hoped they wouldn't now.

6

Urbino picked up the lap desk and the camera, and walked toward the door. He stopped short. The door was slowly opening. Cautiously, stealthily, a head appeared. It was Bambina.

She started when she saw Urbino, and a hand flew up to her heavily painted mouth, accompanied by an involuntary gasp.

Then her dark, round eyes focused on Molly's body. She stared at it intensely for a few moments as if it were important to take in every distasteful detail.

"What do you want, Bambina?"

The harshness of his voice startled even him in this room of the dead.

Bambina, who had paled, seemed at a loss. Her eyes wavered again in the direction of Molly's body. A guarded yet also somehow childlike expression passed over her face.

"Mamma sent me," she said quietly. Then, glancing quickly back at Molly's body, she lowered her voice even more and said, "To keep vigil. She didn't like to think of Molly being all alone. She would have come herself but Mamma—Mamma isn't feeling well. Dr. Vasco is with her. She insisted that I come by. I meant no wrong."

"That's very considerate of you both, but right now we're going to move Molly."

"Move her?"

"To the bed. Then the room will be locked."

"Locked? But why?"

"Out of respect."

"I see. I'll tell Mamma that she's being looked after. It's only because of her that I came. Good-bye."

She went out into the hall. Urbino followed and closed the door behind them. He then took the key from his pocket and locked the door. Bambina watched him. For the first time she seemed to notice his rubber gloves, then, with a puzzled expression, the lap desk and the camera. She said nothing further, but now seemed eager to leave and hurried toward the other wing, where her room was.

Urbino peeled off the gloves and went to his bathroom to throw them in the wastebasket.

Urbino and Milo, the Contessa's chauffeur, managed to move Molly's body to the bed fifteen minutes later. There was no doubt in Urbino's mind now that the scent of perfume was coming from Molly's body. He said nothing to the Contessa, however, who stood solemnly watching them and then placed the little woman's spectacles on the bedside table. She had brought one of her scarves to arrange around Molly's head.

She had no success in keeping alight a small votive candle. The draft from the broken pane—Urbino had closed both the louvered and the glass doors to the loggia—kept blowing it out. When Milo left to have Lucia bring up a candle guard, Urbino mentioned Bambina's visit.

"To keep vigil at Marialuisa's suggestion? Strange," the Contessa said. She sighed and looked down at Molly's body, which was more grotesque lying on the bed, with the Contessa's scarf around the head, than it had been when it was impaled by the glass. "But—but death makes everyone act strangely, don't you find? Out of character, I mean."

Lucia came in with the candle guard. The votive flame was properly set alight.

"I think I'll stay here for a few moments by myself," the Contessa said. She drew her shawl more tightly around her shoulders. "It's very cold in here."

"I've shut off the radiator."

The Contessa looked puzzled.

"But why—?" She broke off. "Ah, I see," she said. "Yes, perhaps that's the best thing to do."

As Urbino was leaving he reminded her to lock the door behind her.

"And I'd like to have the key, if you don't mind."

"There's only the one."

"If you need to go in, I can unlock it easily enough, but Molly should be kept undisturbed."

"Yes, I suppose you're right," she said vaguely. She looked at the broken pane. "But there's no lock on the loggia doors and with the pane broken—Listen to me!" She gave a nervous laugh. "As if anyone would want to come in that way. All anyone has to do is just ask for the key."

"If you want the key to let yourself in, you can have it, but no one else is to come into the room. Do you understand?"

The Contessa might have been about to point out to him that this was, after all, her house, but she held her tongue.

8

In his room Urbino poured himself a whiskey, sat down in the armchair, and opened Molly's lap desk. He first took another quick look at the contract for *The Blood of Venice*, and wrote down the name of Molly's literary agent in London in case he needed to contact him. He then went through the index cards, but found nothing different to add to his original impression. Each contained some episode of Venice's more sensational history.

The small notebook seemed at first to have only more of the same: brief anecdotes about Venice and Venetians throughout history, in which death figured prominently and often melodramatically and grotesquely. Many of the anecdotes had also been on the cards.

From the cards and these entries he could form no opinion of what the book itself would have been like, or might even already be like if she had begun to write it.

But then he came upon an entry with the title "Houses with Pasts." On the list were the Casino degli Spiriti; the "unfinished"

Palazzo Venier dei Leoni, with its history of wild parties both before and after Peggy Guggenheim bought it; the so-called House of Desdemona; the Ca' Rezzonico, where Browning had died, and the Palazzo Vendramin-Calergi, where Wagner had died; the cursed Palazzo Dario. Even the Doges' Palace, which certainly didn't quite qualify as a "house" the way the others did, was on the list.

What surprised him was the last name: the Ca' da Capo-Zendrini. As far as Urbino knew from his own research on the building, it didn't have any bloody or even dubious history, as did the others, but it did have the Caravaggio Room—and the deaths that had taken place in there: the Conte's grandmother, Flora, and Renata.

And now Molly.

She had obviously been interested in the Ca' da Capo-Zendrini before coming to Venice. What had she known about it and where had she gotten her knowledge? And since she had included it on her list of "Houses with Pasts," he assumed that either she had known about the Caravaggio Room—or had discovered something dark about the palazzo that even he and the Contessa didn't know.

Urbino next went patiently through the address book. It must have been redone recently for there were none of those inevitable crossing-outs of defunct names, addresses, and phone numbers. He didn't recognize any of the names, other than that of Molly's agent. There were five "Wybrows" listed, all of whom lived in London, scattered across its various districts.

He got up and went to the window for a few minutes, looking out at the driving rain. The doors to the loggia were buckling slightly inward from the force of the wind. Worries about the Palazzo Uccello came again, and he went to the telephone and picked it up. Still dead.

Urbino poured himself another whiskey and returned to the contents of the lap desk. At the bottom of a pile of envelopes were two folded sheets of inexpensive notepaper. He unfolded them. They were filled with writing.

Urbino's surprise at finding the Ca' da Capo-Zendrini on Molly's list in her notebook was nothing to what he now felt as he read the two pages. The writing was in Molly's hand, but in something approximating shorthand, with initials and abbreviations, dashes and symbols. It wasn't, however, hard to read. It had a breathless, rushed quality, as if Molly had been transcribing something that was being dictated to her or had been writing it down as quickly as possible because she was afraid of being interrupted.

The sheets were filled with information about himself and the Contessa. The circumstances of his parents' death in the fiery crash with the sugarcane truck outside New Orleans. His brief marriage to Evangeline Hennepin. His inheriting of the Palazzo Uccello through his mother, an Italian-American. His decision to live in Venice. His biographies, with the names of the subjects. His amateur sleuthing. And his friendship with the Contessa.

The Contessa's life was also fully if briefly documented. Her education, when she was simply Barbara Spencer, at St. Brigid's-by-the-Sea in England. Her studies at the Venice music conservatory. Her marriage to the Conte Alvise. Her renovation of the Ca' da Capo. The Da Capo-Zendrini summer house, La Muta, in the hills of Asolo. The childlessness of her marriage. The Conte's death from pneumonia. Her patronage of Venetian causes. What gossipy Venetians called her "Anglo-American alliance" with Urbino for the past fifteen years.

Molly's "gift," at least insofar as Urbino and the Contessa were concerned, was here demystified. Urbino dismissed the possibility that the list was the result of some bizarre communion with the past, although its unmistakable air of precipitateness might have been seen by someone more credulous as proof of just that.

But if one mystery seemed to have been solved, another more disturbing and puzzling one had taken its place: Where had Molly gotten her information from? And had this also been the source of what she seemed to have known about the history of the Ca' da Capo-Zendrini?

Although most of the information about himself and the Contessa was in no way confidential, and was in fact a matter of public record, he couldn't believe that Molly had industriously gathered it all by herself by using the skills of a researcher.

The inclusion of the story of his parents' death was the most strange. It was something he kept close to himself, sharing it with few people. But Molly had been in possession of it. Urbino suspected that she had heard it, along with the other details about himself and the Contessa, from someone now at the Ca' da Capo-Zendrini.

But from whom? The only ones at the house party who knew all these things, other than himself and the Contessa, of course, were Oriana and Filippo. Could there be some hidden link between them and Molly?

These speculations led him to consider the possible sources of the other things that Molly had said which had apparently disturbed some of the guests. A vague understanding of what he believed was called Occam's Razor surfaced to support his hunch that Molly's information was all of one piece. There was most likely one—and only one—source for everything she had known about the Contessa, himself, and the other guests at the Ca' da Capo. There was probably an evident fallacy in this, but he nonetheless remained convinced of its truth.

Urbino refolded the two sheets, returned them to the lap desk, and opened the checkbook. It was all that remained to be examined. There were about a dozen stubs. The first stub was dated the last week of October. The neatness and organization evident in Molly's address book were also displayed in the checkbook. Each stub was neatly and carefully recorded.

Checks had been written out to Molly's Harrods account, several charge cards, Thomasina Wybrow (Urbino remembered her name from the address book), Molly's landlord for the November rent, the National Gas Board, and British Telephone for over two hundred pounds. Several were made out to "Cash." These latter were for very large sums, although they hadn't noticeably diminished the unusually large checking balance.

The last entry, however, had come close to wiping out the balance. It was made out to Sebastian Neville.

Urbino barely had time to begin to consider the possible implications of this when a piercing scream sounded above the noise of the storm.

When Urbino went into the hall, Viola and Robert had already emerged from their rooms. Vasco had his door open and was looking out.

Shouts came from the first floor, where the sweep of marble steps stopped before making their even broader descent to the *pianoterreno.* Urbino, Viola, and Robert went to the top of the stairway, where Oriana and Filippo were peering down at the floor below. Bambina emerged from her room and joined the small group.

"My God, what is it now?" Oriana said.

Vasco joined them with a troubled look on his thin, lined face and followed the group down to the floor below. There they found Sebastian and Lucia with several other members of the staff gathered in a circle. Urbino slipped between Sebastian and Lucia.

Lying on the floor on her back was Gemma in her bathrobe. Her eyes were closed.

"Vasco!" Urbino called, but the doctor was already at his side and quickly determined that Gemma was alive, but unconscious.

"Mother!" Robert cried, kneeling down beside her.

Vasco loosened Gemma's robe and the high neck of her nightdress. Carefully, he checked for broken bones and said there didn't seem to be any. Neither was there any sign of blood from the head injury, but in Italian Vasco mumbled something about internal bleeding.

With surprising rapidity Bambina had fetched a glass of water. "Give this to her," she said.

"You know better than that!" Vasco shouted.

In the violence of his reaction he flung out his hand and knocked the glass of water from Bambina's grasp. It shattered against the wall. For the second time in less than twenty-four hours her offer of water to her niece had met with a rebuff. She looked down at Gemma and a tick came and went several times in the corner of one eye.

"What's going on?" It was the Contessa, coming down from the floor above. "My God! Gemma! What's happened?"

"She fell down the stairs," Sebastian said.

"How do you know that?" his sister challenged.

He stared at her with irritation for a few beats before he said, "It's obvious."

"What was she doing up?" the Contessa asked. Before anyone might answer, she said to Vasco, "How is she?"

"She's unconscious. She hit her head when she—she fell down the stairs."

"We can't leave her here," the Contessa said. "Carry her back to her room."

Urbino, Robert, and Sebastian, under Vasco's direction and with the Contessa leading the way, carried Gemma carefully up to her room. The bedclothes were already thrown back and they laid her on the bed.

Viola, Bambina, and Oriana had followed. "My poor niece!" Bambina said. She rushed to the bed and almost threw herself against Gemma, putting her arms around her in an overwrought display of concern.

"Get away from her!" Vasco shouted.

Urbino remembered Vasco's behavior yesterday in the

conservatory when Bambina had offered Gemma some water and then again earlier today when he'd knocked the glass of water she had brought for Gemma out of her hand. Vasco now reached out his hand to pull Bambina physically away from her niece, but Bambina withdrew, her ample bosom rising and falling rapidly.

Vasco, trying to control himself, said that under no circumstances should Gemma be left alone.

"I'll stay with her," said Robert, who seemed oblivious to everything except his mother.

"We'll take turns," the Contessa said. "Let's hope this storm will be over soon and we can get her to hospital. God! Listen to it!"

It was now thundering.

"Maybe not all the telephones are out," Viola suggested. "Is there any way to signal to a neighbor?"

"A neighbor?" the Contessa repeated, as if Viola had mentioned something exotic.

"It's a good idea," Urbino said. "Maybe I can call from one of the windows or go across the *calle*."

"Everyone must be in the same position we are. And no one's boat would be able to go out in this storm. Our only hope is that it's over soon."

"But we should at least see if someone else's phone is working," Urbino insisted, realizing that the Contessa wasn't thinking clearly. "The hospital could surely get an ambulance here."

"The hospital?" Robert said. "Where is it?"

"In the Castello behind Piazza San Marco," the Contessa said.

"But you're forgetting the private hospital near the Madonna dell' Orto," Urbino said. "It's closer."

"I'll go there," Robert said. "Give me directions."

"That's impossible!" the Contessa said. "You'd never find your way in this storm. Just let Urbino see if the telephone is working across the way."

"She's my mother!" Robert shouted.

"Come. Let's go outside and let Luigi look after her while we discuss this."

"There's nothing to discuss," Robert said.

"Listen to Barbara," Vasco said. "Go outside. All of you. I'll watch over her."

"Be sure you do!" Robert said.

"I always have, Robert, long before you came along. She's still a defenseless little girl to me."

Robert had a dubious look on his good-looking face, but he relented and went out into the hall with the Contessa. Urbino, feeling impelled by Vasco's look of irritation and impatience, followed, as did Sebastian and the three women.

"Barbara's right about the hospital, Robert," Urbino said. "You would get lost in a few minutes. You would have no idea of an alternate route when you reached a flooded area."

"I'd go right through the water. I'd get there! I'm not an idiot!" And once again he said, this time with desperation, "She's my mother!"

Angelica, looking anxious, now joined them.

"Has something happened to Gemma?" she asked.

"She fell down the stairs," Robert said. "She's unconscious. I'm going to get help at the hospital."

"I'll go," Urbino said. "I have a better chance of getting there, and you should be here with your mother."

It seemed the inevitable solution. The look on the Contessa's face, however—a look that spoke of fear and abandonment—momentarily checked him. It was with considerable relief that he heard Filippo's voice say:

"I insist on going. I know Venice even better than you do. And Barbara needs you here."

"Don't leave me, Filippo," Oriana wailed. "It's just like that movie! One by one, we'll all be—be snatched away. First Molly, now Gemma! Someone else will be next!"

"Don't get hysterical," her husband said.

"You're not thinking of Gemma! You're not thinking of me! You're just thinking of the Ca' Borelli! You'll forget about us all! I—I hope it gets swept into the Adriatic!"

"It has your jewelry, wardrobe, and love letters, dear, you had better reconsider!"

Filippo went into their room next door and came back a few minutes later wearing his trenchcoat.

"I'll need a pullover cap and some boots."

"Mauro will fit you up," the Contessa said. "Please be careful."

"Don't worry about him!" Oriana shrieked. "He can't wait to escape. Can't you see it?"

Filippo shook his head silently and went downstairs.

"Oriana," the Contessa said in a controlled voice, "I think it would be best if you went to your room. Maybe Luigi can give you something for your nerves."

Oriana stared at her without speaking for several seconds.

"I *will* go to my room," she said with a lift of her well-tended-to chin. "And I'll lock the door and stay there until this nightmare is over!"

She swept down the hall into her room and slammed the door.

10

It was only now that Mamma Zeno opened her door. Her room was next to Gemma's. Several hours earlier she had vehemently proclaimed Molly's death an act of God. Now, with her own granddaughter lying unconscious and perhaps close to death herself, she might not find solace in the same sentiment.

"Is something the matter?" Her voice sounded tired. "I fell asleep. The wind . . . rain . . ." Her voice faded out for a few moments, then came back clearly and distinctly: "I heard voices in my dream. Shouts. I realized they came from out here."

She looked more than ever as if she were on the point of disappearing into the voluminous folds of her clothes.

"It's Gemma," the Contessa said. "She seems to have fallen down the stairs. She's unconscious. Luigi is looking after her."

"Let me go to her." She moved toward Gemma's door. The small group made way for her. "Robert, why are you standing here? Come with me."

"Dr. Vasco said to leave him alone with Mother."

"He did? I'll see about that."

Her obvious weakness didn't prevent her from walking toward her granddaughter's room with an air of command that boded little good for the Zeno family physician. The Contessa put a gentle arresting hand on her shoulder.

"Why don't we all gather down in the library for a few minutes, if you don't mind," Urbino said.

The Contessa, guiding Mamma Zeno, led the rather solemn processional down the staircase to the library. As if under a general agreement to remain silent, they quickly disposed themselves in various chairs and sofas—with the exception of Sebastian, who preferred to lounge near the liquor cabinet, glass in hand, and Urbino himself, who stood on the carpet in the middle of the room.

Urbino felt vaguely uncomfortable as the others stared back at him with what he felt were varying degrees of resentment, nervousness, and puzzlement. He told himself that he had better start getting accustomed to discomfort. It was only going to get worse from this moment on.

"In what can't be much more than twelve hours we've had what seem to be two accidents here," Urbino began. "And—"

"Seem to be!" repeated Bambina. She immediately clapped a hand over her mouth and stared at Urbino, then at the others.

"Yes, seem to be," Urbino said. "You know about Molly. Now there's Gemma and her apparent fall down the stairs. Did anyone see her fall?"

"Why ask us about Gemma first?" Viola said. "If you're going to do things right, you should begin with Molly. I thought you had experience with these things," she added with an attempt at affectionate mockery.

"We'll get around to Molly," Urbino responded more sharply than he intended. Viola's smile disappeared.

"That'll put you in your place, Viola," her brother said. "Do you mind if we have a drink, Mr. Sleuth?"

"Go right ahead," the Contessa said before Urbino could answer. It was as if she were making an attempt to remind them—Urbino perhaps most of all—that she was still in charge of the revels, no matter what bizarre form they were taking. "But please don't smoke!" she added as a further assertion of authority.

"A drink will be sufficient unto the moment." Sebastian poured himself a whiskey. His hand shook slightly. "Can I do the honors for anyone else?"

No one chose to join him. Urbino continued.

"So, did any of you see Gemma fall?"

"I was in my room reading," Angelica said. "I didn't know anything was wrong until I heard Robert shouting." She looked at Robert, who as usual was sitting next to her on the sofa, one arm extended across the back. She reached up and patted his hand. "I'm in a different world when I'm reading. I didn't even hear the storm."

"The pleasurezh—the pleasures of the text," Sebastian said and took a sip of whiskey, which he evidently didn't need. He dropped himself onto an available sofa.

"What about the rest of you?" Urbino asked.

"I was reading in my room, too," Viola said. "I came out when I heard all commotion. I'm afraid I'm not much help."

The rooms in both wings closest to the stairway were those of Angelica, Viola, Bambina, and Mamma Zeno.

"I was in my room, too," Bambina said quickly. "I was daydreaming. The scream frightened me. I guess it was Gemma screaming when she fell."

The twitch was still there in her eye. One hand held the other tightly in her lap. She seemed to be restraining herself from reaching up and touching the twitch.

Mamma Zeno, who had already told them upstairs that she had been asleep, offered nothing more, but just sat there with an inscrutable look on her shrunken face.

"I was at the window of my room, looking at the storm," Robert said. "It was making enough noise to wake the—" He broke off. "I rushed out when I heard the scream. It *wasn't* my mother."

"It was Lucia," Sebastian said with the air of clarifying all from his reclining position on the sofa. "And no, I didn't *see* her scream, but when I hurried from the library she was bending over Gemma."

The library wasn't far from where Gemma's unconscious body had been found.

"And you didn't hear her falling?"

"Afraid not. The walls in these palazzos are thick. But she obviously *did* fall. By the way, I was in the library for a good hour or so. Never left. Needless to say, Gemma wasn't there when I came down."

The Contessa excused herself and said she would be right back. While she was gone, Urbino asked the group if they had seen or spoken with Gemma since at the breakfast table when she had summoned the Contessa. Robert was the only one who said he had.

"I went to see how she was about an hour and a half ago. She was extremely upset at having seen Molly like that. She kept saying that it was her fault. I asked her what she meant, but she just kept saying it over and over again. Vasco's sedative must have disoriented her. I stayed with her until she fell asleep—a drugged slumber is more like what it was." He shook his head. "She—she must have got up for some reason and lost her balance."

The Contessa returned with Lucia. Lucia said that she hadn't heard anything but that she had discovered Gemma when she was going upstairs to speak with the Contessa about that evening's dinner.

"What about the other staff?" Urbino asked her. "Did they hear or see her fall?"

"But of course not, Signor Urbino! They would have called Mauro or the Contessa. None of them were by the staircase for at least half an hour before I found her."

So, unless any of the absent guests had something different to add, there seemed no way of knowing exactly how long Gemma had been lying there before Lucia discovered her.

Lucia left. Urbino, who had nothing more he wanted to ask them as a group, fixed himself a whiskey. Viola came over and asked him to fix her one, too.

"It's been quite a day," she said after taking a sip. "And it's not even over yet."

"Nonetheless, I just might lock myself in my room with a good book and a supply of candles."

"So you're not mad at me. I—"

"Excuse me," the Contessa said, overriding Viola's comment and the quiet conversation Robert and Angelica had begun, "but I'd like to say a few things." Her eyes met Urbino's, and she seemed to be warning him to allow her to speak without any interruption. "It's obvious that we can't consider ourselves in the middle of a house party any longer, certainly not the one we all hoped it would be." She frowned at the inadequacy of her words and began again. "I mean that what's happened to Molly and now our dear Gemma"—she looked consolingly at Robert—"makes even the thought of any further attempt at diversion completely impossible. What has happened has happened in my house and I accept full responsibility. No, please," she said, putting her hand up when there were some murmurs of objection from Robert, "I do feel responsible, and in some way I am. Considering that I feel this way, you might find a little strange what I have to say next. I've decided to throw you on yourselves for the remainder of our time together. What I've had planned for us will be forgotten about. The unveiling of my portrait, the treasure hunt this evening, everything."

There was a note of regret in her voice, which she made an effort to banish as she continued: "You're free to go anywhere in the house you wish"—she glanced nervously at Urbino as if she expected him to disagree—"and to entertain yourselves as you wish, but *please* be careful. I—I mean, of course, that we can't have any more accidents of even the slightest kind. I'll understand if you choose to remain in your rooms under the circumstances and have your meals there, like Oriana, although I don't think we should take her as our example. Perhaps Filippo has already found a telephone that's working and we'll soon have help." She stood up. "I'll be up in my room if anyone needs me."

Urbino felt her parting words as a summons. He quickly finished his whiskey and, to Viola's evident irritation, excused himself and slipped out of the library.

Urbino immediately realized upon entering the Contessa's room that his suspicions in the library were correct. What she had just given them downstairs had been a calculated performance. Here in her private domain, with only himself as audience and surrounded by her most beloved objects—her Fabergé revolving frame with photographs of her dead, her well-worn books, and a half-dozen small Longhi paintings—she could be herself.

All he needed to tell him the true state of her nerves was the glass of gin in her hand, a drink she seldom indulged in and never at this hour. She gripped it tightly as she said to him in a lower voice than necessary, "Do they know what I'm really thinking? What did they say after I left?"

"Very little, since I left right after you. I thought you wanted to talk to me."

"I do want to talk to you, but one of the things I wanted to talk about was their reaction. I thought you would understand that."

"Sometimes you assume I understand much more from what you might or might not say than I possibly ever could."

"I don't know if you're trying to be humorous or carping. We're not playing games! This is serious."

"Exactly. You know how I feel about Molly's death. And I feel even more strongly about it now."

"And why is that?"

He busied himself with pouring himself a gin as he considered a response. He didn't want to mention the check stub made out to Sebastian for a large sum until he had an opportunity to talk with him. And he needed to get his thoughts more in order about Molly's notes on himself and the Contessa. He had barely had time to absorb these things when the alarm had been sounded about Gemma.

When he turned around the Contessa was looking at him with impatience.

"There really wasn't enough blood."

"Not enough blood! The room was full of blood!"

"I'm not an expert in pathology, but when Molly's artery was pierced by the glass of the door, blood should have been sprayed over the room for some distance." When she shook her head as if she didn't want to hear any more, he said, "I don't find this any more agreeable than you do." He fortified himself with a sip of gin and continued. "It was obvious where the glass had pierced her artery, but the piece had fallen out somehow, maybe from the movement of her head and body in the wind, I don't know."

"You don't know! What else don't you know?"

"I suppose it's possible she died from a slow seepage of blood caused by head injuries. And the piece of glass that pierced her artery could have fallen out after her heart had stopped pumping her blood, but I don't think so. The room shows some signs of violent activity. A table and chair in different parts of the room were overturned, but there were no traces of blood near them. If she had been injured by the door bursting open and then moved around the room in shock or whatever, there would be some blood."

"Are you saying that there was a—a struggle of some kind in the room?"

"It's one possibility."

"You're holding something back. I can tell. I want to know everything. I have a right!"

She did, but it was best that he keep her in the dark about certain things for a while. He did tell her, however, about the scent of perfume in the air of the Caravaggio Room and especially around Molly's body.

"I didn't smell any," the Contessa said, "but in the state I was in it's a wonder I was even breathing myself. But what of it?"

"I'm not sure, but it wasn't the perfume in the bottle in her room, and if she was indeed wearing perfume, she put it on after she took her bath. It might mean she was expecting someone to stop by, presumably a man. It's—it's just speculation at this point. Bear with me. There were some other things but I'd rather wait before I go into them. I need to—"

"You need to brood and worry over them! Well, go right ahead, but don't spend too much time about it. We have to get through until—until this storm ends or Filippo gets some help. The way things have been going today, who knows what can happen in the next few hours?"

She started to raise the glass to her lips in an agitated movement, then looked down at it as if someone had just thrust it into her hands.

"So you don't think we're dealing with accidents, either?"

She put the glass down violently on the table.

"I don't know what to think! Everything is starting to look suspicious to me now. Oh, I'm probably making a beam out of a twig"—she often fell into a direct translation into English of Italian idioms—"but when I went to Gemma's room after we found

Molly, she asked me to tell her exactly which room was yours. It seemed such a strange question. She said she needed to be absolutely certain. I thought it was just one of those irrelevant things people say when they're in shock, but I'm not so sure now."

Urbino told her what Gemma had said to Robert—about how she was responsible for Molly's death.

"She said that? It—it just goes to show you how confused she was. She kept saying, 'Poor Molly! To die through no fault of her own.' I did find *that* strange, too, to be honest—that she said 'fault.' I assumed she was hysterical, and she was, really, but it seemed a rather strange way to put it. It made me think of how Molly's death could be said to be *my* fault, but I don't think she was trying to make me feel responsible. Anyway, it was then that she asked where your room was. I said that she shouldn't be concerned about anything or anyone but herself, and just to get some rest."

"But you did tell her where my room was?"

"She insisted. Maybe she had something to tell you. She could have gone looking for you and—and fallen. I don't necessarily mean that she fell because she was coming to see you. I mean, she might have fallen *on the way* to seeing you and—"

She broke off. She was trying to retreat from the implications of her own statement.

"You think Gemma might have been pushed down the stairs by someone because she was on her way to see me."

The Contessa had a defeated look that made her face seem as if she had never spent all that time up in Geneva.

"Yes," she said quietly. "Tell me it's ridiculous."

He went over and took her hand.

"We both have to face something, Barbara. I think you realize it yourself. There's something very strange going on. Even before Molly died and Gemma fell down the stairs, there was a tension in the air and—"

"But of course there was," she interrupted. "Having the Zenos here after all those years, and maybe it was a mistake to have the twins come, and then of course they brought Molly, and she made thirteen, and Oriana . . ."

She trailed off. He was shaking his head.

"I don't mean all that, although Molly's inclusion in the house party by the twins *is* part of it." This was the closest he wanted to come at the moment to discussing Sebastian. "Surely you noticed how both Bambina and Angelica reacted when they first met me. As if they'd seen a ghost. Then Molly's comments caused a bit of a stir—"

"They caused a bit of a stir in you, too! And in me! I don't see what that has to do with all this."

"Perhaps a great deal. Exactly what, I don't know, but if you think Gemma might have been pushed down the stairs because of something she might have wanted to tell me, isn't it even more logical that someone killed Molly because of something *she* knew or someone *thought* she knew? I'll try to find out what I can and—"

"Find out nothing! If what you say is true, then you'd be in danger yourself! Leave the door closed! Just as I should have left the door of the Caravaggio Room locked and barred. There's some truth in the fairy tales! Bluebeard's wife, Pandora, and—and all the rest of them! Just do whatever you can to see that no more accidents happen to anyone else before this storm ends!"

Exactly how he was going to have any chance of effecting this without opening a few doors, the Contessa didn't say.

After leaving the Contessa, Urbino went to the conservatory. Unless someone was concealed among all the plants, it seemed empty and glowed with a strange, green, sickly light.

As he had only a short while ago he went to the cabinet beneath the sink and took out another pair of white rubber gloves. There were still a few pairs left. He stuffed the gloves in his trouser pocket. At the door he paused to consider the storm crashing furiously against the glass. With a shiver he was reminded of the "ghostly hand" he had seen—or, more likely, of course—had imagined he had seen flying past his window last night.

He went directly up to Gemma's room. Vasco was sitting by the bed, holding Gemma's hand. The drapes had been drawn and the room was dark.

"I'll relieve you, Dottore," Urbino said quietly. "Barbara is arranging for the staff to stay with Gemma until we can get an ambulance here to take her to the hospital. Filippo might be close to having one sent soon. Let's hope so."

"We could be hours from any help at all," Vasco said. "I don't see why I have to leave her. If—when she regains consciousness she should have someone familiar by her side."

Urbino, remembering how Gemma had shrunk away from Vasco on one or two occasions yesterday, wasn't so sure that she would necessarily appreciate Vasco's "familiar" face bending over her.

"When you look at her, Macintyre," the doctor was going on, "you see a woman in her sixties. I still see the child she was—and it doesn't seem all that long ago. Not at all."

A melancholy expression passed over his face. He released Gemma's hand and stood up.

"I'll speak with Barbara to see that everything is done properly. I don't intend to be pushed aside when Gemma needs me."

"Of course not. You have done a lot of good for her under other circumstances as well, Dottore. I'm thinking, of course, about the period after her mother's death when I'm sure you were indispensable. I assure you that Barbara has no intention of pushing you aside. She just wants you to get some rest. You'll have a better chance of continuing to help Gemma that way. You'll be called immediately if she regains consciousness or if there's any change."

Although Vasco didn't seem satisfied, he made no more protest. His footsteps receded down the hall.

Urbino didn't know how much time he had to do what he needed to do. He had told the Contessa not to send Lucia in to sit with Gemma for another half hour, but anyone might come in.

He took the gloves from his pocket and put them on. He started to go through the room. Once again the uncomfortable feeling he had had in the Caravaggio Room came over him, even more strongly this time.

He began with the bathroom. The tub, soap, and towels were dry. The blue Murano crystal water tumbler, replaced neatly on the cabinet beside the sink, held some droplets, however. Also on the cabinet were an array of cosmetics and a half-filled plastic bottle containing tablets that, from the name on the label, he recognized as a potent painkiller. The tablets had been bought in London and bore the name of the physician.

He then unstoppered an elaborate crystal bottle of Shalimar perfume and sniffed. It was definitely the scent surrounding Molly's body, but once again it seemed to evoke another association that eluded him.

He returned to the bedroom and went through the clothes in the armoire and checked the pockets. Unlike Molly, Gemma had some expensive items, but, with one or two exceptions—an evening dress and a Missoni skirt—they were not new, but well cared for. He found nothing of possible importance. He had no idea what he was looking for, but neither had he when he had gone through Molly's things.

He approached Gemma herself. She was still wearing the nightdress and robe she had been found in. Vasco had dressed the injury to her head. A blanket was pulled up around her so that she wouldn't lose body heat.

Making a silent apology, he went through the pockets of the robe and nightdress. He felt a strong sense of violation, and kept telling himself he was obliged to do this for Gemma's own sake. He could find something that might answer some questions, perhaps about Gemma's fall, or even Molly's death, perhaps—

He broke off speculating as his hand touched a small, cold,

hard object in the pocket of her robe. He took it out. A peacock of gold, lapis lazuli, rubies, emeralds, sapphires, and diamonds. It was the Contessa's brooch.

He put it in his pocket. That Gemma could have taken it seemed inconsistent with the impression he had formed of her. Yet he had long ago, because of his work as a biographer and an amateur detective—not to mention because of his general observation of others—given up being surprised by people's inconsistencies, or being hard on himself when he was mistaken.

The evidence of the brooch made it less likely that Gemma had been on her way to see him when she had "fallen"—unless she had slipped it into her pocket for safekeeping, not caring to leave it in her room. Perhaps, once having taken it, she thought it best to have it on her person at all times.

Gemma could conceivably have found the brooch and been on her way to tell him, and had been pushed down the stairs by the thief, who wanted to avoid detection at all costs.

Or someone might have wanted to make Gemma look like the thief and planted the brooch on her after her fall. But if this were the case, had the brooch been taken to implicate Gemma? Or had the thief originally stolen it to keep, but then disposed of it in this way to protect himself or herself? Had events made it more valuable as a means of incriminating Gemma?

Was the person who had stolen the brooch—Gemma or someone else—also the one who had murdered Molly? If so, how was it all related?

He put these questions aside for future consideration as he turned his attention to the rest of the room, now even more fearful of a sudden interruption.

He went through a trousseau chest, in which he found only items of clothing, neatly folded, then opened all the drawers and compartments of an escritoire. Nothing. Near the escritoire was a bookshelf with uniform leather-bound volumes of classical European literature in English and Italian translation. He flipped the pages of two or three of the books but found only some pressed wildflowers in an edition of Maupassant's short stories.

He found no passport, no wallet, no purse, no letters—in fact, not even a scrap of paper with writing on it. It wasn't just the contrast with what he had found among Molly's things that surprised him, but the contrast with what one would expect to find in anyone's room.

He picked up a book on the bedside table. A well-worn copy of Vasari's *Lives of the Artists* in Italian. There was nothing between its pages, not even a bookmark.

He was reaching for Gemma's paintbox when he heard footsteps approaching the door. He quickly pulled off the gloves and thrust them into his pocket.

"What do you think you're doing?"

It was Robert. His voice, though quiet, was cold and exact.

"When Vasco told me you were with Mother, this is just what I expected you came for. To put your nose where you shouldn't." He looked over at his mother and lowered his voice even more. "What the hell gives you the right!"

"I understand your anger. Hard though it might be to believe, I'm only trying to help your mother." Urbino then thought about the brooch in his pocket. "You might feel a little different if I tell you that someone seems to have taken away your mother's documents and money—and whatever personal things she might have had. The clothes in the chest over there seem to be all thrown about. Does your mother have much cash with her?"

"What my mother does or does not have is no business of yours, Macintyre—or of anyone else in this place. That's why I took away what you've called her 'personal things.' Vasco was kind enough to leave me alone with her for a few minutes. Now, if you'll excuse me, I'd like to sit with her."

On his way downstairs Urbino met no one in the hall or on the staircase. In the library he found Sebastian, sunk deep in the generous cushions of an easy chair. A copy of Lamansky's *Secrets d'Etat de Venise*, printed in St. Petersburg near the end of the nineteenth century, lay splayed open on his cashmere sweater. A glass of brandy was within easy reach, and the odor of cigarette smoke hung in the air.

Urbino coughed, none too quietly. Sebastian opened his eyes and stared at him, blankly at first.

"Oh, if it isn't the charming Urbino. Is it a book you stopped by for?" His speech was even more slurred than earlier. "Yes, my friend, a book I'm sure it is. For those odd moments when you're not playing Sherlock Holmes. Here you go. Take this one."

He started to hand Urbino the Lamansky, but he lost his grip on it, and it dropped to the floor.

"Excuse me. Hope I didn't split the binding. Don't want to send Barbara to the pauper house. Such an interesting book, even if I did take a snooze in the middle of a chapter! Ah, the intrigues of the Doges! How boring Venice is nowadays. Just another theme park."

He grabbed for his brandy, almost upsetting the glass. He eyed the glass critically.

"Amazing how fast it disappears. Just evaporates. Drink?"

"No, thank you. I've had more than enough already."

This was certainly true—and he had mixed his drinks abominably—but he also hoped, by saying it, that Sebastian would take it as a hint. He didn't, however. He got up and made his way unsteadily to the liquor cabinet, where he filled his glass.

"Dear Barbara does have all the little—and big—accoutrements, don't you find? Sometimes I feel as if I'm in The Old Curiosity

Shop—*très, très* chic, though very much New Bond Street, icons and Fabergé eggs and Brustolon and Hepplewhite and objets d' of all shapes and sizes!" He made his way back to his armchair and almost collapsed into it. Urbino remained standing. "But I ask you? What is a library without a humidor? Not that I smoke cigars, but it's almost a sine qua non. And not an ashtray in sight, so I'm obliged to use this charming champagne glass. Murano?" He blew a stream of smoke into the air. "The faint smell of smoke will be my contribution to the improvement of the room. In my humble opinion, Urbino, you have one major flaw that gives me pause. You don't smoke, and probably never have. How can you find a permanent place in my heart unless you do?"

More than ever Sebastian seemed to be hiding behind a screen of persiflage. This, along with his less than sober state, made Urbino realize that it wasn't a good time to bring up the checkbook stub. But perhaps he could lay the groundwork.

"Tell me how you met Molly," he said before Sebastian could go off again.

Sebastian snuffed out his perfectly viable cigarette, deposited it with all the others, and lit another.

"I already have. Is this one of those sobriety tests? If it is, you can stop wasting our time. I plead guilty, guilty, guilty!"

"You and Viola met her for the first time on the *Orient Express*, you said."

"So we said and so we meant and so we did."

"Humor me. Tell me what the circumstances were."

"Only since you have that earnest quality that makes fools of a certain kind of woman—and man, I might add! Let me see. I met Molly shortly after we left Paris. Viola was in her compartment and I was at the bar. There I was, lifting my elbow, and there was Molly. She was babbling away about her so-called gift. I took to her right away, maybe it was the alcohol, but when Viola joined us, she found Molly as cute and as—as—amusing as I did."

"You said her 'so-called gift.' You never considered it a real one?"

"What do you take me for? One of those fools who follows the sign to the 'egress' looking for some kind of bird?"

He used his own joke as an occasion to go into a spasm of laughter. When he finished, Urbino said, "Did she say anything about you that made you wonder? I mean, made you wonder how she knew about it if she *didn't* have a gift?"

Sebastian's green eyes, so disturbingly similar to his sister's, stared at the Baroque ceiling as though he were deliberately weighing Urbino's question. He pulled his gaze back and looked at his glass.

"As a matter of fact, there were a few things that gave me pause. She said that Viola had fallen very hard once, and she *did* when we were eleven. Down from a tree we were climbing." He smiled faintly. "But all children have falls. She also said that I had a problem with my tutor at Cambridge. What student worth his salt doesn't? But what was strange was that I never told her I went to Cambridge."

"I see."

Urbino thought for a few moments and then asked him how he came to invite Molly to stay at the Ca' da Capo.

"You mean Viola and me. Oh, Molly was saying how she didn't have a reservation and did we think she'd have a hard time finding a place and did we know of any hotels. It only seemed natural to invite her to join us. And it was Viola who did the asking."

"Did you have any reason to stop by to see Molly last night after we all went upstairs?"

"You must be kidding! A midnight rendezvous with Molly? Entertaining though she was, hers would be the last door I'd tiptoe to for some divertissement. I have my own pleasures *and* my reputation to consider. Now I hope you're finished because I find that Mother Nature is calling me most desperately to a fine and private place."

He got up. As he was walking past Urbino, he swayed slightly and seemed in danger of losing his balance. Urbino reached out and grabbed his elbow. For a brief moment Sebastian clung to him, standing closer than necessary, then disengaged himself. His smile made Urbino even more uneasy than the sudden physical contact between them.

"Don't worry!" Sebastian said as he continued to the door. "I won't tell a soul what's just happened between us. Especially not Viola!"

Urbino lingered in the library for a brief moment, trying to make some sense of his encounter with Sebastian. Among many other things, he wondered if he had made a tactical error in not having mentioned the check stub.

He had reached no conclusions when he met Viola coming down the staircase to the dining room. He led her into the picture gallery through a large doorway above which was a marble coat of arms of the Da Capo-Zendrini family. He closed the door behind them.

Only three Venetian walnut divans and a gilt chest competed with the offerings of the room. The lacquered walls were covered with portraits of various sizes, although the full-length monumental predominated. There were several pastel portraits by Rosalba Carriera, mainly half-lengths of old women with fans and gentlemen in wigs. But their delicacy was more than a little overwhelmed by the more dramatic offerings of Titian, Lorenzo Lotto, Tintoretto, Veronese, and Van Dyck. Soon Gemma's portrait of the Contessa would take its place among the portraits by the great and by those only slightly better known than their subjects.

The different styles in dress and art could in no way disguise the characteristic Da Capo-Zendrini features—the aquiline noses, shrewd eyes, pale Venetian skin, and unmistakable air of unconsidered privilege. Even those who were Da Capo-Zendrini by marriage and not birth seemed to share these features, perhaps by that peculiar sympathy and transformation wrought between husbands and wives through the years.

This couldn't be said for the Contessa, however, whose portrait was soon to hang on these walls; exactly where, given their crowded condition, was far from clear.

Urbino thought that he and Viola would retire to one of the divans, but the portraits were initially too much temptation for her. She preferred to walk around the room, examining them silently. Urbino wondered how much of them she was taking in, for she had the air of having just awakened. Her eyes were dreamy and slightly out of focus, and her angular face seemed as pale as the powdered face of the eighteenth-century woman she was now standing in front of.

"Would you tell me again how you came to meet Molly?" he asked quietly, as if afraid of disturbing her train of thought.

She said nothing at first but passed from the pastel to the dark, passionate Tintoretto of an elderly bearded man with the mien of a biblical patriarch.

"So you think Molly's death wasn't an accident."

It was a statement, not a question. Before he could respond, she went on: "And you probably think that Gemma's fall is related in some way to Molly's death."

Her directness reminded Urbino of how different she was from her twin despite their unsettling physical similarities.

"I've been doing a lot of thinking myself, and I agree with you," she went on, treating his silence as a tacit agreement. "The more we know about Molly, the better position we'll be in."

Urbino didn't fail to note the "we."

She walked over to the bright silks and brocades of a Veronese lady. On the bodice of her gown was pinned the peacock brooch. Viola bent closer to look at the way Veronese had rendered it. Still looking at the portrait, she described how she and Sebastian had met Molly on the train. It matched what Sebastian had already told him in every detail, even down to how she had been the one to suggest that Molly join the Contessa's house party.

"It seemed the right thing to do," she said, turning to Urbino. "Barbara has always said that Sebastian and I could come down with one or two of our friends. I didn't think she'd mind—and I really don't think she did, except for the number thirteen, that is, and because she had to use the Caravaggio Room."

"Did Molly give any indication that she had an ulterior motive in accepting?"

"I've been going over all my conversations with her with just that in mind, but I can't come up with anything. I've been thinking of something—Oh, it's silly, but you know what it's like when an idea gets lodged in your head!"

"What is it?"

She stared with a little frown at a nineteenth-century portrait of a woman with all the Da Capo-Zendrini features, displaying the peacock brooch on her black bombazine.

"It's just that I was wondering if—if she could have known who the other guests were? Other than Sebastian and me and—and you and Gemma, that is. You see, Sebastian and I mentioned you both. Don't you see what it might mean if she knew ahead of time who was going to be here?" She gripped Urbino's arm. "That all her spouting away about the past was arranged ahead of time! She seemed to know such a lot of strange things," she continued with a touch of what sounded like wonder in her deep voice. "But why did she do it and what does it have to do with everything?"

That Viola's thinking so closely paralleled his own was only marginally less surprising to him than that she was so freely expressing it. Was she trying to gain some kind of advantage? For what purpose? Urbino still felt sufficiently disconcerted from his encounter with Sebastian in the library to be sure of his own responses. Something of what he was feeling must have communicated itself to her.

When she looked at him, her eyes seemed wounded. It wasn't

just their usual melancholy cast, but something different, deeper darker.

"You don't trust me, do you? Oh, I know how it is! Everyone's a suspect—everyone except the detective and his sidekick! And that's indisputably Barbara, isn't it? You've got to follow the rules. But don't get too clever or—or you might fall into a trap of your own making! I don't care what you think about me—or what you *think* you should think about me, which is more to the point—but I'm going to do whatever I can to help you find out what happened to Molly. Whatever we manage to discover we can turn over to the police, once this bloody storm is over. Agreed?"

Urbino, who felt that there was much to ponder in her behavior, said, "I think you should stay out of it."

"But I'm already right in the middle of it, aren't I?" She looked around the room at all the portraits of the dead Da Capo-Zendrinis and seemed to shiver.

15

Lunch was strained. Oriana and Mamma Zeno stayed in their rooms, and Robert was still with his mother. Looking around at those who had come down, Urbino wondered if they had done so only to show they had nothing to hide from the others' scrutiny and to remove any suspicion that might be generated if they chose to be alone.

Of course, there was also the very real possibility that they were afraid to be alone—all, perhaps, except one, who only wanted to give that appearance and had come down for that very purpose.

The Contessa used a lot of nervous energy seeing that everyone got what they wanted at the sideboard, and then sat down with a small plate. As if in imitation or comradeship with Angelica, she only picked at it for form's sake. Her eyes kept darting from one guest to another as she carried on what turned out to be a monologue about how she was sure the storm was abating and how Filippo must have reached the hospital or another source of help by now. They needed to wait only a short time more.

No one pointed out that the storm seemed to have renewed its strength during the past hour and that they should have started fearing for Filippo a long time ago. Surely if all had gone well with him he would have managed to get Gemma some help before now.

Only Bambina, who made three trips to the buffet—twice for herself and once for Vasco, who seemed drained of all energy—ventured to utter anything longer than a sentence. She said that Molly wouldn't want them moping around just because she was lying upstairs dead. She somehow seemed to think—and expressed herself vividly on the point—that Molly had been a game sort and that her "gift" had made her as philosophical as Socrates. As for Gemma, she had known her since Gemma was a child and was sure that she'd want the party to go on.

"Or at least to have her portrait unveiled," she said, directing this to the Contessa. "In honor of her."

"Little Gemma's not dead," Vasco said, showing more energy than he had since entering the dining room.

Bambina looked as if she were about to snap something back at him, but instead popped a piece of bread into her mouth, then got up and began to prepare another plate, this one for her mother. Vasco excused himself and said that he wanted to look in on Gemma.

When he had gone, Sebastian, in his inebriated state, came close to shouting that he agreed with Bambina. He got unsteadily to his feet, made a self-conscious gesture of throwing back his thick auburn locks, and raised his wineglass. "To each his hemlock! Let the revels go on!"

Urbino, who throughout lunch had preferred close observation of the others to conversation, noted the look of disgust on Viola's face and the shocked one on Bambina's.

"You've had more than enough to drink, Sebastian," the Contessa said.

"But there you're absolutely wrong, dear cousin! I intend to get thoroughly soused before the cavalry ride in—or should I say float in!"

16

"Never! Not one single, solitary word!" the Contessa insisted in a low voice. Urbino and the Contessa were alone together in the *salotto blu* after lunch, the others having gone their individual ways. He had just asked her if she had ever said anything about his parents to either Sebastian or Viola.

He had told her about his searches of Molly's and Gemma's rooms, his reading of Molly's journal and other writings, and his conversations with Vasco, Robert, and the twins. He hadn't told her, however, that Viola had expressed strong doubts about Molly's accident or that Molly had apparently written out a large check to Sebastian. The twins were family, and he wanted to get a clearer picture before he spoke to her about them. Neither had he told her about having found the brooch in the pocket of Gemma's robe or his belief that the scent of perfume surrounding Molly's body was the same perfume Gemma used.

"And neither Viola nor Sebastian knew about the Caravaggio Room before you told them about it," she was saying. "It's been a well-kept secret, as you know."

"Yes, but as I also know, secrets are shared with a select few."

"Never the twins or anyone in my family at all!"

"You never said anything to Gemma?"

"But she didn't need to be told about the Caravaggio Room. Oh, you mean about your parents. No, not a word."

Urbino thought for a few moments, then said, "But Oriana knows."

"Of course she knows! She has for years! You're not suggesting any connection between her and Molly?"

"No, but Oriana isn't the most discreet of people, and she and Gemma spent time together."

"A couple of visits to the Guggenheim, that was it. Oriana appreciates all that insane art, and you know how I hate that place even more since the murder."

The Contessa was referring to one of his previous cases that involved a Dali painting at the Guggenheim and a beautiful young artist's model whose body had been discovered floating by the water steps of the museum.

"Let me ask her," the Contessa went on after giving a sigh that seemed to evoke all the personal sorrows for her at that time. "I know how to handle her. She's a bundle of nerves at the moment." She shook her head slowly. "But aren't we all?"

Together they listened to the rain driving against the window, as it had so many years ago during the original house party.

"I hope Filippo is all right. He should have reached the hospital long before now."

"True, but maybe even the ambulances can't get out. They might be sending someone on foot."

Surely she, too, must realize this was an unrealistic hope, but she said nothing to contradict him.

Without in any way preparing her, Urbino took the brooch out of his pocket and put it on the table next to her collection of ceramic animals.

"My brooch! Where did you find it?"

When he told her, she was speechless.

"Gemma took it?" she eventually said. "But why?"

"It's not at all definite that she took it. It was in her pocket. Someone could have put it there before or after she fell. Or maybe she found it in someone's room and was bringing it to me."

"When the thief pushed her down the stairs? The person who murdered Molly? Because that's what you're thinking, aren't you? That the theft and the murder are somehow related?"

"Yes, but maybe they aren't at all."

"But that would mean that there are two maniacs around—one pushing a woman's head through a door, if that's what happened to poor Molly, and another one pushing an ill woman down a flight of stairs! No, they're one and the same, you can be sure of that."

"Unless Gemma did steal it and was the one to murder Molly."

"The only comfort that would give me was that we wouldn't have to sleep with our doors locked. Gemma's in no condition to do anyone any harm."

"But that doesn't mean that someone else might not carry through what she set in motion."

"An accomplice?"

"Or someone who might want to protect her. And there's another thing. Remember I mentioned the scent of perfume from Molly's body? Well, I'm almost convinced it's Shalimar. Gemma used Shalimar."

"I could have told you that! And so does Bambina!"

Urbino now realized where his other association with the scent came from: the flask that Bambina carried with her all the time.

The Contessa stood up abruptly.

"I'll leave you to sort it all out and go up to talk with Oriana and get some real work done!"

"Here," Urbino said. "Take your brooch."

He handed it to her.

"I'd prefer if you kept it," she said. "I know it's unlikely that it would be taken twice, and if what you suspect about Gemma is true—"

"It's only a possibility," he interrupted. Before she could launch another exasperated stream of retorts, he quickly told her what he wanted her to do with the brooch. Her gray eyes opened wide.

17

After the Contessa had gone, Urbino sat thinking. His intuition told him that there was a link between Gemma and Molly other than the perfume, which was as much of a link between Bambina and Molly.

There very likely could be some evidence of this, some clue, among Gemma's personal things, which Robert had removed to his own room. Robert might be aware of a connection between his mother and Molly that he preferred to keep hidden, perhaps for his mother's sake or for his own. Urbino would try to persuade Robert to let him look through Gemma's things.

He was convinced that Molly—the apparent stranger at the feast, the thirteenth guest—had been murdered because of something she knew about the immediate or the distant past. Urbino had become conditioned to think of murder as seldom a random act, even though he knew that in the world at large it usually was.

Everything indicated that the situation was the same now. Molly's gift for the past, which, if he was to judge from her notes, had only appeared to be extemporaneous and inspired. Her death in the Caravaggio Room, the scene of so much tragedy for the Da Capo-Zendrini and Zeno families. The disappearance of the peacock brooch, also with its associations with the histories of the two families, and the brooch turning up in Gemma's pocket. The scent of perfume surrounding both deaths—a scent that the Conte had referred to in his memoir as the "odor of sanctity." The gathering of six people all related directly or indirectly to the mysterious death of Renata Zeno Bellini in the Caravaggio Room: Mamma Zeno, Bambina, Dr. Vasco, Gemma, Robert, and Angelica.

There were also the Neville twins, the extent of whose relationship to Molly was still very much in question. Exactly what had Molly paid Sebastian for? Only to get her into the palazzo? Could Sebastian be working with Gemma in some way? And what role might Viola be playing? Urbino had to confess to himself that the twins disconcerted him enough to make him dubious of his own responses.

Those who remained were Oriana and Filippo, who were friends of Barbara, unconnected to her family, and whom he didn't even remotely suspect.

Whenever Urbino hit a snag in his writing or his cases, he would put it out of his mind and take one of what the Contessa liked to call his "long vague walks." Very often this activity would result in his seeing things more clearly. But he didn't have the opportunity for a rambling walk in the storm-ravaged city, and if he had, he certainly didn't have the luxury of time. He needed to get to the bottom of things as soon as possible. The air of the Ca' da Capo was charged with menace.

His eye wandered to the velvet-shrouded easel holding Gemma's portrait of the Contessa. It was to have been unveiled that evening. Bambina, provoking Vasco's anger, had suggested at lunch that it still should be. Urbino got up and walked over to it. He suddenly realized that he had not been giving sufficient attention in his thinking to one detail. The portrait itself. It had been the Contessa's commissioning Gemma to paint the portrait that had set the present house party in motion. She had intended to use it as an occasion to "heal old wounds" between the two families. He remembered what the Contessa had said at Florian's a month ago. Some wounds never heal.

The velvet draping was slightly askew. He started to rearrange it, wondering if, after all, Bambina might be right. Perhaps it would be a good idea to unveil the portrait this evening. Consumed with a desire to see the portrait, he drew away the draping.

He was appalled. A vicious slash angled down to the left-hand corner from the Contessa's face.

He heard footsteps approaching the door and tried desperately to cover the portrait, but the door opened before he could.

The Contessa stood motionless, looking at her mutilated portrait. A strangled sound came from her throat. Urbino hurried to her side and guided her to the sofa.

"Someone wants me dead."

She said it without any emphasis but with as much conviction as if she had herself just been stabbed.

After calming the Contessa, Urbino convinced her to say nothing about the slashed portrait to anyone. They spoke with Mauro, Lucia, and some of the other staff. No one had seen anyone going in or out of the *salotto* when the Contessa or Urbino weren't in it themselves.

"I don't know exactly what to think, Barbara," Urbino said when they were alone again. "It could have been done by someone with a hatred for you. Someone who wants you to know that he—or she—is out there and is prepared to strike at you personally. Or it could be a warning for you to turn a blind eye to things."

"Turn a blind eye to what things? To what's going on under my own roof? Even if I wanted to pretend to be deaf, dumb, and blind, there's Molly's dead body lying up there in the Caravaggio Room—and maybe we'll have another death in the house soon if Gemma doesn't recover. I have no intention of being intimidated!" she cried, her voice quavering.

"It could also be a way of trying to get me to stop poking around."

"I absolutely forbid that! I might be afraid, but fear is not going to dominate my actions—or yours! We may be close to some real answers now. That's probably why this—this maniac slashed my portrait. I spoke with Oriana. She's still a bundle of nerves, lying in bed under the covers with ear stoppers. The whole place could fall down now and she wouldn't know it! But listen to this! She did tell Gemma about your parents the first week Gemma was here."

"Unsolicited?"

"Let's say that Oriana was maneuvered into it. They were at the Guggenheim. Gemma brought up your inheriting the Palazzo Uccello through your mother. She knew that from me. She asked Oriana if she had ever known your mother. Oriana took it from there. Oriana tried to use her fears of the storm and worries about Filippo as a cover, but I could tell that she probably said even more than that. Probably about your marriage and divorce from Evangeline, and most definitely quite a lot about *me*. So it's obvious. Oriana told Gemma, and Gemma told Molly. There must have been some relationship between the two of them long before Gemma came to paint my portrait."

"Gemma might have told someone else what she knew, and that person could have filled Molly in."

"You're thinking of Robert. Because he wouldn't let you go through Gemma's things."

Urbino was also thinking of Sebastian, but he was reluctant to mention this suspicion. Instead he said, "Robert might be only protecting his mother's privacy. I'd do the same in his position, but—" He broke off and shook his head slowly. "A distasteful business, when I have to do things that I don't like to do, that I'd criticize someone else for doing."

"This is not a time for scruples," the Contessa said, more than a little uncharacteristically since she was the most scrupulous person Urbino knew.

"And rather late in the game, too, I'd say," Urbino added wryly.

"You know, there's another aspect to the slashing. The person who did it might be trying to implicate someone else."

"The way the same person might have tried to implicate Gemma by putting the brooch in her pocket?"

"Yes, and perhaps Gemma is once again the target."

"How do you figure that? It's her creation!"

She looked over at the easel, now reshrouded in velvet, and shivered as if it held a monstrous creation.

"Artists are considered temperamental, subject to sudden and violent tantrums. People always remember Van Gogh, not painters like Sargent or Renoir. But artists sometimes *have* been known to destroy their own creations. And if the brooch was put in Gemma's pocket, the person who did it—probably the same one who stole it, who murdered Molly, who pushed Gemma down the stairs, who slashed your portrait—wanted it to be taken as a sign of Gemma's dislike and resentment of you."

"Dislike and resentment of me for what?"

"For the past. For what happened here back in the thirties—"

"But I had nothing to do with that house party! I was in England! Just a young girl myself, like Gemma. Even younger!"

"The person doesn't have to be thinking rationally, Barbara. In fact, I believe we're dealing with someone who is very irrational at times. Not just in the way that we can say all murderers are, but beyond that." He thought for a few moments, then added: "And I have little doubt that this has to do in some way with the past."

"If Gemma isn't the one who's having the finger pointed at her through the slashed portrait, then who?"

"We'd be better able to answer that question if we knew exactly when the painting was slashed. Remember that Bambina mentioned at lunch that you should unveil it despite, perhaps even because, of what happened to Gemma."

"So you think it could have been Bambina?"

"Bambina would appear to be the most likely—but it could have been anyone else at the table who heard what she said. He or she might have got the idea to slash it, hoping you would unveil it tonight and then we'd all think of Bambina's suggestion."

"But would Bambina have wanted the painting unveiled if she had slashed it?"

"She—or someone else—could have wanted just that. Sitting there, knowing the painting was slashed and waiting for the moment the draping was taken off. I rather find it consistent with the kind of person who would slash it in the first place."

"But then we're limited to Bambina, Vasco, and Angelica," the Contessa said. She had an almost disappointed expression, which, however, quickened into something more like unease as she added, "I assume you in no way intend to include Sebastian and Viola!"

Urbino didn't reply immediately, and the Contessa said, nervously, "Well, there's also Robert and Mamma Zeno even if they weren't at the table!"

"I'm well aware of that." He didn't develop this any further but instead asked, "Is it true that you've never looked at the portrait?"

"It certainly is! I promised Gemma. She insisted on it. Oh, I was tempted, just to see if she had made me into a fright, but I didn't. It wasn't all that hard. I'm not in the habit of gazing at my own face—whether it be in a mirror, a photograph, or a painting!"

Urbino smiled to himself at the obvious falsehood of this.

"But you should, Barbara. It's such a lovely face." He couldn't resist adding: "And it always has been, even before Geneva."

Evidently embarrassed and just as evidently pleased, she tried to cover both emotions by turning her face quickly in the direction of the shrouded easel again and asking, "So what are we to do with the portrait?"

"The same thing we're going to do with the brooch."

"You don't mean—!"

She stopped and looked at him in disbelief.

"Exactly!" he said.

PART FIVE

The Curse of the Ca' da Capo

1

It was still more than four hours until dinner. Urbino returned to his room. There, he reread the Conte's memoir, which he had retrieved from a drawer in the *salotto* where he had placed it after reading it to the twins. He paid close attention to what the Conte said about Vasco, Mamma Zeno, Bambina, Andrew Lydgate and his fiancée, the doomed Renata, and her eight-year-old daughter, Gemma.

He took out a sheet of paper and a pen from the desk and made a list of Molly's provocative comments yesterday. He had an excellent memory and it served him well now.

When he had finished, he read it over several times. The large majority of Molly's comments had been about the Caravaggio Room and the death of Renata Zeno Bellini. She had even named the specific date of the house party. If the death of Renata had always struck Urbino as strange, it now, after his rereading of the Conte's memoir and his reconsideration of Molly's comments, became sinister. He had to face the very real possibility that someone had murdered Renata. It could be someone now under the roof of the Ca' da Capo. And the person who had murdered Molly could be either the same person or someone who was willing to go to extreme lengths to protect Renata's murderer.

He had no proof that Renata had been murdered, only the strongest of suspicions, but it seemed imperative that he not leave it out of the equation.

For the next few minutes he filled another sheet of paper with a diagram of the layout of the two bedroom wings of the Ca' da Capo. The only rooms beside the Caravaggio Room that had access to the wide loggia were those of the Contessa, Bambina, Angelica, Urbino, and Robert. It was perfectly conceivable that despite the storm, Molly's murderer had gained entry to the Caravaggio Room through the loggia itself. The storm would have been a perfect camouflage, for no one would have been inclined to take an airing as long as it had gone thundering along.

He fixed himself a drink and stood staring through the window and across the loggia at the foaming gray clouds, the lances of rain, the high, choppy waters of the Grand Canal.

He needed to know more. But in this case perhaps more than any of his others, because of the hothouse atmosphere and the storm still malevolent outside, to search for more information could be extremely dangerous.

Possibly two people—Renata and Molly—had already been murdered in the palazzo, and another was lying close to death.

All of them women. Two were mother and daughter, and the third, Molly, had surely been murdered because of what she knew—or seemed to know. She had penetrated the Ca' da Capo, she had ended up in the notorious room, she had not left it alive after her first night.

Could the person who had gone to so much trouble to put Molly in the house have been the one who had murdered her? Had she paid such a large sum of money to Sebastian not only, perhaps, to be admitted to the Ca' da Capo, but also to end up being murdered by his hand?

And how had she come to carry the scent of the perfume that both Gemma and Bambina used? Had one of them visited her during the night and murdered her? Had the scent been planted—the way the brooch might have been planted on Gemma? Or had Molly borrowed some of the perfume from one of the women in expectation of a special guest? If so, who had she had her assignation with? Dr. Vasco immediately came to mind, but perhaps Sebastian had stopped by to collect more money, this time in the form of cash. Or Robert, to warn her away from his mother. For that matter, why should Urbino assume that she had applied perfume for a man, and not for another woman?

It was almost like a nest of Chinese boxes or Russian dolls.

How many more were there to discover? Who else might be in mortal danger? Who else, that is, other than himself?

Urbino's reflections were interrupted by a knock on his door. It was Mauro. The elderly majordomo, who took his responsibilities seriously, looked tired.

"The Contessa said that I should give this to you," he said. "It was on the tray in the downstairs hall."

He handed Urbino a long white envelope. It was addressed in Molly's now familiar hand to her agent. Urbino looked at the back, where Molly's engraved London address was crossed out and the address of the Ca' da Capo-Zendrini written beneath it.

Before he could ask Mauro anything, the majordomo started to speak in a weary voice:

"I'd like to explain as I did to the Contessa, Signor Urbino. Last evening before dinner Signora Wybrow asked me where she could put letters to be mailed and where she could get stamps. I told her to put her letters on the tray in the hall and not to worry about the stamps. We would take her letters to the post office at the earliest opportunity. She thanked me." He glanced down at the envelope in Urbino's hand. "I noticed that letter on the tray a short time later, but because of the—the confusion in the house, I forgot about it until a few minutes ago."

"There's no problem, Mauro. I'll take care of it."

As soon as Mauro left, Urbino slit open the envelope. He had no qualms at all, although he reminded himself, too late, that he should have been more careful about not destroying whatever fingerprints other than his, Mauro's, Molly's, and possibly the Contessa's, were on the envelope. He carefully withdrew what was inside by one corner.

On a sheet of Molly's engraved stationery was written:

Dear Harold,

Well, I'm on the inside just as I said I would be. And not just "inside" but in the cursed room itself! Never fear when Molly's here!

I know you're worried about me, but there's no need. So far it's been all fun and games with me as the ringleader! I've been promised the whole story at the end of this, and it will make a great chapter, and the chapter will make the book. You'll see!

This won't be the last of my missives from bloody Venice, dear. I intend to linger on after this weekend. I give you only this consolation for not being with me in these splendid digs: It's raining here too!

Cheers!

Molly

Urbino carefully put the letter back in the envelope. It confirmed his suspicions. Molly had had an accomplice. "I've been promised the whole story at the end of this," she had written. By whom?

Most likely Gemma, who it seemed had already told her so many things about Urbino and the Contessa. Could Gemma have murdered Molly for some reason? If she had, what had led Gemma to this ultimate act of violence? In what way could it all be related to the events of the house party back in 1938?

Yet someone had tried to murder Gemma, too, it seemed.

Could Gemma have engaged Molly as an instrument of vengeance against whomever had murdered her mother? But why now? And could she have known or suspected all these long years who the murderer was? Perhaps even seen the actual murder? Urbino remembered how Sebastian had joked that Gemma might have been a "bad seed" and murdered her own mother.

Then something occurred to Urbino that scattered all these speculations. He might be going in the wrong direction completely because of his assumption, almost his conviction, that Renata had been murdered. He had no doubt that Molly had been, but if Renata had died a natural death then he had put something into the equation that was disastrously misleading. The theory of Renata's death by foul play meant that he was obliged to consider Vasco, Signora Zeno, Bambina—and very remotely Gemma—as major suspects since they had all been present at the original house party, and were now here at the Ca' da Capo, when Molly had been murdered.

But if Renata hadn't been murdered, someone could be very eager to take advantage of that suspicion to point the finger of blame in the wrong direction. Molly's death could have nothing at all to do with the distant past. He should be considering more proximate causes. He might be in danger of falling victim to his own ingenuity.

In fact, someone could be trying to exploit his lively imagination—his creative imagination, as he so often liked to think of it.

He cast his mind over those people in the palazzo who might have encouraged this tendency in him. The names he immediately came up with were Sebastian and Viola. Each in his or her own way—by banter in the one case and intimacy in the other—had planted ideas in his mind. And Sebastian and Viola had been an all-too-willing audience for the story of the Caravaggio Room.

Urbino realized that he had to be even more wary of the twins, who, either together or individually, could be taking malicious advantage of the past, which, any way he seemed to look at it, was almost a palpable presence in the Ca' da Capo.

A short time later, Urbino found Robert sitting alone at the dining room table, staring morosely at a plate of food.

"How is your mother?" Urbino asked as he seated himself across from him.

"The same."

Robert offered no more.

"She'll have help before long," Urbino said, although he didn't feel optimistic.

"What the hell happened to Borelli? I should have gone myself."

"If Filippo is having problems, you or I would be having more. You're much better by your mother's side, as Barbara said."

"Barbara seems very concerned with pacifying me! But she can save her efforts. Neither my mother nor I is the kind of person to sue for an accident."

"Why do you assume it was an accident?"

Robert's short-cropped head snapped up from his contemplation of the still uneaten food. The contrast between his sharp blue eyes and dark olive skin had never seemed so manifest to Urbino. It reminded him of the contradictory sides of this man, with his English and Italian heritage and his respect and skepticism for medieval relics.

"Of course it was an accident! My mother hasn't been well for months. Overwork, she says, but I think she's quite ill. Painting Barbara's portrait and—and this house party have taken away her reserves of energy. She lost her footing. But what are you suggesting? That someone pushed her down the stairs? That's absurd!"

Urbino sensed that he didn't really think it was, however.

"Is that why you want to look through her things? What do you expect to find? A will? As far as I know, I'm the only beneficiary other than some art program in London. I hope you don't think I pushed my own mother down the stairs!"

"Would anyone here want to see her come to harm?"

"You must be mad! Of course you mean either my great-grandmother or great-aunt Bambina or Vasco. They all adore her! You can see that!"

Urbino, remembering Robert's own caustic words to Vasco when Gemma had been injured, didn't respond.

"Or is it Angelica you're thinking of?" Robert went on more heatedly. "Lurking around a dark corridor on the off chance she can shove her fiancé's mother down the stairs so that he'll inherit a fortune?"

"Is it a fortune?"

Robert looked embarrassed.

"My father was very well-off. Inherited money and good investments. But how much of it's left after ten years, I have no idea."

Urbino doubted this since Robert was an only child with an apparently good relationship with his mother. Surely she would have kept him informed about her financial situation.

"Perhaps you'll reconsider and let me look through your mother's things?" Urbino risked asking. "I assure you that I don't ask to satisfy my own curiosity—"

"I'm glad to hear that, but the answer is absolutely not!"

He pushed his plate away and got up.

"Did your mother talk much about the past?"

Robert gave a slight start.

"Why do I feel you don't mean the cheerful anecdotes a mother shares with her child, but something sordid and painful? I assume you're talking about the death of my grandmother?"

"That—and other things," Urbino added vaguely and, he feared, a bit lamely.

"Strange as it may seem to you—and disappointing as I suspect it will be—my mother told me very little about that weekend. She was only a child at the time."

"An adult can usually remember a great deal from that age. Eight, I believe she was?"

"You forget it was traumatic. She probably blocked the whole weekend out. I would appreciate it if you kept your nose out of it."

"Are you afraid of something, Robert?"

Robert's mouth took on an unpleasant twist.

"If it's not already apparent to you, Macintyre, let me spell it out: I'm concerned about anything that will disturb my mother. Do you understand?"

"Perfectly. I saw how angry you became with Molly because some of her comments disturbed Gemma."

"What are you implying?"

"I'm just stating a fact. Molly was describing a beautiful young woman lying at the foot of the bed in the Caravaggio Room. Obviously your mother assumed she was referring to her mother, Renata."

"It was a stupid thing for Molly to say."

"But surely she had no idea of how it might affect your mother—or anyone else. And your mother became upset later in the evening when Molly was going on about Boccaccio and cats and some other things."

"I only barely restrained myself from going over and shaking the silly woman."

"Do you have any idea why your mother reacted so violently at that point?"

Urbino thought he knew exactly why she had, and why she had shouted that Molly was saying too much.

"Unless you care to make something out of the fact that Mother has always hated Boccaccio and loved cats. She was fed up with Molly. I'm sorry the woman had such an accident, but I confess that I'm happy not to have her adding to the din of this bloody storm!"

Urbino stared at Robert for a few moments. If Robert suspected—or knew—that Molly had been murdered, this outburst might be much more calculated and less naive than it seemed.

"At any time during the night did you hear anything unusual coming from Molly's room?"

The Caravaggio Room was next to Robert's.

"Did you? Your room is on my other side!"

"Why didn't you or your mother object to your being put so close to the room where your grandmother died?"

"Because neither of us is a sentimental fool—or a superstitious one! Yes, I'm interested in relics. I've given part of my life to them, but if you think that I give any credence to nonsense like curses and superstitions, you're completely wrong!"

Angelica had transformed her already comfortable and well-appointed sitting room into something resembling a Victorian boudoir. Urbino took in the calculated placement of embroidered cushions and flowered scarves, period novels, a box of Belgian chocolates, and a jar of potpourri. Incense drifted in the air, originating from a ceramic censer whose painted design of cats peering from behind fronds in no way reflected the Contessa's taste.

Urbino seated himself in an armchair across from Angelica, who had tucked herself in on the sofa beneath a Victorian quilt.

Angelica cultivated an air of frailty. It was there in her pale makeup, her unemphatic clothes, her hair pulled back and parted in the middle with tendrils curling on the sides. Urbino wondered what the attraction was between her and Robert—on both sides. Could it be found somehow in the relationship between his grandmother and her great-uncle, which death had ended so abruptly? How had the two of them met? These were questions whose answers might help him unravel the mysteries so thick in the air of the Ca' da Capo.

Angelica, in her turn, was scrutinizing his face in a way that made him feel uncomfortable. It reminded him of her reaction when she had met him yesterday. Perhaps too abruptly, considering the kind of woman Angelica appeared to be, he said, "How do you think it came about that Robert's mother fell down the stairs?"

Her bemused and even slightly affectionate stare faded. In its place was now an ironic smile.

"Until you asked I assumed that she tripped and fell. But I see that you think otherwise or else you wouldn't ask. You think she was pushed?"

"I think it's a possibility."

"You could say that of almost anything," she came back with.

Given the woman's cultivation of the high Victorian, he wouldn't have been surprised if she now quoted something appropriate from Tennyson or Browning. Instead she said, "But you seem to be the kind of person interested in probability, especially in the present situation."

"Which is?"

She sighed with affected weariness.

"I might have my nose in a book much of the time, Mr. Macintyre, and I'm not a brave sort of person even in my thinking"—she offered a small, shy smile—"but you think that there have been too many accidents in the palazzo recently, don't you? And that there's some connection, shall we call it, between them?"

Urbino was amused by her unexpected way of turning the tables. Perhaps Robert had more of a match than at first seemed to be the case.

"It had occurred to me. Did you hear or see anything out of the ordinary since retiring last night?"

"Not really. I tried to read but the noise of the wind was most distracting. I had to read sentences over and over again. Eventually I drifted off to sleep and was awakened by what sounded like breaking glass. I know this room isn't very close to the Caravaggio Room but I have very sensitive hearing. It must have been when—when the door blew into the room and hit her."

"You were able to distinguish that sound with all the noise from the storm?"

She nodded her head.

Angelica's room was at the far end of the hall from the Caravaggio Room. Urbino had not heard the sound of breaking glass, even though his room was closer to the Caravaggio Room.

"Would you know what time that was?"

"Three forty-seven. I looked at my watch and was surprised at the hour. I got up and went to bed."

She frowned slightly and seemed about to add something. She remained silent, however, and examined her bracelet, turning it around on her wrist.

"Was there something else, Miss Lydgate?"

"I suppose it's nothing," she said in the time-honored manner of those who thought very much the opposite. She looked at him directly with her warm brown eyes. "It's just that I have a very highly developed sense of smell. That and my hearing. My eyes are as weak as a newborn kitten's. Anyway, when I went to the door to be sure it was locked, I smelled perfume. Shalimar."

"You could smell it from the hallway?"

"Oh yes, it came right through the door. The person had put a great deal on."

"You're sure it was Shalimar?"

"I know my perfumes very well. I must. I'm allergic to most of them. Not, fortunately, to Shalimar."

"You say 'fortunately.' Is that because you particularly like the scent or because your future mother-in-law wears it?"

Angelica seemed only mildly surprised.

"For a man you're very perceptive about a woman's perfume. Robert had to ask me what perfume she wore. Maybe you also know that her aunt wears it, too."

"There's one other thing I'd like to ask you. It's about your great-uncle Andrew Lydgate."

She seemed amused when Urbino brought up his name.

"Of course you would! I've been waiting."

"I'm afraid I don't understand."

"You're becoming less and less perceptive by the minute, Mr. Macintyre. I thought you knew."

"Knew what?"

She surprised him by lifting off the gold chain and locket she had around her neck. She opened the locket, which sprang noiselessly outward into three oval frames of slightly diminishing size. He was reminded of his earlier image of Chinese boxes.

"Please look."

He got up and went over. She handed him the locket and chain.

He looked at the three frames. Each held the black-and-white photograph of a different man. One was Robert. Another was a man who faintly resembled Angelica. The third was a man about his own age, perhaps somewhat younger, who stared back at him with intelligent eyes. The man would probably have been considered by most to be attractive in a refined, vaguely insolent sort of way, but this wasn't for Urbino himself to say, for the man in the photograph could almost have been his twin. The similarity gave him a brief but intense feeling of uneasiness, jolting that sense of complacency most people have about their own supposedly unique self.

Urbino now knew why Angelica had looked at him so strangely when she first met him. Bambina's reaction had been even more marked, but of course she had known Lydgate when he looked like this photograph.

And what of Gemma? Had she noted the resemblance between Urbino and the man who almost had become her stepfather?

"Of course I didn't know him like that," Angelica said. "I remember him when he was in his seventies, but he never really lost the look he has there. Sort of ironic and disdainful. So what is it that you wanted to ask me about Uncle Andrew?"

"Do you remember your uncle saying anything about the time when his fiancée—Gemma's mother—died in the Ca' da Capo-Zendrini? He was here at the time."

"Oh my, Mr. Macintyre, have you been reading the same kind of books as I have? Surely you aren't suggesting that there's some kind of relationship between our accidents and that long ago time? If you are, I can't be of any help. Dear Uncle Andrew would entertain me with oh-so-many stories but not one of them was about Gemma's mother. It wouldn't have been a suitable topic for a little girl, would it? The death of a mother who had a daughter my own age? But I must tell you, Mr. Macintyre, that once I grew up and learned that he had lost his fiancée, I remembered the sadness on his face whenever the past was mentioned. And one time when I asked him to look through a picture book on Venice with me, his eyes filled with tears. I asked him why. He said that Venice was beautiful but also very sad and melancholy.

"Once, though, he did mention Gemma," she went on. "Oh, not by name, but he said that he had once known a little girl who was very sweet and who had always been brave even though she had troubles, and that she was now very happy and successful. It was when I was frightened one night by some childish fear. I was jealous and I stopped crying right away, I remember."

"Have you ever confided this to Gemma?"

"Never! I know she doesn't want to be reminded about that time."

"Robert warned you?"

"Warned me?" She gave a little laugh. "We've spoken about it on occasion. He knows how much I think of his mother. I liked her long before I even knew him! I met Robert through her after I went to her London exhibition three years ago." She imparted this piece of information with a reminiscent smile. "I went out of curiosity more than anything else. I knew her name from family gossip. The sad little girl who grew up to be an artist and who was almost my—my step-aunt, I suppose she would have been. I immediately loved her work. It reminded me of Whistler and Sargent, don't you agree? So old-fashioned, in the best sense."

She got up and lit a kerosene lamp that deepened the shadows in the room and made her eyes seem to recede more deeply into their sockets.

"I introduced myself," Angelica went on, "and told her that Andrew Lydgate was my great-uncle. She gave me a big kiss and told me that if it hadn't been for my great-uncle, she never would have been an artist. He paid to send her to school in England when she was eighteen, you know. He was a very generous, kind-hearted man."

"How old were you when he died?"

"Seventeen."

"What did he die from?"

"He was an old man, Mr. Macintyre. He got pneumonia one winter and died." She paused as if expecting him to say something. When he didn't, she went on in a slightly higher voice, "I've always been timid about illness and death. I'm afraid I don't know anything more specific than that."

Urbino asked a few more questions, but her responses became increasingly noncommittal and a contrast to her recent forthrightness. Maybe it was weariness. He had never considered that she might be anything more than a woman inclined to bookish swoons and vapors, but now he seemed to see the sign of something else in her pale face.

Not knowing if his stronger feeling was one of having imposed himself on her or of having been used for her own obscure ends, he thanked her and left.

Viola was standing in the hallway.

"Making the rounds of the ladies' chambers, I see," she said. "I insist on being next."

She took his arm and led him across to her room. It was the best bedroom after the Contessa's, with Venetian furniture in the Chinese style and two paintings by Longhi. Urbino seated himself in—or more precisely was almost pushed into—a satin and lacquer armchair. Viola ostentatiously took possession of an ottoman and looked up at him, her eyes shining.

"I've just remembered something! I've been cudgeling my brain. It's about Bambina. Remember how we both agreed"—as he had earlier Urbino took note of her choice of pronoun—"that if we know more about Molly we'll get to the bottom of things? Last night when she was having her tête-à-tête with our resident Dr. Caligeri I overheard them talking about somnambulism. He said that Bambina had been a sleepwalker when she was a young girl. She claims that she occasionally does it now, but he doubts it since it's usually outgrown. Molly seemed to find it immensely amusing. She looked over at Bambina and laughed. I don't blame her! Just picture Bambina walking in her sleep along a roof edge or over one of the bridges here, padding along on her tiny little feet with her hands sticking straight out like timbers! Maybe she's his minion or his agent that he sends off during the night to do his evil bidding!"

When Urbino didn't join in her amusement—even to the extent of a smile—she said, "I hope you don't think I'm treating all this lightly. I'm very serious."

"I'm sure you are."

"You probably think I should have remembered it before, don't you? But we should both be thankful I remembered it at all. With so much happening, who knows what else we've forgotten—even you!"

Bambina entered the conservatory warily and peered around. The storm beat against the panes of glass and the plants swayed.

"Signorina Zeno, how kind of you to come," Urbino said as he appeared from behind a screen of plants. He spoke in English because it was his experience that people found it difficult to lie in another language and when they did, they often gave telltale signs.

"Bambina," she reminded him. Her bright red lipstick looked freshly applied, and the aroma of perfume wafted from her—the same one, he was now sure, that had hung in the air of the Caravaggio Room. "Your note said that you'd like to see me as soon as possible. I've never been the kind of girl to keep a man waiting."

"I'm hoping you can help me. You seem to be an observant person."

"I've always been praised for it. I could have made a writer, like yourself—or even a painter like poor Gemma. How is she?"

"Still unconscious."

"Oh, I hope she regains consciousness soon! The longer she doesn't, the more chance that her memory will be impaired, isn't that right?"

"I really don't know. This house has had its share of troubles this weekend."

"Accidents," Bambina quickly corrected him. "Terrible accidents."

She reached up to touch one of the bows in her hair but seemed to think better of it and pulled her hand back and clasped it with the other in her ample lap.

"I hate to see Barbara torturing herself," Urbino said. "You know how responsible she feels."

"But Gemma just lost her footing and Molly's death was an act of God! How can we control them? Look at this storm."

"You're probably right, Bambina." He paused and smiled at her sympathetically. "You're being very brave. I want you to know that I realize it."

"Brave? I don't understand."

"Brave because Molly died in the same room your sister Renata did. It must bring it all back to you."

"That was so long ago. I was only a little girl."

"You were young, Bambina, but Gemma was the little girl. They say the past never dies."

"I hardly remember what my sister looked like."

"Very beautiful, I've heard. Exceptionally so."

Bambina held her head a little higher.

"Beautiful, they say, but I was younger."

"I think you remember what Andrew Lydgate looked like, though."

"Oh yes!" For a moment there was an unmistakable tenderness in her gaze. "How funny you mention Andrew."

"Because I look like him?"

She giggled.

"So you know! I wondered if you did. You could be brothers—or twins!"

"It's sad that your sister died right before they were to be married. He must have taken it very hard."

"Of course, he was very upset," she said slowly as if she were reciting something imperfectly learned.

"Did your family see much of him after that?"

"For a few months." Her face clouded. "Just listen to the storm! It's surprising it hasn't come crashing through the windows here."

"I think it's dying out. We'll get help soon."

"I hope nothing has happened to Signor Borelli. That will be one more accident Barbara will have to add to her list."

"I was wondering if there was something you could satisfy my curiosity about, Bambina."

"Oh, you writers with your curiosity and your—your imagination! They must carry you far away at times."

"You're very perceptive."

Bambina preened under the glow of the compliment. It made him feel not at all pleased at what he was doing.

"My curiosity involves your cat, Bambina. You see, I have a cat, too. I found her shivering her little heart out in a park here. Serena's her name. I couldn't help noticing how disturbed you were when Molly mentioned your cat. Her name was Dido, wasn't it? I found that Molly did have a gift at times. She seemed to know some very personal things about me. How sad that her gift died with her. What happened to your cat? That is, if Molly was right about what she said."

She stared at Urbino and this time didn't restrain her hand from straying up to one of her ribbons.

"Yes," she said in a low voice, "she was right. I did have a cat. She died. A long time ago."

"As long ago as the time your sister died?"

Her eyes started to fill with tears and spilled out onto her heavily rouged cheeks. He took out his handkerchief and gave it to her.

"Thank you." She dabbed at her cheeks. The handkerchief came away pink. "A month or two before."

"Perhaps if you tell me about it, you'll feel better. I know how it is."

Hating himself, he reached out and touched her hand.

"Yes, her name was Dido. I had just read the *Aeneid.* I've always been such a reader. All the classics! I—I could have been a professor. Oh, Dido was so pretty—all white and fluffy—and as sweet as could be. She wouldn't leave my side. How devoted she was! She would follow me everywhere. Poor, poor Dido!"

The tears started again and she was forced to do further damage to Urbino's handkerchief.

"It was some strange cat disease. I'm sure it has a name these days but all I knew was that she got very sick and died. So quickly. Horrible! I stayed by her side every minute. Molly's comment brought it all back. Oh, look at what I've done to your handkerchief! I'll wash it and give it back to you. It will be my pleasure."

She quickly stuffed it into her pocket before he might reclaim it.

"I guess this room hasn't changed much since the last time you were here at the Ca' da Capo, has it?"

"Not much." Her eyes shifted in the direction of the sink and cabinets. "Barbara has done a wonderful job of improving what needed to be improved and—and leaving other things alone. Mamma and I were talking about it. Barbara is such a marvelous woman."

"She takes such good care of the roses," Urbino said. "No aphids or anything. Let me get you one."

"Oh, please don't bother!"

He went to the sink, where he took shears from the cabinet containing other small implements and various plant foods, sprays, insect killers, gardening mittens, and the remaining rubber gloves. He cut off a full-blown rose, returned the shears to the cabinet, and brought the rose to her.

She stared at the rose with a little frown and dropped it in her lap.

"You're a sensitive man, Signor Urbino. Do you think I could ask you a personal question?"

"What is it?"

"Do you walk in your sleep?"

The question, coming after what Viola had just told him, surprised him.

"Sensitive people often walk in their sleep," Bambina continued. "*I* do! I wouldn't be surprised if someone saw me walking around one of these nights. But if you do, remember: You mustn't wake me. It could be dangerous. Just take me right back to my room."

She gave him a grotesquely suggestive smile. She put the rose to her nose and sniffed it.

"I'll remember that. But no, I don't walk in my sleep. By the way, Bambina, what kind of perfume are you wearing? My cousin is visiting me at Christmastime and I think it would be just the thing for her."

A sly, guarded look came into her eye.

"Shalimar, but I warn you it's very expensive! Mamma berates me for spending so much money on it, but she splashes some on herself from time to time, although I pretend I don't know."

"It's such a nice scent. Did anyone here ask to borrow some of it?"

"No, of course not!" she said. She seemed to regret her quick denial, however, and added, "But—but maybe someone borrowed Gemma's. She uses the same perfume. She's always said it smelled so nice on me."

"Do you mind if I smell some of it from the little flask you carry around?"

"Oh, you do notice details, Signor Urbino! Do you do it especially because you know we women love it? Of course, I mean only when the details involve *us!* My little flask you say? Pure silver with a craftsman's mark on the bottom. I've had it for the longest time. But how unfortunate! I don't have it with me now. I wish I did, because you've been so kind and it's so unusual to see a man interested in these things. Oh my, look at the time. I should take a little rest before dinner. You'll excuse me, won't you?"

Urbino waited until she had time to return to her room and then went upstairs to see Dr. Vasco.

As he sat across from the octogenarian physician, Urbino felt entombed by the past.

From over the massive bed a full-length portrait of Doge Renier Zeno by a minor thirteenth-century Venetian painter dominated the dark chamber, which was known as the Doge's Room. It had the air of a museum, and was directly across from the Caravaggio Room.

Doge's hats, engravings of the doge's annual marriage with the sea, replicas of the gilded Bucintoro, ducal seals and codices, small modeled hands of wood and gold used for the reckoning of secret ballots—yes, the room was very much a museum and its atmosphere, though enlightening, was oppressive.

Vasco had managed to put his personal imprint on the room, although not as extensively or as calculatedly as Angelica had on hers. His was a matter of disarray, with cast-off clothes, bottles of pills and tubes of ointment, and medical magazines.

Then there was the odor, a stale one, despite the strong draft from the loggia doors, of medicines, mustiness, and exhaled breath.

Vasco offered Urbino a whiskey, but Urbino declined. He wanted to be as clear-thinking as possible and regretted the drinks he had already had.

Urbino got the feeling that he had interrupted the physician's dark thoughts. Rather than resent the intrusion or see it as an opportunity to escape their disturbing implications, however, Vasco immediately drew Urbino into them.

"Do you believe in the power of the mind, Signor Urbino? Little Molly did." His face clouded. "I have since I was a young man. I look at sweet Gemma and try to communicate all the strength of my mind to her. Get up, Gemma! Wake up! We're all waiting for you." He shook his head. "Nothing. But the mind's power to do good should be equal to its power to do wrong, yes? I try very hard to concentrate my mind on the good, but sometimes the bad has a power equal to ten—a hundred—a thousand times its force! I—"

He reached for a glass of whiskey on the cluttered table and drank most of it down.

"I'm an old man, Signor Urbino. Listen to the old, they say. It's very bad advice. We have seen too much—ah! *done* too much—to offer any hope."

Vasco's words carried a heavy burden of not just pain but guilt. This was consistent with his behavior on other occasions, and Urbino couldn't help linking it with what he had just said about the power of the mind to do evil. What proofs of this might he be torturing himself with? Did they have anything to do with Renata's death? Molly's? Or with Gemma's fall down the stairs?

Urbino needed information and he could see that he might be able to play on Vasco's apparent feelings for Gemma to get it.

"I hope you won't think that I'm asking you to betray a professional confidence, Dottore, but is Gemma ill? Aside from her accident, I mean?"

"There's no confidence to betray. I'm not her personal physician. I agree that she hasn't been looking well lately. So disturbing to see it. She's always been healthy."

"She wasn't a frail child, then?"

"Not at all! Very healthy. Perfect in every way—and so intelligent!"

"How did she take the death of her mother?"

Vasco picked up a ducal medal from the table next to him and examined it.

"Children are resilient. Sometimes it can be disturbing how resilient they are."

"She must have had many questions."

"Not very many. We told her the things you tell a child. That God wanted her mother for an angel."

"She must have had more specific questions later."

"Actually, she didn't." He put the medal down. "And none of us ever spoke of that time. I'm sure she has only vague memories now, if any."

Urbino, who couldn't have agreed less, said, "Tell me about her mother."

Without hesitation Vasco embarked on a long encomium. Renata had been the brightest, the kindest, the most generous, the most beautiful, the most sincere, the most everything, as far as Vasco was concerned. Yet, according to the Conte's memoirs, Vasco had expressed resentment against Renata and had told Alvise that he didn't intend to be made a fool of. None of that animosity seemed to have survived her death. Urbino wondered if Renata had encouraged Vasco only to drop him when Lydgate had come along. What had their relationship been like? Why had she preferred first Bellini and then Lydgate to him?

As he was trying to think of some way to get this information, Vasco surprised him by seeming to show his awareness of Urbino's thoughts.

"Bellini started to come round when she was barely fifteen! Almost three times her age and with a mountain of lire! He made his offer and Renata was obliged by her parents to accept. She didn't care a fig about money, but she was just a girl and couldn't stand up to them. Especially to Marialuisa. She's got a will of iron! When Bellini died, I thought that we might marry. I already loved Gemma like my own daughter. But then Lydgate came into the picture," he said bitterly.

"Renata must have been independent enough by then. She had inherited Bellini's money, I assume."

"He had lost much of it. Renata and Gemma were left with very little. With what I could earn, we would have been comfortable enough. But—but Renata had Gemma to think about then, and in those uncertain times she felt she should make a marriage that would secure Gemma's future. She was only thinking of Gemma, I tell you! Lydgate was rich. Renata sacrificed herself—sacrificed us, the life we could have had—and accepted Lydgate."

Although Urbino knew very little about Renata, this picture of her as a self-sacrificing young woman didn't ring true. He doubted if Vasco believed it now or at any time. The man seemed driven by a desire not so much to remember the past as to revise it.

Vasco got up and replenished his glass. This time Urbino joined him.

When Urbino asked Vasco how Renata and Lydgate had met, the doctor confirmed what Urbino already knew from the Conte's memoir. Lydgate had been a friend of the Zenos' English tutor.

"There was some expectation that he might marry Bambina at first. Marialuisa encouraged it, but then Bellini died and the next I knew, he was courting Renata."

It was an old-fashioned term, but Vasco was in many ways an old-fashioned man.

"How did Bambina take it?"

"She eventually came to accept it."

Urbino decided to change his tack.

"Did Molly confide anything in you during the time the two of you spent alone together?"

"We were never alone together!"

"I didn't necessarily mean completely alone, but you retired with her to a corner on one or two occasions."

"Only to talk about the power of the mind. But I don't see

what this has to do with anything! We were talking about poor Gemma."

"Yes, about Gemma and her mother. But one more question about Molly, if you don't mind. How do you think she died?"

"How? An accident! Just like Gemma."

"I don't think so, and neither do you. Surely you noticed the same thing I did. There was only a pool of blood around Molly's head. None at any great distance. And yet her artery was pierced by the glass of the door. In all probability she was dead before her head went through the glass."

Vasco looked lost and frightened.

"There could be other explanations."

"Possibly. It's your field of expertise, not mine."

Urbino took a last sip of his whiskey and got up.

"But I'll tell you one thing, Dottore. With this death in the Caravaggio Room there *will* be an autopsy. Whatever might have stopped one from being done on Renata—money, influence, whatever—isn't going to have the same result this time around."

Urbino expected Vasco to defend himself against the implications of this, but he remained grimly silent. Urbino thanked him for the drink and bid him good-day.

As he was going to his room to rest and mull things over, Lucia approached him with a little silver tray. It held a white envelope.

He opened it and found a soiled visiting card. On it was engraved "The Signora Marialuisa Zeno" and on the reverse side was the handwritten message in Italian: "Signor Macintyre, I would like to see you at once, in my room, if it is convenient for you."

Mamma Zeno was staying in a room with less apt associations than Vasco's. Known as the Room of the Courtesan, it took its name from the Contessa Querini-Benzon, who supposedly had slept in it after her dalliance with Byron when she had been in her sixties. A painting of her by Longhi hung on the damasked wall.

Mamma Zeno was seated on a massive chair at the far end of the room, her thin black cane like a scepter in one hand. She was so small and frail, and the chair so large, that it was improbable she had climbed into it herself; more likely she had been helped into it or even carefully placed and arranged. Feeble light struggled through a crack between the drawn drapes.

"Sit down, Signor Macintyre."

An almost imperceptible nod indicated which seat it should be: a low one with considerably more history than comfort. Urbino seated himself and had the peculiar sense of having to look up at the tiny, perched woman.

As his eyes accustomed themselves to the dimness, he saw that she had already changed for dinner. Her shrunken body was once again overwhelmed by her clothing—by the stiff black and gold dress, the gray shawl, and the black Burano lace wound around her head that artfully concealed whatever hair she still might claim. No jewelry except for her worn gold wedding band. She resembled one of those effigies of saints, pinned with lira notes and carried through the streets of Italian towns on a litter.

"Best to have come to me first with your questions about my family, Signor Macintyre," she said in Italian without any preliminaries. "A man living in my country as long as you have should understand these things."

Her voice, although at the mercy of her shallow breathing, had a peculiar command. It seemed to issue not from the old woman in front of him, but from another, much younger one inside.

"You have been rude," she went on, "but you yourself have suffered most. Only *I* can answer your questions. Only *I* know the truth."

Urbino couldn't have been more on his guard if he had seen the hilt of a stiletto glinting in the ample folds of her dress.

"My dear, dead daughter Renata still seems to have the power she had in life. The only immortality we have. Ah, yes, the effect we have on others . . . yes, on others . . . I will tell you."

She remained very still, her little head cocked to one side as if she were listening to something beyond the room, beyond the storm outside.

"Wait until you are an old man, Signor Macintyre. If you are so lucky—or unlucky! My eyes water and my mouth is always dry. And my joints are on fire! There's some virtue in dying young, especially when you are beautiful like my Renata was. You want to know about her. Because she died in the same room . . . that silly woman, Signora Wybrow . . . dead and there's an end to her life. We still have it."

Her voice faded in and out like some distant, poorly received station on an old wireless. She took several shallow breaths, all the while peering at him with her small dark eyes. The expression on the tiny patch of face visible between the lace head-covering and the high neck of her dress was pained and determined. No doubt she was willing her voice to be steady, and as she continued, the success of her efforts was immediately apparent.

"Yes, my daughter died in the same room. A bubble in her brain or a defective heart. All this poking and Renata's life ran its natural course. A happy life, despite her husband's death. Happier than mine, than Bambina's. A mother doesn't expect her children to die before her, but what can be done? You are listening to me, aren't you, Signor Macintyre?"

She glowered at him and her hand tightened around her cane. She seemed completely capable of striking out at him with it—and with considerable force.

"I didn't want to interrupt you, signora."

"I see," she said, relaxing her grip on the cane. "You'd rather have me run on until I tire myself out, is that it? Then what good will I be to you?" She pressed a shriveled hand against her breast and shook her head slowly. "I can only do so much with this body of mine. Better to ask your questions. I'll either answer them or not."

Urbino rapidly considered all the things he would like to ask her. He then looked very hard at her as he said, "Tell me about Dido."

There followed a brief silence. Mamma Zeno took several shallow breaths and dropped the lids of her eyes partway.

"Dido? Testing an old woman's education? That isn't very cavalier of you. I thought that Barbara had smoothed away most of your hard American edges." She gave several quick little choking sounds that might have been laughter or something more pathological. "Dido was some barbarian queen who killed herself for the love of Aeneas. Burned herself to death, wasn't it?"

"I wasn't asking about Virgil's Dido, signora, but your daughter Bambina's cat."

"She had so many."

"Dido was the one who died a few months before Renata did. On the last evening of her life, Renata mentioned Dido's death. She said that Bambina was unlucky in things that she loved."

"How do you know these things? Not from Bambina!" The old woman's frailty seemed to fall away from her like some rotted garment. "If it was Luigi—!"

Her hands, gripping the arms of the chair, looked as hard and tense as the rococo carvings.

"It was neither Bambina nor Luigi, signora."

Urbino thought it best not to tell her that he knew it—and more—from Alvise's account.

"That stupid, meddling woman! How did *she* know?"

Since Molly was beyond danger now, Urbino encouraged Mamma Zeno's mistake by saying, "Signora Wybrow mentioned Dido last night. She said that she had suffered a lot. Bambina got very upset."

"Sentimental fool! Yes, I remember Dido. Long white fur that flew all over the house. She would let Gemma carry her around like a doll. I think Gemma cried more over that cat than over her own mother. What else did that woman tell you?"

Urbino decided to take full advantage of Mamma Zeno's misconception, if this was what it was.

"She said that Andrew Lydgate had no intention of marrying Renata. That he was going to marry Bambina."

Mamma Zeno's reaction to this fabrication was to twist her thin lips into a smile.

"Now I know the woman was an idiot! Lydgate not marry Renata? He was mad about her."

"But I heard that he was originally interested in Bambina."

"That woman again? Well, even an idiot can hit the mark sometimes. Lydgate and Bambina came to nothing."

"Once Renata became available, you mean."

"He was mad for her, I said, and a good thing he was. I made it clear to Bambina. A woman with another man's child doesn't have an easy time finding a husband. Marry Bambina when there was Renata needing a good husband? I wouldn't have had it! I had a plan for my family."

"But after Renata died? What about Bambina's chances then?"

"Lydgate was never free of Renata. Never! You see the power that Renata has even over you, who never knew her! Unless that mad woman convinced you that you knew her in a former life! Did she tell you that you—"

She didn't continue but stared at him with an almost scornful smile.

"That I resemble Lydgate? Is that what you were going to say?"

"What does it matter? I once resembled Renata. Many people took us for sisters back then. But, yes, you do look like Lydgate. I wouldn't advise you to try to make much of it, though. The resemblance is only skin deep." She paused, then added: "He wasn't a man of particular intelligence."

Urbino didn't know what to take more note of in what she had said: the implied compliment or the distant warning. He looked into what he could see of her face, and tried to bridge the years between now and when that wrinkled face had resembled Renata's. He couldn't do it. It wasn't that his imagination failed him, but that something in the old woman made the effort futile.

Mamma Zeno, despite her frail physical condition, was a strong woman, perhaps stronger than any of the other guests isolated this weekend at the Ca' da Capo. Urbino thought it unlikely that she had ever done anything she didn't want to do. It was therefore perfectly consistent with his thinking that he now asked her why she had decided to come to the Contessa's house party.

"For Gemma's sake" was her answer. It was when she apparently felt the need to clarify that he sensed she wasn't telling the truth. "Because of the portrait."

"She urged you to come?"

She nodded.

"She wanted Bambina and me to be here for the unveiling. And Luigi," she added, anticipating his next question. "He's been like a father—an uncle—to her."

"So she obviously wanted all four of you to be here again together after all these years."

Mamma Zeno stared at him coldly.

"Don't you think you should say that it was Barbara who wanted us all here?"

He felt the need to shock the old woman.

"Suppose I told you that I believe Molly didn't die in an accident, signora?"

"I would say that you're as insane as she was and not as intelligent as I thought! I don't think that you are qualified to give a professional opinion. We have a physician in the house. I'm sure he didn't say anything of the kind."

"I find it interesting that you're so certain of what Dr. Vasco did or didn't say to me about Molly's death."

"I don't know what you mean by that statement, and I'm not even going to try to—"

"Oh, Mamma, excuse me" came Bambina's voice from the door. "I didn't know that you had a guest. Signor Urbino, what a surprise!"

Bambina started to flutter nervously around the room, making it obvious that she was looking for something.

"I seem to have misplaced my copy of *Gente*. I wanted to read it before dinner. Have you seen it, Mamma?"

"It's not here. Leave!"

She raised her cane threateningly.

Bambina came to a quick halt in her movements around the room and, with an embarrassed look at Urbino, she retreated with almost comical rapidity.

Mamma Zeno waited until the door had closed behind Bambina before she said to Urbino with an unmistakable valedictory air:

"My family's affairs are private, signore, even if you are Barbara's intimate friend. And remember that she herself isn't a Da Capo-Zendrini, certainly not a Zeno! I am a Zeno not only by marriage but by blood! By blood! It would be much better for you to devote your time to figuring out ways for Barbara to make this drafty building safe for a person to walk and sleep in. She and she alone is responsible for what has happened under this roof!"

Immediately after leaving Mamma Zeno, Urbino went to see the Contessa in her boudoir.

"What's the matter?" she asked. "You're not even dressed for dinner yet."

She, however, was—in a silk dress printed with designs inspired by San Marco's mosaics.

"Nothing's the matter," he said. "I just stopped by to be sure that you weren't having any second thoughts."

"Second and third and fourth! I hope you know what you're doing! What you're asking!"

He put his arms around her and kissed her forehead.

"You'll be fine. You'll see." As he said it, all he could think of was what she was going to have to go through before everything was all over. He looked down into her frightened gray eyes.

"I take full responsibility—for you and everyone else," he reassured her. "Just remember that I don't want you to sit down at the table until I already have. Everyone will be there, as we agreed, won't they?"

"Yes." She disengaged herself from his arms and looked at herself in a mirror. She trifled uneasily and unnecessarily with her hair. "Even Oriana, although much help she'll be! All she keeps moaning about now is that the 'curse of the Ca' da Capo' must have followed Filippo. Ridiculous, isn't it?"

She turned to Urbino with a worried, quizzical look.

The only comfort he could give her—and a cold one at that—was "Ridiculous, yes. No one has left the Ca' da Capo but Filippo himself."

His hair still damp from a quick, cold shower, Urbino slipped into his accustomed seat at the end of the dinner table as the last gong sounded. Everyone was down except for the Contessa.

Urbino's entrance had made no interruption in the rhythm of Sebastian's patter. Sebastian had either sobered up considerably or was in that transitional stage before the total oblivion of inebriation descended on him. For the time being, however, he was functioning very well, except for less than precise pronunciation and more violent gestures than were called for.

The other guests, with varying degrees of bored or irritated expressions—or, in the case of Bambina and Angelica, uneasy ones—seemed content to let him run on as long as they weren't expected to join in.

". . . and so I said to the fellow, if you really believe this is a

Raphael, then it's time for you to close your shop and take up another trade. It made me wonder what other fakes he had all over the place, and I was going to help him out by poking around and telling him, but Viola dragged me out. Then, a couple of weeks later, I was in another shop, this one in New Bond Street, and I took one look at a painting that everyone was *ooh*-ing and *aah*-ing over—a Rubens, they all thought—"

He broke off as the Contessa swept into the room, murmuring apologies. The peacock brooch was pinned to the front of her dress, its gold work and colored stones a perfect complement to the tones and shapes of the mosaic-print of her dress.

If her smile was a bit tight and her voice strained, no one needed any more explanation than the ones already at hand. One guest was lying dead upstairs, another was unconscious, and a third was somewhere out in the storm, possibly incapacitated.

Only Urbino and the Contessa knew that she was feeling like an actress whose imminent performance risked more than just jeers and scathing reviews. But what Urbino hadn't told her was that, in order to get as true a performance as possible from her, he had been obliged to keep her in the dark about some essential points.

The Contessa seated herself, not risking a look at Urbino. Mamma Zeno, on Urbino's immediate left, gave a gasp as she noticed the brooch.

Bambina's and Vasco's attention was also riveted on it. Bambina pulled her eyes away to stare at her mother, and suppressed what sounded like a nervous giggle.

"It's the brooch from some of the portraits in the gallery!" Viola said. She was sitting to Urbino's immediate right next to Bambina, and had most of her hair artfully wrapped in a piece of Fortuny fabric. "Where have you been hiding it?"

"In some deep coffer," Sebastian immediately jumped in to say. "Ha, ha! She probably has so many bijous she has to rotate them like the V & A. She won't get around to this particular bauble again until the next millennium."

Angelica, who had been staring at the brooch with unusually keen interest, said, "Is it art nouveau?"

"Can't you tell, my dear?" Oriana said. "It's older than that."

"A lot older," said Bambina. "It's from ancient Constantinople."

"Ancient Constantinople?" Sebastian repeated with a grin. "'Hammered gold and gold enamelling' done by Grecian goldsmiths to keep a drowsy emperor awake? Ah yes, 'an aged man is but a paltry thing,'" he went on, quoting Yeats but completely mystifying Bambina and most of the others. "Set there on the golden bough of Barbara's bosom"—here he hiccuped—"singing to us lords and ladies of Venice of what is past, or passing, or to come."

He rewarded himself after this effusion by draining his wineglass and reaching for the carafe to refill it. He almost upset one of the candelabra.

"Yes, it belonged to an emperor!" Bambina burst out with almost evident relief, apparently seizing on the one thing she had understood in what Sebastian had said. All it earned her, however, was a glare from her mother.

"I have an idea," Sebastian said. "Let's chase away our fears and blues and have Barbara tell us the story of the brooch!"

"The Conte's memoir!" Viola said softly. "Someone told a story about a brooch back then."

No one but Urbino seemed to hear her. Sebastian was hitting his water glass with a spoon.

"Here, here, Barbara! The story. We insist."

"I—I'd rather not," the Contessa said. She looked at Urbino, then away, as if she wasn't quite sure this was what she should have said.

"Oh, let me!" piped up Bambina as she pushed her dish of shrimp away. Her mother stared at her silently but nonetheless thunderously from her beady eyes. "It's really a Zeno story as much as a Da Capo-Zendrini one. Excuse me, Barbara, but you're not really a Da Capo-Zendrini—not a blood relation—even though you have the brooch."

The Contessa paled. The immobile Mamma Zeno looked angry, and Vasco monumentally disapproving. Oriana, who didn't seem to be registering what Bambina was saying and who, like Urbino, had in any event heard the story of the brooch before, ate her shrimp with an abstracted air. Angelica was smiling expectantly, until she noticed that Robert's brow was creased with worry. The expression on her heart-shaped face then more closely approximated his. Sebastian was looking very hard at Bambina.

Viola said softly, "The Conte's memoirs! Bambina told the story of the brooch then, too, didn't she?"

The question was addressed to Urbino, who said nothing. He wasn't going to intervene unless it would advance his own scheme, but he took everything—and everyone—in. He had a habit that had grown over the years of holding himself aloof and watching, even when he himself was most actively in the middle of the fray. It had left him open to the charge of coldness and restraint, but without it he would be far less able to navigate the troubled emotional waters he so often found himself in.

And so he waited now and watched in his characteristic fashion. It was to his credit that so few people at the table were aware of the power behind his withdrawal. The Contessa, who knew him so well, was one of them. The only other was Viola.

Bambina interpreted his silence and smile as nothing less—or more—than anticipation of her soon to be revealed charms as a Scheherazade. But eager though she appeared to be to begin, she waited until the course of *risottino verde* was set on the table. Then, in a hushed tone and with a faraway look in her eyes, she began the story she had told at the same table almost sixty years before.

"A long time ago a Venetian ship on its way to Constantinople was sunk by a cannonball by the evil Turks, who were taking over that part of the world. The captain was cut up into little pieces and all the other men on the ship had their heads chopped off. All of them," she said with a satisfied little smile, "but Alvise da Capo-Zendrini, a very, very distant relative of the Conte Alvise and me! With the help of a Turkish woman who fell in love with him, he made his way, after many adventures, to the court of the Byzantine emperor."

"Constantine. The emperor's name was Constantine," Sebastian interjected. He shoved a forkful of rice into his mouth and washed it down with some wine, then looked around the table with self-satisfaction.

"Of course it was. The city was named after him," Bambina said incorrectly. "Anyway, the Byzantine emperor gave Alvise all kinds of rewards for his bravery, and he was allowed to live in the palace—"

"Topkapi," Sebastian interrupted again.

"No, Mr. Know-It-All," Viola said. "Topkapi was the Turks' palace *after* the fall of Constantinople."

"More's the pity. I was settling in for an amusing caper. The first Alvise da Capo-Zed descending into the museum from the skylight to steal the jewel-encrusted brooch à la Peter Ustinov. Too bad."

He consoled himself with some wine.

"*Allora*," Bambina said, after taking a few dispirited pecks at her rice, "at this same time a Venetian merchant arrived in a galley with some supplies for the emperor. His name was Marco Zeno. Also a distant blood relative of mine and," she added somewhat grudgingly, "of the Da Capo-Zendrini family, too, because of subsequent marriages. When he was at the palace he was surprised to see his old friend Alvise sitting next to the emperor. But they barely had time to renew their acquaintance when the Turks started battering against the walls. It was at this bloody and unfortunate time, when men were dying all around the two friends, who were so far away from their beloved Venezia, that the brooch—*la bella spilla*—entered their lives."

She gave a quick look at her mother, who was sitting motionlessly and showing no interest in the story or the meal.

"The peacock brooch was a gift, you see," she continued, tilting up her chubby chin an inch or two and narrowing her eyes as much as their roundness allowed. "The emperor gave it to Marco—yes, to Marco Zeno—because he bravely refused to seek his own safety and insisted on fighting alongside the emperor and his friend Alvise, his trusted friend Alvise," she emphasized. "Not long afterward the poor emperor, who realized the end had come for his empire, threw himself against the Turks and was killed. Marco and Alvise escaped miraculously and swam out to a Venetian galley. Marco had pinned the brooch to his shirt. A strong southern wind blew the galley away from the city back toward Venezia and—"

"Northern wind," Sebastian said. "It would have to have been a northern wind, old girl, or they would have gone all the way up to the Black Sea."

"Really, Sebastian, does it matter?" Viola said.

"I'd say it damn well does!" he almost shouted. "Who knows what other details she's getting all upside down, and here we are hanging on her every word as if it's gospel!"

"Bambina is telling the story just as it was passed on down to Alvise," the Contessa said calmly and with an air of evident relief. "Perhaps you should switch to mineral water."

"Give me sermons and soda water—the day after!"

Bambina had a blank look on her face and waited to see if he had any more to add. When he didn't, she finished up her story with nervous haste: "On the ship, Marco became feverish and delirious. Late one night, he and Alvise went up on deck for fresh air. Alvise said that Marco insisted on being left alone. *Marco was never seen again.* And—and that's how the Da Capo-Zendrini family came to have the valuable peacock brooch. The same one that Barbara is wearing at this very moment."

The Contessa was stunned. The Da Capo-Zendrini version was that Marco Zeno, feeling near death, had given the brooch to Alvise, then wandered up to the deck and been washed overboard by the heavy sea.

When disagreement came, however, it wasn't from the Contessa, who was confused as to what reaction would be appropriate given Urbino's instructions to her before dinner. It came, perhaps not so unpredictably, from Sebastian, who seemed determined to play the role of fractious chorus to the very end.

"Oh, come now," he said with a mixture of irritation and sarcasm. "Are you suggesting that the Conte's great-grandfather to the hundredth power stole the brooch and tossed your own great-grandfather to the hundredth power into the wine-dark sea?"

Bambina was totally lost until Urbino, to the Contessa's evident dissatisfaction, translated the gist of Sebastian's comment. Bambina made a motion with her hand of zipping her lips together.

"But surely this story didn't come down from the original Alvise da Capo-Zed," Sebastian said. "And this Zeno fellow was a feast for fish."

"An English sailor aboard informed the Zeno family when the ship reached Venice," said Robert coldly.

His comment served to unzip Bambina's mouth.

"You see how even Roberto, the youngest of our family, though perhaps not for long"—she smiled meaningfully at Angelica, who throughout the story had maintained an aloof air—"how Roberto knows the whole story. Our Gemma learned it from Renata. She used to think that her mother called her Gemma because of the brooch. Silly how children think, isn't it?

Anyway, little Gemma—our sweet and sparkling jewel—could tell the story of the brooch over and over again herself when she was only six or seven. Fascinated by it, she was."

"Not only with the story of the brooch," Urbino ventured to say, "but surely with the brooch itself."

The Contessa drew in her breath, and Mamma Zeno and Vasco exchanged a quick glance.

"Oh yes, you're so right, Signor Urbino," Bambina said eagerly. "And she—she still is. She just loves to look at it."

"I don't see what you mean at all, Bambina," the Contessa said. "I never showed Gemma the brooch in all the time she's been here. You must be mistaken."

Urbino was proud of the Contessa. Uncoached and unprepared for this eventuality, she had nonetheless said just what he wanted her to say.

Bambina's confused look became overlaid with fear. She opened her mouth to speak but nothing came out.

"Aunt Bambina is speaking of the other time my mother was here at the Ca' da Capo-Zendrini, Barbara," Robert said. "The Contessa—your predecessor—was wearing it. My mother remembers the brooch from then."

"Yes, that's exactly what I meant. Gemma remembers it from back then. She always talks about it. She'd do anything to have one just like it."

"Bambina!"

Mamma Zeno's voice startled them not only because of its uncharacteristic loudness but because the old woman had been so silent for so long. Her watery eyes slid in the direction of the Contessa's bodice, then back to her daughter, where they took on a harder look.

"It's Barbara's. Just as it should be," she added with a rictus of a smile.

The Contessa and her party had retired to the library for barely ten minutes, with coffee or drinks according to their preference, when there was a quiet knock at the door. It opened.

Mauro guided in Milo and a young member of the Contessa's staff. As the three men carried in the easel and the velvet-draped portrait, a silence struck the guests. Only a moment before they had been in strained and fitful conversation about the storm, which seemed to be giving signs of abating. At least the rains had ceased and the winds were considerably weakened. Sebastian, however, took obvious pleasure in insisting that the storm was just lying low for a final, treacherous assault.

The two men carried the shrouded portrait reverently as if it were a corpse and placed it on the easel in front of the fireplace. Sebastian settled more deeply into his armchair and jiggled his slippered foot. A smirk crawled across his lips, which he attempted to conceal by taking a sip of brandy.

The Contessa waited until Mauro and the two men had left. Then, in a voice whose tremors she hoped would be seen as signs of a nervous vanity and nothing else, she said, "My dear friends and—and family"—her gray eyes took in not only the twins but also Mamma Zeno, Bambina, and Robert—"a proud and yet a sad moment has come. We're all going to see dear Gemma's portrait of me. I've decided to do Gemma this—this honor, and to do it with all the prayers in my heart for a speedy and complete recovery. All of us, including myself, I might add, will be seeing the portrait for the first time. I respected Gemma's wishes not to give so much as a quick glance at it while she was doing it—or, in fact, after." Urbino, who feared she was about to gild the lily even more, was relieved when she quickly brought her comments to an end: "Gemma's great talent will speak for itself. Surely she will go on to exercise it on subjects far better than I."

The Contessa started to untie the tasseled cord securing the velvet, her hands trembling. Urbino, who had positioned himself alone in a corner, looked at the guests. Everyone's eyes but those of Sebastian were riveted on the shrouded portrait as the Contessa gradually unworked the knot and started to draw the velvet away.

Sebastian was looking at the Contessa's face.

Urbino knew exactly the moment when the portrait was uncovered from the gasp that filled the library. It was as if one collective breath had been caught. Whatever reaction—or reactions—were feigned among the guests was completely lost in the sound.

A few moments later the individual responses began.

"Barbara, you *poverina!*" Oriana said as if it were the Contessa herself who had been disfigured.

The Contessa's face was white. This wasn't acting, but the real thing. It was as if she were seeing her slashed portrait for the first time.

"Gemma's lovely work," she said. "Oh, you can see how lovely it was." Her voice, empty of all vanity and pride, communicated only regret. "Who could have done such a thing?"

"Maybe Gemma didn't think it turned out well and took her palette knife to it," Sebastian said.

"This is no time for joking!" Robert shouted, getting to his feet. "Not with my mother lying unconscious upstairs! This is an attack on her."

"Looks more like an attack on Barbara," Sebastian said.

"The person who did this," Robert went on, "is the same one who pushed my mother down the stairs! Yes, I said *pushed.* I agree with Urbino now. She no more fell down the stairs than—than . . ."

He trailed off, apparently unable to come up with an appropriate analogy. It was supplied, however, by Urbino, who got up and went over to the Contessa.

"—no more than Molly was killed accidentally by the door of the loggia blowing open."

The Contessa, who seemed to be experiencing each revelation for the first time, swayed on her feet. Urbino took her arm. Viola rushed up to help, and together they guided the Contessa onto the sofa. Then, with her Swinburnish eyes brimming with anger, Viola picked up the velvet draping and carefully covered the mutilated portrait as if she were covering the face of a dead woman.

"You have to put a stop to everything," she said quietly but urgently to Urbino before joining the Contessa on the sofa. There she and the Contessa sat, staring at Urbino.

In fact, everyone in the library was staring at him as he stood in front of the reshrouded portrait. So silent was it that he could hear a candle spattering on the other side of the room.

"Do tell us what's going on, Mr. Macintyre," Angelica said in her gentle voice as she reached up to touch Robert's sleeve. "It's all right, dear. The only thing that matters is that your mother completely recovers."

Robert reseated himself next to her on the sofa.

"We're waiting with baited breath," Sebastian said from the depths of his armchair. "You could say you've thrown down the gauntlet."

And so he had, Urbino realized. The two Zenos, Vasco, and Oriana had no trouble understanding Sebastian's idiom, which was identical in Italian. Yet, if there had been any confusion, Sebastian's next words would have dispelled it: "Urbino is saying that one of us did in poor little Molly and tried to do the same to Gemma—and is now sitting here hoping she doesn't pull through."

"One of us a murderer?" Angelica said with a puzzled, ingenuous look.

"He's not serious, my dear," Vasco said. He gave Mamma Zeno, who was sitting bolt upright in her chair and still staring at Urbino, an apprehensive look.

"Oh, he is!" Oriana wailed. "It's all because of the curse of the Ca' da Capo!"

"We'll have no more of that nonsense, Oriana!" the Contessa said in an effort to get some control. "We're all going to sit here like sensible grown-ups and listen to what Urbino has to say. I—I insist!" she finished feebly and looked at Urbino with round, frightened eyes.

Before beginning to speak, Urbino briefly regarded each of the guests: Viola, who had one long arm cradled protectively around the Contessa; Oriana, her eyes frightened behind their Laura Biagiotti glasses; Angelica, pale, her fingers loosely intertwined in her lap; Robert, his olive skin shining with perspiration; Vasco, a truculent expression on his bone-thin face; Mamma Zeno, whose small dark eyes seemed to look at something far beyond the room and who was grasping her black cane more tightly than usual; Bambina on an ottoman in front of her mother, staring unblinkingly and guilelessly back at Urbino; and Sebastian, his long fingers lost in his thick auburn hair and wearing, as he so often did, an insinuating smile.

"No, Oriana," Urbino began, "it's not the curse of the Ca' da Capo. And there's no haunted room, although someone here would like us to believe there is. Yes, the Caravaggio Room has seen death several times, on two occasions very violent death, the second time as recent as the early hours of this morning. But if Molly had been staying in any other room, she would be just as dead." He paused for a beat, then added: "And so would Renata Zeno if she had stayed in one of the other rooms."

"Renata!" Bambina said. "What does Renata have to do with this?"

"Everything," Urbino said.

A little smile quivered at one corner of Bambina's mouth.

"Mamma, what does he mean?"

Mamma Zeno, without even glancing at her daughter, pulled her gaze back from wherever it had been and directed it with startling clarity at Urbino. He held it steadily for a few moments before going on:

"I intend to explain everything. Before I ask some of you to help me out with your information, let me tell you a few things as I see them. No one came to the Ca' da Capo with murder on the mind. Or perhaps I should clarify and say that the murderer had murder on the mind, but not the murder of Molly."

"My mother!" Robert cried. "She was the real target."

"No, Robert, she wasn't on the murderer's mind either, but as events quickly developed, she soon was."

Everything wasn't completely clear to Urbino. There was a small but crucial area within which he was still feeling his way. By articulating things he was better able to sort them out, but he was well aware of the risk of doing it in this way. There were still people in the room who were in danger from the murderer. He was one of them.

"Then what you're saying is that Molly's murder wasn't premeditated," Viola said with the air of trying to clarify things for herself and the others. "It was a *crime passionnel*."

She held the Contessa closer and tighter and looked in her face with an uncharacteristically gentle smile, as if a crime of passion under her roof alleviated a great deal of her burden. The Contessa's expression, which had proceeded to darken the more Urbino spoke, gave no indication that she was in any way consoled.

"Not a crime of passion either," Urbino said, not looking at Viola. "Let's consider various things," he went on quickly. "In fact, there are a great many, and each plays a part in the tragic events. For example, there's the story of the peacock brooch, which Bambina has just been kind enough to grace us with." His nod in her direction was met by a self-satisfied smile. "This story, with its glimpse into history—"

"The fall of the Byzantine Empire from the point of view of a brooch," interjected Sebastian. No one paid him any attention and Urbino continued without even glancing at him.

"Bambina told the Zeno version of the story, of course. What the Da Capo-Zendrini version is and which one is the true one"—the Contessa was about to protest but restrained herself—"is not really important for us right now. What is important is that the bad blood between the two families goes a long way back."

Vasco took advantage of Urbino's pause and said, "I believe you are trying to tell us that you believe little Molly was murdered because of this bad blood? Because of the brooch?"

There was a faint note of relief in Vasco's voice.

"I didn't say that," Urbino responded, but he didn't then add what he had meant. It would soon become clear and he needed to do it in the way he had planned.

"By the way," he began casually, "none of you know that the brooch was stolen—none of you but Barbara and the thief, that is." He studied them closely. "It was stolen some time between when Barbara came down for drinks before dinner last evening and when she returned to her room after her bridge game with Oriana, Filippo, and Dr. Vasco."

Everyone but the Contessa looked surprised, and at least one of them was doing a very good imitation.

"Stolen?" Bambina said. "But she's wearing it right now! How silly of you, Urbino!"

She stared at the sparkling ornament with avidity.

"Maybe it's paste," Angelica said. "Or maybe the one that was stolen was paste, like in that French story."

A look of dismay came over Bambina's chubby face. She looked at her mother, who remained silent and impassive.

"That was a necklace," Robert said, "and it was lost, not stolen. Maybe that's what happened. Barbara mislaid her brooch and only thought she lost it."

"Oh, it was gone, all right," the Contessa jumped in, only to wonder the next moment why she hadn't kept her mouth shut. "And it's not paste. It's the real thing."

"Then where did you find it?" Viola asked.

"I didn't find it."

"What the hell is going on?" Sebastian said. "I thought last night was the time for playing games!"

"What Barbara means is that I found it," Urbino said. "In the pocket of Gemma's robe."

Robert got to his feet, his mouth open, and for several moments no sound came from his lips. When it did, he was shouting.

"In the pocket of my mother's robe? And what business did you have going through her pockets?"

He started across the room toward Urbino, but was stopped by Urbino's next words: "I'm not saying that Gemma stole the brooch. I said that I found it in her pocket. I believe it was put there by the thief, so that we would assume she had stolen it."

Robert looked around at the other guests, searching out the thief among them who had tried to cast suspicion on his mother, who might have pushed her down the stairs.

"Come back here, Robert," Angelica said. "Let Urbino finish."

Robert returned to the sofa, mumbling something indistinguishable under his breath.

"So we have the theft of the brooch, planted on Gemma by the thief," Urbino continued, "and Barbara's slashed portrait, which also in its way—as Robert pointed out earlier—involves Gemma since she painted it. All of you knew where to find the portrait and all of you knew about the existence of the brooch. Some of you from as long ago as the thirties and even earlier, others"—he looked first at Viola, then at Sebastian—"only since yesterday afternoon when you heard about it in the memoir left behind by the Conte."

"Alvise left a memoir?" Vasco said with a gasp. "What do you mean?"

"A memoir he wrote for Barbara about the Caravaggio Room and about Renata's death. He left instructions that it was to be given to Barbara upon his death. I shared it with the twins yesterday afternoon."

"A questionable form of entertainment," Robert said.

"What did Alvise say in it?" Vasco asked.

"Many things," Urbino said, "and one of them was about the brooch, as I've said. He described how Bambina, so many, many years ago, was the person who told the story of the brooch to the dinner guests."

"History repeats itself, they say," Sebastian said. "And those who don't know it are condemned—isn't that the word?—condemned to repeat it, poor, benighted souls."

He finished his brandy, got up, and replenished his glass.

"It's more appropriate, given the events here at the palazzo in the past twenty-four hours," Urbino rejoined, "to say that those who *do* know history are in a perfect position to see that it *is* repeated—or to create that impression."

"I see what you mean," Viola said. "Someone wants us to believe in the curse of the Ca' da Capo, as you said before."

"Yes, someone was very pleased to be able to take advantage of the superstition surrounding the room—a superstition which all of you were also fully aware of, just as you were about the brooch. And although I keep saying 'you,' let's not forget to include our absent guests, too: Filippo, out in the storm somewhere, and Gemma, who even at this moment might be regaining consciousness"—his eye swept over them all as he said this last—"and, finally, also Molly."

"Molly!" Vasco broke out.

"Were you entertaining her, too, with the story of my grandmother's death?" Robert asked.

"I may be wrong," Urbino said quietly, "but I believe it was your mother herself who told Molly about her mother's death, the Caravaggio Room, and the brooch."

Before Robert could jump up again, Angelica put a restraining hand on his arm and said, "Why would Gemma ever have done such a thing, Mr. Macintyre? Molly was a stranger to her. Gemma barely breathed a word about the past to me."

"She didn't have to tell you anything. You learned what you know from your great-uncle Andrew Lydgate and, of course, from Robert. Molly knew more than you although she understood less."

"Riddles, again!" Robert said contemptuously.

"I suppose they are, but like all riddles they only seem to be confusing. Their answers are relatively simple. You see, Molly was writing a book. She was to call it *The Blood of Venice.* All about strange happenings, mysterious disappearances, bloody deaths—historical and otherwise—associated with Venice. In the course of her research she must have come across something about the Caravaggio Room. The Ca da' Capo is famous enough—on the Grand Canal, designed by Cominelli, frescoes by Zugno and Cignaroli—to appear in many of the guidebooks. Although Barbara and I don't know of any that specifically mentions the Caravaggio Room, one might exist—"

"It doesn't say much for your research skills," Sebastian said.

Urbino realized that, for the moment, it was best to ignore Sebastian, who had been downing his brandy as if it were water.

"—and this guidebook, with perhaps only a brief reference to the Caravaggio Room, could have been enough to cause Molly to add the Ca' da Capo to her list of subjects. I found some papers among Molly's things—a book contract, the name of the Ca' da Capo along with other buildings in Venice with mysterious or violent pasts. At some point and in some way Molly and Gemma managed to get together and Gemma told her what she knew."

"But why would my mother do such a thing? As Angelica said, she's close-mouthed, especially about the family and most especially about the death of her mother."

"But what about other things that Molly said?" the Contessa stepped in, perhaps sensing that Urbino wasn't ready to answer Robert's question yet. "Things that had nothing to do with the family or the Caravaggio Room—personal things about Urbino, for example. The death of his parents. I never told Gemma."

The Contessa's eyes, almost involuntarily, moved in Oriana's direction.

"Why don't you and Urbino just say it, Barbara? It's my fault! That's what he's working up to, isn't it? My fault that Molly is dead! My fault that Gemma might die! Everything's my fault! Even this storm and poor Filippo lying senseless somewhere! Yes, I admit it! I told Gemma some things about you and Urbino. She might have been close-mouthed, Robert, but she was very curious just the same. Does this make me an—an accomplice before the fact?"

"No one's blaming you for anything," Urbino said. "What you told Gemma and what she then passed on to Molly didn't result, even indirectly, in her death."

"You're off the hook, Oriana," Sebastian said.

"You must listen to Urbino closely, my dear brother, although in your condition it's a wonder you can hear anything. He didn't say that Oriana wasn't a murderer—but of course we all know that already," she added quickly when Oriana made an exclamation. "What he said was that what she told Gemma didn't lead to Molly's murder. Urbino is keeping all options open, you see. To keep us all guessing, especially the murderer, who is bound to wonder if he really has it all figured out."

"Ah, yes," Sebastian said, "the rules of the game. I know a bit about them myself. Isn't this where Urbino is about to stun us with his knowledge of the Bhagavad-Gita or the sumptuary laws of old Constantinople as he answers the burning question: Who under the humble roof of the Ca' da Capo did Molly in? Years ago, maybe around the time of the first fatal fete here, it would have been Mauro, the old family retainer and that sort of thing. Then I believe there was a distinct preference for the professional authority figure, the man—always was a man, wasn't it?—everyone's depending on. Guess that would be old Vasco here. And then there's the straightforward chap who wants to get to the bottom of things and no nonsense about it. That's obviously me. And what about the languishing heroine, whom we have in the pale flesh of Angelica?"

Urbino wasn't inclined to interrupt Sebastian and in fact

wished he would go on, for it was a good opportunity to observe the guests as he named them. But Sebastian had tired of his exercise and returned his attentions to his brandy glass.

"So let me get this right," Robert began with an edge of sarcasm. "The twins meet Molly on the *Orient Express* and invite her to a palazzo that she's writing a book about. Then my mother, for some unknown reason or a reason you aren't prepared to share with us quite yet, drags Molly into a dark corner of the Ca' da Capo and makes her the repository of our family history and some anecdotes from your own life. Then the brooch is stolen. Then Molly is murdered. Then my poor mother is pushed down the stairs. And at some point someone slashes her portrait of Barbara. Have I missed anything?"

Bambina tried to suppress a giggle. One chubby hand was clapped over her mouth and she stared at Urbino, then at her mother, with almost merry eyes.

"For one thing," Urbino said, "Gemma didn't inform Molly yesterday, but some time before she ever got on the *Orient Express.*"

"But it was the twins who invited Molly," Angelica said in a cool, calm voice.

"Yes, they did. The circumstances of that invitation have a bearing on what happened to Molly. Sebastian?"

Sebastian straightened up in exaggerated fashion, in the process spilling brandy on himself.

"*À votre service!*"

"Why don't you tell us how it was that Molly came to be invited?"

"Again? Don't press my admiration of you too far! Oh well, just let me get a spot more of Barbara's inestimable cognac to wet my whistle."

When he had reseated himself, he began: "Once upon a time about three days ago as the *Orient Express*—most unfortunately the ersatz *O.E.*—was easing out of the City of Lights, I—"

"Don't you think you should begin before the *Orient Express?*" Urbino asked.

"Before the *Orient Express?*" Viola echoed. "Whatever do you mean?"

"Sebastian knows very well. You knew about Molly's book, didn't you?"

Resentment blazed in Sebastian's green eyes.

"Molly never said anything about a book!" he said.

"Molly kept very good accounts in her checkbook. Names and dates and amounts. What she didn't put down on the stub that particularly interested me, however, was why she had made the check out to you. For a very large sum."

"What is the meaning of this?" the Contessa said. It wasn't clear if she was addressing Urbino or Sebastian. What was clear, however, was the anxiety in her voice.

Sebastian appealed to the Contessa with a nervous, embarrassed grin, like a schoolboy caught out in a prank, then sobered as he turned his long-lashed gaze on Viola. Brother and sister, so close to being mirror images that it was disturbing, exchanged a long, silent look. Seeming to take some courage or caution from the depths of her green eyes, Sebastian squared his shoulders and looked at Urbino directly.

"I suppose you think that I lured Molly here to murder her and she was kind enough to pay me for it! So she wrote me out a check! That doesn't mean I killed her or that anyone else did. She died in a freak accident! This idea of yours about murder is—is pure egomania. You're quickly losing whatever charm you held for me."

He got up and stalked over to the window. He drew aside the drape and stood gazing down at the garden.

"Your garden looks torn to pieces, Barbara," he said, almost inconsequentially, then turned around and looked a bit sheepishly at the Contessa. "I hope you'll forgive me. I would have told you everything once the weekend was over. Molly made me an irresistible business proposition. She was willing to pay for it. Handsomely." He put his brandy glass down and lit a cigarette. He puffed at it reflectively. "Who was I to say no? I figured she'd be a lively addition to the festivities. Yes, I knew her before the

O.E. I was giving tours at the British Museum. A little extra money and a chance to meet people who might see their way to helping me out. Molly gave me a generous tip and invited me out for a coffee. She started in on Venice, how she was going the next week and didn't have reservations, how she wished she had planned far enough ahead to rent a flat in a palazzo because that was the only way to do it. I said that renting that kind of place would cost a fortune, but she said money wasn't a problem. This was her first visit to Venice and she wanted to do it up in style. She said she was taking the *O.E.* Of course, it was only natural to tell her that Viola and I were coming here on it, too. She wanted to know when and it turned out we would be on the train together. One thing led to another, and—and I told her about Barbara's house party. Oh, I talked it up big, Barbara. *La grande fête* of the season and all that. She was pea green with envy and—and, well, I ended up inviting her. She made it clear she was willing to pay a lot for the privilege. More than enough to get me out of the red and to finance a jaunt to Morocco this winter—which I thought I'd ask you on, Urbino, until this public humiliation you've subjected me to!"

"How could you!" Viola looked at her brother in astonishment. "What a position you put me in!"

"Don't go moralistic on me, Vi. You know I've had a hard time of it. I could plaster these walls with dunning letters! I even owe you a pound of flesh! What's funny is that you went right along as if you were in on it yourself." He extinguished his cigarette and took a sip of brandy. "So there you have the whole sordid truth. That's the extent of my liaison with poor little Molly."

Urbino thought for a moment, then said:

"There's no way to tell if she made the entry in her journal about the Ca' da Capo before or after she met you. If it was before, it means that she probably didn't just happen to meet you at the British Museum. She knew who you were. She knew about your relationship to Barbara—and, through her, to the Ca' da Capo. What did you tell her about the Ca' da Capo?"

"The little I knew. That it was a palazzo on the Grand Canal and that my cousin had made it her mission to restore it to its former glory. I told her nothing personal about Barbara, except that she had married an Italian count."

"Has it occurred to you that someone might have set you up?"

"Set me up?" Sebastian repeated as if it were in a language he didn't know.

"Told her about you—your relationship to Barbara, where you worked, your plans to come to Venice for the house party, maybe even your financial straits."

The Contessa glanced nervously at Robert and said, "I—I told Gemma about Sebastian and Viola. But I didn't know anything about his money problems."

Sebastian gave a short laugh and tossed off the rest of his brandy.

"Just the fact that a young man of good family and high talents was obliged to babble on about the Elgin Marbles and Halicarnassus might have tipped her off."

Bambina, who had been following all of Sebastian's revelations with increasing interest and with even a strange kind of glee that lit up her round eyes, said, "Maybe Sebastian took the peacock brooch! It must be worth a lot of money!"

"And if he did, Bambina," Urbino said, "why do you think he would have put it in Gemma's pocket?"

"Hold on! I had nothing to do with that!"

"Oh, Sebastian, I hope not!" Viola said with what sounded like real distress in her voice.

"Answer the question, Bambina," Urbino said, paying no attention to the twins. "We'd like your opinion."

The look Bambina gave her mother was a strange mixture of fear and supplication. But Mamma Zeno didn't choose this moment to break the silence she had wrapped herself in since entering the library. She once again made a point of not even glancing at Bambina, but instead held Urbino's gaze for several long moments. He tried to read everything in her dark pools but so much eluded him. He wondered if Bambina, with her many decades of experience, was more adept.

"I don't know. Maybe he got frightened or regretted taking it, since it belongs to Barbara, his own cousin, who's so kind to him and—and to everyone else."

She threw a look at the Contessa that was meant to be all gratitude but looked more like a scowl.

"But why in Gemma's pocket? He could have done any number of things with it."

"Stop right there!" Sebastian said, his face red.

Viola got up and went over to him. She whispered in his ear. He angrily extinguished his cigarette, then immediately lit another. Viola seated herself on the carpet beside his chair.

"He could have dropped it into an urn," Urbino continued. "There are enough of them around. Or hidden it among one of the plants in the conservatory." He put a special emphasis on this last word. "Or gone out onto the loggia and thrown it into the Grand Canal."

"He would never do that!"

She smiled benignantly at Sebastian, as if to assure him that there were some things she believed were beyond him. He puffed away furiously at his cigarette as Viola peered up into his face with a worried look.

"You still haven't answered my question, Bambina," Urbino persisted. "I really would like to know. You strike me as a very observant and resourceful woman."

Flattery had worked with her earlier today and he hoped it would again.

"I do? *Tante grazie*. Let me see." She put a finger to her cheek. "Why would—why *did* Sebastian hide the brooch in Gemma's pocket? I—I suppose he could have wanted to catch two pigeons with one bean! He got rid of the brooch—which he never, never should have taken—and he makes my niece look guilty, because—because he wants us—wants *you*, Urbino—to think even worse of her."

She beamed like an apt pupil waiting for her praise.

"What do you mean? Even worse than a thief?"

Bambina made her characteristic zipper action across her mouth with her thumb and forefinger.

"By the way, Bambina," Urbino began, "there's one more thing you might be able to help me with."

"What is that?" she asked with every appearance of wanting to be of help.

"Did you see anyone on the loggia last night after we all went up to bed?"

"On the loggia? Oh no! With the storm I was afraid to even peep out. And good thing I didn't. Look what happened to Molly. I—I've never been out on the loggia at all!"

"That's strange, Bambina, because I found this out there this morning."

From his pocket he took the pink ribbon and held it out in the palm of his hand. He could almost feel the intensity of Mamma Zeno's stare burning into his hand.

"How do you account for this being there?"

She stared at the ribbon. He went over to her and placed it near one of the matching ribbons in her hair. To her credit, she answered quickly.

"Oh, I forgot. I—I went out to the loggia before the storm. A lovely panorama! It was getting windy and the ribbon could have flown away." She paused and said, with a little concentrated frown, "Or—or maybe someone took one of them from my room—I have so many, how would I notice?—and threw it on the loggia to get me in trouble. It could all be a plot against poor Gemma *and* me. The brooch in her pocket and my ribbon on the loggia."

Sebastian, who had been so loquacious and intrusive in his comments in the earlier part of the evening, somehow held his tongue. Viola was once again whispering in his ear.

"Let's forget about the ribbon, Bambina. I suppose it could have just blown out of your hair, as you say. Barbara, would you ring for Mauro?"

"Mauro?"

"Please. He's expecting to be called."

She pulled the cord and within a moment there was a quiet knock on the door and the old majordomo entered. Urbino hoped he would remember exactly what he had told him to say. The man had at first protested, assuring him that he never lied, but had quickly relented when Urbino had pointed out how important it was to the Contessa.

"Excuse us for taking you from your duties, Mauro, but would you tell us what you saw last evening?"

"Certainly, Signor Urbino. It was some time after the Contessa came down for drinks before dinner. I can't say exactly what time it was because with the storm there's been so much to do. Some windows up in the attic story wouldn't stay closed. It's been very difficult."

Mauro was not only remembering his lines, but also embroidering on them. Everyone was listening intently, none more so than the Contessa, whom Urbino hadn't told about his plans to use Mauro in this way.

"Go on, Mauro," Urbino prompted, when the man's pale Venetian skin turned even whiter after seeing the disturbed look on the Contessa's face.

"I—I had occasion to go out to the loggia. I was afraid that we had left some chairs there. I was outside the Contessa's bedroom. Her shutters were open. I looked through the door-pane to see if everything was all right, and I—I saw a woman in the room. She—she was standing by the Contessa's dressing table."

"Who was it, Mauro?"

"It—it was the Signorina Zeno."

Mauro avoided Bambina's eyes as he said this.

"She had the Contessa's peacock brooch in her hand. When no one said anything was missing, I—I thought it best to mind my own business."

"You did well, Mauro. Thank you. You can go now."

When the majordomo had left, no one broke the silence that

reigned in the library until Robert said, his face livid, "How could you do such a thing, Zia Bambina? Put the brooch in Mother's pocket like that?"

Bambina, who had looked stunned during Mauro's account, gave her great-nephew a tremulous grin.

"It was a joke. I got caught up in the spirit of our charades. I thought it would be amusing to have it disappear and then turn up in an unlikely place. Like a treasure hunt. That's all. I meant no harm."

She put her hands over her face, then latticed them and peeped out at Urbino.

"It was a foolish thing to do, Bambina," Vasco said sternly, his sharp eyes shooting disapproval. "It could have had serious consequences, joke or not. You see how it's misled Urbino to think that someone was trying to make trouble for our little Gemma."

It was perhaps a strange comment to make since it had been Bambina herself who had apparently tried to mislead Urbino. Vasco glanced at Sebastian, surrounded by a cloud of cigarette smoke and an air of barely subdued anger.

"It's interesting that you mention my being misled, Dottore, because you tried to do that to me yourself, didn't you? You insisted, drawing on your professional knowledge and experience, that the cause of Molly's death was a piece of broken glass from the loggia door which pierced her throat, and that she died instantly."

Vasco nodded his head.

"Instantly—or relatively so."

"But as we discussed this afternoon in your room, if Molly died in that way, blood would have spurted around the room because of the pumping motion of the heart."

"Only if the carotid artery had been pierced."

"As we both observed, it had been. This leads me to wonder how—or perhaps I should say, why—you made such an error. Did you really want me to believe it was an accident, or did you want me to see through your deception? I can come up with one reason why you might not want to believe it actually was an accident—and that's not because of any sympathy with Barbara's position as the *padrona* of the Ca' da Capo. It's because of your belief in the powers of the mind—your belief that if we direct our energies in a certain direction, we can affect the course of the natural world and maybe even behavior. Am I right? Accident or murder. You're not comfortable with either alternative. But better that Molly's death is determined to have been an accident than murder, for there's much greater culpability there, a much more frightening example of the power of the mind. The power of a mind focused consciously on ending the life of another person."

Urbino paused, and for a moment his eyes locked with the frightened, pleading ones of the Contessa.

"Surely, when the Caravaggio Room was examined and the autopsy was done," he went on, "there would have been no doubt that Molly didn't die in the way that you said. I can only assume that you hoped to gain time, perhaps to make some changes in the room so that her death would seem more like an accident."

The old physician's expression had become dazed, and the silence surrounding the immobile Mamma Zeno now seemed to spread over him. Without a word spoken between them or so much as a brief glance exchanged, they had an unmistakable air of complicity.

"Why did you want me—and later the police—to believe that Molly's death had been an accident? So that no one would associate her death with Renata's except to say that they both died under strange circumstances in the Caravaggio Room? Maybe you were afraid that your past had caught up with—with who? Yourself? Who, with your skills as a physician and your long-standing interest in mesmerism and the powers of the mind, has remained devoted to the Zeno family? Or maybe it had caught up with Gemma, whom you seem to cherish as if she were still the eight-year-old girl she was when Renata died. Or Signora Zeno, so long a widow and so long a mother burdened with the greatest sorrow a mother could have: the death of her child. Or Bambina, with all her energy and love of pranks and pink ribbons and cats and—many years ago—Andrew Lydgate. I suppose I should add Robert, Gemma's son, to the list, and his fiancée, Angelica, Lydgate's grandniece."

As Urbino had named each of these individuals, he had treated them impartially with his glances, but now his eyes returned to Mamma Zeno and rested on her, still so silent, sitting there on the sofa swaddled in midnight satin, her only adornment the gold wedding band worn as thin as a thread.

"You married a Zeno, signora, and you yourself are by birth and blood a Zeno, the cousin many times removed of your deceased husband."

The old woman said nothing. She didn't even move except for the slight rising and falling of the bodice of her dress and the nervous tapping of her fingers against her cane.

"I've noticed, signora, that you prefer not to wear any jewelry—no earrings, no necklaces or bracelets, no brooches of any kind, no rings except your wedding band."

"Mamma has been like that ever since I can remember," Bambina said quickly. "I always—"

She was silenced by a look from her mother, who then immediately returned the full power of her eyes to Urbino. He waited, as everyone else around him was waiting. They all sensed that the time had come for her to utter her first words since she had reprimanded Bambina in the dining room about the brooch.

Her thin voice was very clear, and as was her habit when using English, she spoke slowly and precisely.

"Young man, I have observed you and listened to you all this weekend. I have even indulged you in the privacy of the chamber that has been put at my disposal. Among other things I have been curious to see how far you would go—how far you *could* go. Very far, I now see. Too far. I suggest that you go no farther. It would be one more indignity, and life is full of too many."

She paused as if to catch her breath, all the while looking at

Urbino. When she continued her voice was even stronger than before.

"I see why you and Barbara are such good friends. Two *ficcanasi!* Meddlers! And you, Barbara, La Contessa da Capo-Zendrini"—she jerked her withered head slightly from side to side as she uttered each of the syllables of the Contessa's title—"more than a meddler! An intruder! But for you Bambina would be the contessa, the *padrona di casa.* Wearing your shoes and your gowns and your jewels. Ha! Your jewels, did I say? Bought with Da Capo-Zendrini money! Or stolen from the Zenos! I laughed when you told me you wanted to heal the wounds between the families this weekend, to bring us together. That was to have been Bambina's job, except that you put yourself into the picture like a well-bred *puttana!*"

The Contessa stood up. She was dead white. Urbino went over to her before she could say or do anything and guided her back to the sofa.

"Let her speak. Say nothing," he whispered.

Mamma Zeno stared at the Contessa with an ugly smile.

"Your portrait! Your portrait of your new, rested face to hang in the gallery of the Ca' da Capo-Zendrini, where Bambina's should have! Never! And to think that Gemma was a party to it! Never!"

She raised the cane and made a slicing motion with it. Although Urbino doubted it, he almost thought that if he grabbed the cane and twisted the ferrule, a foot or two of sword-stick would appear.

"Never!" Mamma Zeno repeated. "I'm still strong enough for some things!"

"You did it, Mamma? *Brava! Brava!*"

Mamma Zeno looked at her daughter and shook her head slowly. She now spoke in Italian:

"You poor fool! It's all over, don't you see? You'll die like me, never having had one single thing you wanted! You wanted Lydgate but he didn't want you. You wanted Alvise and see what happened! When the time was right for you both—*she* came along!"

Bambina, who had been so enthusiastic a few moments before, now looked distressed.

Vasco started to get up. Mamma Zeno waved the cane at him and he retreated back to his seat.

"Sit down! I said I wanted to bring things to an end with dignity, not have *il signore americano* point his finger at me. You have been a fool, Bambina, but I've loved you. All these years you've had me to thank!"

"Oh, Mamma, you are wonderful! Calm yourself, please. Cool yourself with some perfume."

Bambina sprang up from the ottoman and went over to her mother. She extracted her silver flask from the deep pocket of her dress and unscrewed the cap.

"Knock it out of her hand, Vasco!" Urbino shouted, hurrying across to where Bambina was about to pour the liquid against her mother's neck.

Vasco flung out his hand and sent the flask flying through the air. It fell and spilled its contents on the Aubusson, far from any of the guests. The scent of Shalimar began to drift through the library.

Mamma Zeno looked up at her daughter with shock.

"Your sister and even me, your own mother?"

But Bambina didn't hear. All her attention was now riveted on the door, which, unnoticed by the others because of this little drama, had opened in the last few moments. Standing framed in the doorway as if she were posing for one of her own portraits was Gemma. Her hair was wild, her face white, her eyes blazing.

Oriana screamed.

Gemma remained in the doorway for but a moment, trembling. Then, with an indistinguishable cry that seemed to come from her very soul, she rushed between Urbino and Vasco to Bambina and fell upon her, knocking her to the floor.

From down the hall a telephone suddenly shrilled its message that there was, after all, still a world outside and that they were once again connected to it.

EPILOGUE

Telling the Contessa

"I feel as old as Noah," the Contessa lamented to Urbino. Considering what she had recently suffered through, the sentiment was understandable and certainly sincere.

But an observer less aware than her good friend of the events at the Ca' da Capo-Zendrini might have accused her of exaggeration, if not disingenuousness. For the Contessa's Ararat was at the moment her customary maroon banquette in the Chinese salon, and her face, though obviously that of a woman of a certain age, was far less obviously that of one of her particular years, especially since exposure to the rejuvenating winds off Mont Blanc. In fact, if you wanted to see any signs of the ravages of time and the elements, you would have to turn your eye away from the Contessa, and out through the windows of Florian's into Piazza San Marco—where the Contessa's and Urbino's gazes were now directed.

Pools of water reflected the stones of the surrounding buildings, some of whose windows had been shattered by the storm. The mosque-like basilica glowed deceptively in the late afternoon light. Only the kind of close scrutiny architects had been giving it during the past few days would have revealed the damages to its recently restored facade and to the mosaics on the floor of the vestibule. Although late in the year for an orchestra in the Piazza, Florian's had set one up beneath a canopy to celebrate the city's survival of the second worst storm of the century.

The city was assessing its damages, licking its wounds, and preparing to face an uncertain future—activities not unlike what Urbino and the Contessa were doing at Florian's this afternoon.

They had already, as was their way and their need, gone over some of the more salient points of the murder of Molly Wybrow and that of Renata Bellini, to which Molly's was so closely, if also so distantly, related. Their knowledge wasn't, however, complete. Some details had been passed on to the Contessa by a friend at the *Questura.* Others had been somewhat grudgingly revealed to Urbino by Commissario Gemelli, with whom Urbino had cooperated on some past murder investigations.

Bambina was in custody, about to undergo psychiatric evaluation. Originally arrested for the attempted murder of Gemma, she had within hours made the mistake of accusing, in succession, her mother, Dr. Vasco, and Gemma of the killings of both Molly and Renata with the kind of detail that only the murderer herself would be in possession of. Whatever shielding of her Mamma Zeno and Vasco had done over the years was at an end. Much was now known but much was also unclear and indeterminate.

The greatest light had been shed by Gemma, now hospitalized for her injuries and for her more serious condition, which had been exacerbated by her fall. She had given a statement to the *Questura* from her hospital bed and, in a rush of heartfelt confession, repeated it all for the Contessa's and Urbino's benefit the other day.

Her revelations had corroborated much of what Urbino had already pieced together and had made use of in the library. Over the years she had harbored a suspicion that her mother's death hadn't been natural. She based it more on the silence that surrounded Renata's death than anything she had heard or seen that weekend back in the thirties: no startling flashbacks, no gradual piecing of things together, but a vague suspicion that grew as the years went by. Any possibility of resolving things through an exhumation was futile, since her mother's body, buried near Naples, had been among those destroyed in the bombardment of the cemetery during the war. What she began to strongly suspect was that there was some kind of conspiracy at work, that her grandmother, her aunt, and the family physician knew something incriminating about her mother's death and were protecting one another—or one of them was being protected by the others.

It was the crisis of her own serious illness that had set in motion the events that had had such tragic consequences for Molly at the Contessa's house party. Gemma had met her at the Victoria and Albert, quickly seen the uses to which she could be put, made her the repository of some crucial details and suspicions, and pulled the unaware Sebastian into the plot. It was her intention to watch, to observe, to evaluate the effects of Molly's observations. Beyond this she hadn't thought clearly, something she now regretted, as she keenly regretted having been indirectly responsible for the murder of Molly, who had never been informed of what Gemma was fishing for.

Yes, Urbino thought, she should have told Molly more and Bambina less. If she had made the one privy to her suspicions and pretended more with the other, Molly might still be alive and Gemma herself might not have been pushed down the stairs on her way to enlist Urbino's help.

Urbino, who had been reviewing all these details as he and the Contessa looked out the window, was surprised to discover that the Contessa had been thinking along parallel lines when she broke her silence. Surely Vasco would see it as a manifestation of the powers of the mind, which—from his point of view—had played such a role in the murders of Renata and Molly.

"Gemma, poor thing, acted irresponsibly, didn't she? To think that all of this was roiling around in her head while I was sitting for her. It's a wonder none of it came out in the portrait."

From her intonation and the quick look she gave him it was clear that she wanted—needed—some verification of this. He fortunately could give it.

"None that I could see. And I'm sure that when it's repaired you'll be proud to hang it in the gallery."

"Ah, but the memories behind it, *caro!* What of those?"

"You're a brave woman, Barbara. And so is Gemma. Dwell on those memories—on those associations. It's such a lovely portrait. Alvise wanted a portrait of you in the gallery. In its own crooked and sad, but, yes, perhaps even inevitable way, this is the fulfillment of that wish."

The Contessa didn't seem convinced, but he was fairly sure that, with time, she would see it this way. Her thoughts this afternoon could only temporarily remain on herself, as was evident when she said, after a short pause to take a sip of tea:

"I hope Gemma will stay with me when she's released from hospital—despite the Ca' da Capo's bad associations. I went to see her today—and Filippo, too." Filippo had suffered a severe concussion not long after leaving the Ca' da Capo when he had been hit by a stone dislodged by the storm. "He's bounced back, thank God. Oriana is by his side every minute, driving the hospital staff mad. His accident seems to have done wonders for their relationship. Gemma has regained some of her color and a lot of her energy. She's refused to see Luigi, you know."

"It comes as no surprise. You must have noticed yourself that she doesn't feel comfortable around him."

"But surely that was only because there was a doubt in her mind whether he might not have murdered Renata."

"Perhaps only partly. She's very sensitive and susceptible. Vasco has been hiding so much, feeling so much, torturing himself so much over the years that I wouldn't be surprised if Gemma responded to it at some level. I mean aside from the fact that she suspected him along with Signora Zeno and Bambina. Vasco himself, from what I hear, still insists that he's responsible for the deaths of Renata and Molly."

"But it was Bambina!"

"Yes, she did kill them, but Vasco wanted both of them dead. The desire, the wish, and the will were all strong, and you know what stock he puts in those things. He was furious at Renata for preferring Lydgate to him. She had given him reason to hope. Then years and years later Molly comes along, apparently in the know about the events of thirty-eight. He was attracted to her but also wanted her out of the way as a threat. The wish is father of the deed. Bambina, he came to realize, had killed Renata. Had the thought been planted in her mind by his own dark thoughts? Was he responsible? He tortured himself in the same way over Molly. Viola said that Vasco reminded her of Dr. Caligeri, who had a minion to carry out his evil bidding. I guess Viola wasn't far wrong, not from Vasco's own opinion of himself and of the power of the mind."

"But what about Marialuisa? In the library I thought that she had done everyone in with a rapier concealed in her walking stick!"

Urbino smiled to himself as he recalled his own fleeting suspicion about the special properties of the old woman's cane.

"So how much did she know about what really happened to Renata?" the Contessa asked.

"She probably knew everything right away, but didn't let Bambina know that she did. What would she have accomplished by turning in her own daughter? Scandal. The end of any hope of advancing the family through marriage. Remember: Bambina was not even eighteen back then. Lydgate was now free, and Alvise was a very attractive possibility. Then, as the years went by and she saw her plans turn to dust, she clung in her way more and more to Bambina. Dominating her, yes, but needing her. Rather classic, really. No, Marialuisa never would have turned in Bambina. Now she's revealing the secrets of the past because she has no other choice. And I suspect she might be worn out by having had to conceal them for so many years."

"And Bambina did try to kill her," the Contessa reminded Urbino, "and then at the *Questura* she accused her of the two murders. Bambina was as desperate as a person can get—and still is, I'm sure."

"Desperate and unbalanced. I don't think there's much doubt about what the psychiatric examination will turn up. I admit I was going on the assumption that we were dealing with a disturbed mind from almost the beginning. The slashing of your portrait seemed to be one more proof, but of course—"

"Of course you were wrong there because it wasn't Bambina but Marialuisa."

Not only that, Urbino said to himself, but he had even fleetingly thought Sebastian had done it. There had been that expectant smile on his face as he stared at the Contessa right before the portrait was unveiled. A now repentant Sebastian, who had remained in town after his sister's departure, had confessed to Urbino that he had taken a peek at the portrait after it was slashed and had been waiting for the unveiling with amusement. Urbino had thought it best not to mention this to the Contessa. Nor had he yet told her about something else concerning her young cousin.

"And you know," the Contessa broke in on Urbino's thoughts, "Marialuisa might be as disturbed as Bambina. *Telle mère, telle fille!*"

"Not really" came Urbino's somewhat deflating response. "I suspect that Marialuisa is most *compos mentis.* And she still has a will of iron."

"I wonder what will become of her."

"Oh, I'm sure that Vasco will look after her."

The observation was, perhaps, a bit unrealistic since Vasco was himself in his eighties, but the Contessa didn't disagree. She instead asked:

"Did you know from the start how Molly was killed?"

"Not for a moment did I think she had been killed because her head went through the glass—either because of an accident or because she was pushed through. Since there were no other visible wounds, I suspected poison. The lingering scent of perfume confused me at first. Why would Molly douse herself with it after she had taken a bath?"

"The obvious answer to that is that she could have been expecting a visitor. Didn't it occur to you that Vasco might be dropping by?"

"That's exactly what I did think at first: him or someone else. But when I didn't find a bottle of that perfume among Molly's things—the same kind that Bambina and Gemma wore, and which Mamma Zeno filched from time to time from Bambina's bottle—the picture started to change. Then I saw the tin of rose spray in the cabinet in the conservatory. I remembered how you said that nothing had been changed in the conservatory since the days of the house party and how you insisted on getting the same nicotine-based rose spray from the old pharmacist in the Dorsoduro quarter. I know enough about nicotine—pure nicotine—to know how it works. Very fast, especially when administered directly to the skin, faster than when it's ingested. I remembered how Alvise was disoriented by the scent of perfume surrounding Renata's body. He called it the 'odor of sanctity.' Murderers seldom change their methods, even over such a long period of time. I had a hunch that both Renata and Molly had been killed in exactly the same way."

"But how did you know it was Bambina?"

"In many ways she was the most likely suspect from the start. She was infatuated with Lydgate. Jealous of Renata. Jealous, even at her advanced age, of every female in the house. Then there was her cat, Dido, who died a painful death a few months before Renata. Jealous of little Gemma, whom Dido became so attached to. Bambina probably poisoned the cat, too. Kind of a dry run for Renata."

The Contessa shuddered and shook her head.

"And of everyone Bambina seemed to be in the least touch with reality—"

"Ah, reality!" the Contessa interrupted. "As if any of us have been on such close terms with it! If I had had more sense, this weekend never would have taken place, and if you had been thinking clearly, you would have discouraged me!"

"No one is responsible for what happened this weekend, except Bambina herself. And Gemma, of course, for endangering Molly the way she did."

"Of course you're right, but nonetheless I know I'm never going to be able to get rid of a feeling of responsibility in it all. And there are so many reminders! The portrait, as I've already said. The brooch. The Caravaggio. The room itself. What am I going to do about all of those?" she almost wailed.

She was to be forgiven as her thoughts strayed back to the personal. Urbino tried to reassure her, by first repeating what he had said earlier about the portrait and then by saying, with what experience had taught him was the right combination of banter and force to use with her:

"You'll wear the brooch as often or as seldom as you did before. It was Alvise's gift to you, and it's surely in better hands with you than Marialuisa. Remember, she gave Bambina the task of stealing it this weekend. She was determined to have it in the family. She'd probably have it in her possession now, if Bambina hadn't decided to plant it on Gemma. And don't think of giving it to Gemma. I doubt if she'd want anything to do with it, and you can be sure Angelica would shrink from it if you made it a wedding gift. You see I know how your mind works! You're probably thinking of Viola, too. But everyone will think you're trying to pass on bad luck—nonsense, of course!—so you must keep it."

"You must feel the same about the Caravaggio. I was considering giving it to you. There's that corner of your library just waiting for it."

"Thank you, Barbara, but I can't accept it." The look that came over the Contessa's face was not so much disappointment or hurt as fear. "Not because of any preposterous superstition, but because I don't want to feel that I've benefited in any way from what's happened."

A skeptical look passed over the Contessa's attractive features, and Urbino himself wondered exactly how selfless his rejection of the Caravaggio was. Despite his belief in rationality and logic, deep inside him was lodged a small, dark corner of superstition that the recent events at the Ca' da Capo had far from swept clean.

"No," he quickly went on before the Contessa might say anything, "what I suggest is that you either put it somewhere else in the Ca' da Capo—some less private area, like the entrance hallway or the *salone da ballo*. If that doesn't suit you, donate it to the Accademia or the monks on San Lazzaro degli Armeni. After all, it was one of the monks there who recognized it as a Caravaggio when Alvise's father brought it to be cleaned."

"That's a good idea. I think that just might be the solution. But if anything were to happen on San Lazzaro after I gave it to them, I'd—"

"As for the Caravaggio Room," Urbino interrupted, "why don't you completely redo it? After all, it wasn't part of your renovations after you married. Now's the time to do it. We can plan it together. Decide on a theme, choose a Fortuny fabric for the walls, scout around for some items. Maybe Milo can take us out with the Bentley and we can make our way as far as Naples. I know some shops there that have beautiful rococo furniture."

"And when the room's done, it can be yours whenever you happen to stay over. How's that?"

A teasing but also slightly sad smile played at the corners of the Contessa's lips.

"We'll see" was the extent of Urbino's agreement.

"Maybe you'll feel more easy about staying in it if you completely exorcise it."

"What do you mean?"

"If you re-create exactly what happened to Molly in the room that night. It would be good for me, too. What I imagine can't be worse than what actually happened." She paused, a worried expression on her face, and added, "Could it?"

Urbino preferred not to respond to the question and took a sip of his Campari and soda. The orchestra now started to play, for the second time since Urbino and the Contessa had come into the Chinese salon, that Neapolitan favorite, "*O Sole Mio.*" In case anyone missed the intention behind this choice, any ambiguity was removed by a red-faced man, fortified with Veuve

Clicquot, now singing—or rather shouting—of "serene air" after the "*tempesta.*" His spirited apostrophes to the sun, shining again on the lagoon city, were joined in by his equally fortified and vociferous companions.

When the orchestra went on to play an arrangement of Verdi arias and the singers had returned their attention to what remained of their champagne, Urbino began to describe how Molly had met her death in the Caravaggio Room.

"Some time after everyone was in their rooms, Bambina must have crept down to the conservatory to get some of the rose spray. Earlier in the day she searched through the cupboard for a glass to fill with water when Gemma became ill. The glasses are above the sink but she could have looked in the cabinet beneath it and seen the tin of rose spray and the white rubber gloves among the gardening tools. That night she put on a pair of the gloves, poured some of the rose spray into a container—probably into her flask—and went back to her room, where she mixed it with a quantity of her perfume. Then, on some pretext or another, she paid a visit to Molly. Poor Molly, for all her dark and bloody pronouncements, was a trusting soul. Exactly what transpired between them, we're not going to know unless Bambina decides to tell, but somehow Molly got thoroughly saturated with the perfume laced with rose spray. Death through skin absorption can be as rapid as five minutes. Bambina probably waited until Molly was dead and then left the room."

The Contessa shook her head slowly.

"No, I was wrong," she said. "It isn't better to know exactly what happened. Not at all."

"But some of this is speculation, remember," Urbino said by way of soothing her.

"Just finish, if you don't mind."

"Bambina returned to her room and probably didn't stir for the rest of the night—except to go out to the loggia."

"In the middle of all that wind and rain?"

"To throw away the gloves. I was looking out my window and

thought I was seeing things. It looked like a white hand riding on the wind. It shook me up at the time. You know I don't believe in such things," he said with more insistence than was warranted if he actually didn't have a touch of superstition. "It must have been one of the gloves. And the next morning I found one of her ribbons on the loggia, as you already know."

"I see."

"And I have a feeling that if anyone had seen Bambina walking around that night—down to the conservatory, in the conservatory itself, back up to her room, back and forth from Molly's room, and out on the loggia—she would have claimed she was walking in her sleep. Although how she would have explained the plastic gloves is something else! But she was very quick to admit to being a sleepwalker when I spoke with her in the conservatory the afternoon after Molly's death."

"So clever in her madness, and so perfectly mad in her cleverness," the Contessa said.

"I'm afraid so," Urbino agreed. "She just left Molly's body where it had fallen near the doors to the loggia. The storm must have forced open both the glass doors and the louvered doors. Somehow Molly's head was in a position to receive the blow of the glass door and to be pushed through it. That's the way she was found. It was only logical at first to assume it had been an accident, but the blood—"

"Yes, yes, I know all about that. You needn't go into any more detail." The hand holding her teacup was shaking slightly. "Maybe we'll all be stronger because of what we've gone through. Just like the city."

She glanced out into the Piazza, where "the finest drawing room in Europe" was, this afternoon, remarkably empty of tourists or anyone who remotely resembled one. Instead Venetians went to and fro with parcels, or gathered in dry spots for conversation, or stood alone gazing about them, thankful that the old stones had survived the recent terrible onslaught. Several couples, one of whom Urbino recognized as the middle-aged brother and sister who owned a nearby bookshop, started to dance when the orchestra finished Vivaldi and began Rodgers and Hammerstein. Oblivious to the puddles, they swept across the stones and among the pigeons.

"Oh my, look who's coming," the Contessa said.

It was Sebastian. He made his way around the edge of the dancers and stepped under the arcades. His arms were full of books and brochures. He grinned broadly at Urbino and the Contessa and continued walking toward the entrance.

"I wonder what the boy is burdened down with?" the Contessa said with a mischievous gleam in her eye.

Urbino took a sip of his drink as a prelude to telling her, but before he could say anything the Contessa went on.

"If I were forced to guess—just off the top of my head, of course—I'd say that he's staggering under the weight of the realm of Morocco! So when are you two off?"

"The day before Christmas," Urbino admitted a bit sheepishly.

Sebastian now stood in the doorway of the Chinese salon, trying to get a better grasp on the books and brochures before proceeding to their table.

"Until when?" the Contessa asked.

"We're not sure."

"Well, Sebastian's a good boy, despite everything. He just needs a bit of direction."

Urbino gave the Contessa a smile of gratitude. He hadn't needed to tell her anything. She had known all along.

But the Contessa, being the Contessa, had something more to say:

"Just don't forget to go Dutch, *caro!*"